WHAT THE NANNY SAW

BOOKS BY KAIRA ROUDA

The Second Mrs Strom

KAIRA ROUDA

WHAT THE NANNY SAW

bookouture

Published by Bookouture in 2024

An imprint of Storyfire Ltd.
Carmelite House
50 Victoria Embankment
London EC4Y 0DZ

www.bookouture.com

Storyfire Ltd's authorised representative in the EEA is Hachette Ireland
8 Castlecourt Centre
Castleknock Road
Castleknock
Dublin 15 D15 YF6A
Ireland

ISBN: 978-1-83525-699-2
eBook ISBN: 978-1-83525-698-5

To the good guys out there, including my husband, my three sons and my son-in-law, who are all nothing like Paul. Thank goodness.

PROLOGUE

Two women randomly meet at a bustling coffee shop in Malibu.

One woman, a stunning beauty who seems to have everything money can buy, needs help with her baby who has upended her life and who seems to be at the end of her rope.

The other woman is a natural helper, a nanny, who is looking for a new position, a step up in life with a dream to create, one day, a loving family of her own.

It's a perfect set-up. They need each other.

Except it's not a random encounter, and both women are hiding secrets and will do whatever it takes to protect the life of their dreams.

Anything.

ONE

LIZZIE

That's the thing when you're a nanny for an uber-rich family. They think they own you, every minute of your time, even if your contract says otherwise. They also raise their children to think they are in charge of you, not the other way around—especially once the children become teenagers. You're the least powerful person in the household, sometimes even less valued than the pets. You're only the nanny.

Case in point, Kathie and Kimmie, ages 11 and 13, two of the four kids I'm taking care of for the Johnson family. I'm in the kitchen—lovely and spacious, with sunshine pouring in at large windows, a view of the Pacific Ocean sparkling in the distance, all the best high-end stainless-steel appliances—loading the dishwasher. It's about 10 minutes before I leave the house to begin dropping the angels off for school. Jimmy, in third grade, is my favorite. He's still young enough to be sweet, while his older brother Johnny, age 10, is slowly becoming his father. Not a good development, not at all.

"Lizzie! I can't find my new pink Prada purse," Kimmie says, stomping into the kitchen in a designer outfit that must have cost thousands of dollars, even without the purse. "You know, the one I got when you took me last weekend?"

I turn around and smile at her. "I do know the one, of course, but I haven't seen it," I say.

"I need to carry it to school today, to show my friends," Kimmie says. Her sandy blonde hair is straightened and shiny. She's started to wear makeup, too, I've noticed. Too young for all of that, in my opinion. But again, I'm not really in charge.

"You'll have to pick a different purse. We're leaving in five minutes," I say. I dry my hands with a dishtowel—plush, all cotton and linen blend, grey and white to match the tones of the kitchen, of course.

"Help me! Please," she says, desperation seeping into her voice over a designer purse she's too young to own.

"Sure," I say and follow her as she races upstairs to her bedroom. Each kid has his or her own room, complete with en suites and amazing walk-in closets. All the rooms have a theme, of sorts, and either a view of the ocean or of the pool in the back-yard. Nice digs if you can get them.

Kimmie shoves the door of her room open, and the mess literally takes my breath away. I know what I'll be doing for the next few hours. Cleaning up after this spoiled one.

"What were you doing? Tossing everything you own out of the closet?" I ask, shaking my head.

"Just out of my accessories closet." She pouts, standing in the middle of shoes, purses, even necklaces and scarves scat-tered across the room. Her room is purple and white, with a plush white rug where most of the things have landed.

Of course, she has two closets. One for clothes and the other for accessories and shoes. I take a deep breath and try to control my anger.

"How about this Gucci bag? It matches what you're wearing, with the cute silver studs," I say, picking a bag up off the white rug.

"They've all seen that one, Lizzie, that's the point. I want to show off something new," she says, frustration clear in her voice.

I step into her accessories closet and take one look around. "I can't see it in here. I don't know what you did with it. I'll look for it when I clean up this mess. But we have to go now."

I walk out of Kimmie's room just as Kathie steps out of her pink-and-gold-themed bedroom. The faucets in her bathroom are real gold, if you can believe it. She's dressed head to toe in Chanel. It's ridiculous. I don't think I can take this life much longer.

"Ready?" I say to Kathie. "Kimmie, come on."

"Yes, don't I look ready?" She smiles as she walks past me.

This overt display of wealth should make me feel worse about myself. I know that. But it doesn't. I know who I am and what I want. These girls, well, I guess if they're lucky they'll be spoiled all their lives and never have to worry about a thing.

But things happen, as I learned the hard way. I was sort of wealthy once, had everything I could ever want. Until my dad slammed his car into a tree and killed himself along with my 3-year-old sister, Sally, when I was only 10 years old. Everything changed that night. The whispers round our small town were that he knew he was about to lose everything and decided to just take them out of their misery, him and my mom. She'd suffered his temper for years before this happened. My poor little sister's car seat flew out the window and landed face down in a ditch. I can barely stand to think about it now.

Some people thought he was driving drunk, and it was an accident. I'm not one of those people. All I know is that's life—it's a bitch.

As we reach the bottom of the stairs, Mr. Johnson greets us, cup of coffee in his hand. He's dressed for a workout in the home gym, wearing a tight t-shirt to show off his biceps.

"Have a great day at school, kids," he says as Kimmie,

Kathie, Jimmy and Johnny rush out the door. "Oh, and Lizzie," he continues.

I stop. "Yes?"

"I'm going to need the house spotless by this afternoon," he finishes. "The kids' rooms are a mess, don't you think?"

"I agree. I was going to have the girls clean up after themselves once they're home from school," I say. "They need to learn to pick up after themselves. They're old enough to do it."

"Maybe, someday, but today you'll do it," he says with a bright, smug smile. "See you later."

I am just about over this job, I think, as I stomp to the car. This family is on my last nerve. I've been with them a little over two years now. I could change families—I've done it before. I open the door to the minivan and slip inside. My next family is going to be the right fit, it just has to be. I feel tears welling up but I hold them back. I will not cry in front of the Johnson kids.

I reach down and turn up the volume on the radio before pulling out of the driveway. The girls must know they've pushed me too far. No one says a word as I make the rounds to the various school drop-offs.

Jimmy's the last one to be dropped off. I plan it that way. "Have a great day, little man," I say.

"Sorry you're sad," he says with a sweet expression on his face as he scoots out the door.

And that does it. I can't stop the tears. I push the button to close the minivan door and drive away.

TWO

CECILIA

Evan promised to be home before the baby wakes up from her nap, which is usually about two in the afternoon. Right now, it's 1:47 p.m. and he is not home.

I text him. No answer.

I call him. No answer.

This is how he's been ever since Peyton was born, her birth a torrent of pain that lasted almost twelve hours. Come to think of it, that's when he started tuning out of our relationship, our entire life, and especially our daughter's life. She's over 5 months old now.

Five months of an absentee dad. I don't know how much longer I can handle this.

Over the baby monitor I hear Peyton's waking up sounds; I know the vague shuffling and stirring noises will eventually build to uncontrollable tears. I brace myself, and try to focus on the beautiful retreat I created for her. Her nursery is a lovely mixture of peach and pink, soothing soft colors. The rug is plush and peach, as soft as the skin of the fruit itself. The lighting is an antique crystal chandelier I had sent over from France, and it sparkles in the center of the room. The crib and rocking chair and changing table are all French, and terribly expensive, but she is worth it. I hand-painted the art on the walls, puffy clouds of serenity, hoping it would bring her joy. The entire room was my design, with the help of the interior decorator, of course. They even photographed it for a glossy magazine, a two-page spread titled: *Fit for a princess, the best nursery money can buy.*

Truth be told, the pregnancy was an accident. But I came to terms with it, and when I found out she was a girl, well, I started to get really excited. Thus, the over-the-top nursery, in my equally over-the-top Malibu home. We're both little princesses.

Peyton begins to wail. She didn't even wind up to it. I stand up from the kitchen table where I'd been enjoying gazing out the window to the pool and the sparkling ocean beyond, but I move too fast. A spasm grips my back, sends shooting pain down both legs. I grab the table to steady myself, my heart thudding in my chest as Peyton cries even harder over the monitor.

Every step is torture, but I must comfort my baby. *Where is Evan?* I reach the stairs and look up. Climbing the stairs will be agony. I use the railing to pull myself up a couple steps before collapsing to my knees. I crawl the rest of the way up the stairs and down the hallway to the nursery, grateful for the plush runner cushioning my knees.

"Mommy is here, Peyton," I call as I reach the door. I grasp the knob and pull myself to standing. I force a smile on my face and step inside.

Poor baby girl is bright red from screaming and crying, her cheeks soaked. She stops and blinks. It's as if she's deciding what to do.

I walk carefully to her crib, knowing I'll need to lean forward to pick her up and that it might cause more spasms. Ever since I broke my sacrum in a fall my back has been terrible. My labor with Peyton exacerbated everything. I'm smiling. I'm cooing. But I'm an idiot because I forgot to bring her bottle up with me, although so far, she's still watching me. She's so beautiful, chubby cheeks, blonde fuzzy hair and bright green eyes, just like mine.

I reach the crib. Peyton begins to cry again, an unbelievably sad and pitiful sound.

"No, baby, I'm here, it's OK, Mommy is here," I say, bending forward, reaching for her. The pain explodes down my spine as I pick her up.

And then we're both crying, inconsolably, in the most beautiful nursery money can buy. It's pathetic. I'm miserable, she's miserable. I'm a failure at this, at motherhood. I make my way to the rocking chair and sit gingerly, resting Peyton on my lap. This is not how I imagined things going, not at all. Everyone tells you motherhood is challenging, but they don't tell you about this. There's no manual, there's no practicing, it's just boom, here's a person to take care of forever. Good luck.

Maybe if I had a partner I could count on, things would be different. But I don't. In fact, Evan has proven to be the opposite of dependable and loyal. I'm going to need to do this better, on my own. For the life of me, though, I'm just not sure how.

THREE

LIZZIE

I'm sitting at my favorite Malibu coffee shop people-watching, and that makes it a perfect day. The sun is shining, the celebrities—or people who look like they should be famous—are out in droves, and my latte is heaven in a cup. I'm considering ordering a snack, something small that won't dip into my limited budget, when my phone buzzes.

When I see who it is, I frown. What does he want? I've done all of my chores, the kids' rooms are all cleaned up, which took two full hours thanks to the girls. The kids are tucked away at school. This is my time. Me time. *Grr*. I send the call to voicemail but before I know it, he's calling again.

"Hello, Mr. Johnson," I say. It's hard to keep the anger out of my voice, but I'm trying.

"Beautiful day today, isn't it?" he says. I picture his perfectly coiffed hair, the speckles of gray at his temples, the crinkles beside his blue eyes that make him look sophisticated instead of old. He thinks he's a catch, and I guess, with as much money as he's made in the movie business, he is to some women. To me, he's just my annoying employer.

"It is," I say. "What's up?"

"Ha, well, funny you ask. It's just that I need some help here at the house and thought if you wouldn't mind coming home, now, that would be great," he says.

"So nothing's wrong with the kids?" I take a sip of my latte and deflate. A nanny is supposed to take care of the kids, not the parents. I don't know why these people don't get that. "I've cleaned up their rooms, everything is as it should be."

"I mean, you aren't busy with anything, are you?" he says. "I didn't think you would be."

He doesn't think I deserve a life outside their house. "Actually, I'm with a friend, having coffee." Yes, it's a little lie, but he deserves it. He really does.

"Well, wrap it up. See you in say ten minutes?" I can feel him grinning through the phone. He wins. Men like him always do.

I consider getting that snack and savoring it for a while, but instead I finish my latte and drive back to the Johnsons' home. I'm surprised to see a few cars in the driveway. They aren't big entertainers, in fact with the four kids and his busy work schedule and whatever it is she does all day—which I'm starting to figure out, and it's sketchy—they barely have time for anything.

I think about Mrs. Johnson. She should be happy. She has a huge house, loads of money, four kids she gave birth to and therefore should enjoy spending time with. She has jewelry and ocean views, and she has me to do everything around the house that she doesn't want to do. But she's miserable, I can tell. I don't know why, but her presence is like a black cloud that dampens the energy for everybody, including her kids. I suppose it's a blessing she locks herself away in her bedroom most days, enjoying movies on demand and bottles of wine from the stocked fridge built into the cabinets. Meanwhile, I handle the kids and the house. How do I know about her day-drinking? I'm the one who stocks the wine. Chardonnay is her favorite.

I'm also the one who takes out the trash, empty bottles clanking as I dump them into the recycling bin.

I park in my usual spot and let myself in through the mud room. The kids' stuff is all put away, by me of course, in their designated baskets, and the laundry is clean and folded. The Johnsons really don't deserve me.

I hear a woman laughing and then a shriek. Strange music with a reggae beat starts up. I hurry into the kitchen and look out the window to the backyard. The swimming pool is filled with people, well, women to be exact.

Naked women, to be even more exact.

"What the hell?" I can't stop myself from saying as Mr. Johnson walks into the kitchen with just a towel wrapped around his waist. He's usually travelling. I realize now I've been lucky he hasn't been around much.

"There you are," he says. He's smiling and clearly proud of himself for the crowd he's assembled out back. "I knew you'd come home. You're so dependable. And prettier than you know."

"What did you need?" I ask, trying to avoid looking at the scene outside the window.

"What I always need. To spend some time with you," he says. I notice a puddle of pool water forming at his feet. He's making a mess. "Have you always been such a good girl?"

I look at him, see his smirk. I meet his eyes, and I hope there's a hard expression in my own even though I can feel my heart hammering in my chest. "Yes. I have."

"Well, that's boring. Just ask Mrs. Johnson. Where is she anyway?" he asks. "I'm assuming her therapist? It's her usual day. Besides, she wouldn't care if you had a little fun."

I shrug and take a step back. "I really need to get back to work," I say.

"Nonsense. All work and no play makes, well, people boring. And you're not boring. I can tell." He takes a step toward me, expanding the puddle on the hardwood floor. "You know, I've always wanted to see you naked. Join us?"

My mouth drops open. I cannot believe this guy. "No. I won't. And you do know the kids will be home from school in an hour?"

"Oh, I know," he says. "I'll clear the ladies out by then. Come on, change your mind. Let's have some fun. Don't you want to have some fun?" He walks toward me as a chill rolls down my spine.

"No," I say, backing away from him. "I'm calling Mrs. Johnson."

"Don't do that, there's really no need to involve her," he says.

"She's your wife," I say. "Of course she's involved."

I call Mrs. Johnson as I hurry out of the house. Of course, like always lately when I try to reach her in the middle of the day, I'm sure it's going to roll to voicemail, but for once, she picks up.

"Hi, Mrs. Johnson. The kids are fine, but, um, well, Mr. Johnson is home, and... well," I say. I try to stay strong, but I lose my nerve. I'd love to tell her that her husband is having some sort of naked pool party in the middle of the day. But instead, I say, "I think you should come home. Right now." And hang up.

These people. I need another job. I am sick of this entitled man and his absentee wife who focuses solely on self-care or tucks herself away in her bedroom, numbing herself out daily. And now he is blatantly hitting on me. As much as I like the kids, and I do, especially Jimmy, this is too much.

FOUR
CECILIA

I cannot believe I let this happen to me. My life is basically consumed by this tiny person. I'm exhausted, and I'm barely functioning. I know this is what all new parents go through, but I'm not sure I can take one more night. It's three in the morning, her usual time for full-on distress crying, and I know if I don't get out of bed and hurry to the nursery, she'll work herself into a complete tantrum.

Peyton may only be 5 months old, but she rules my world, and has since the night she arrived in a flurry of pain followed by something I hadn't expected: a surge of overwhelming emotions that felt like, yes, love.

I climb out of bed, my back aching, sending waves of pain down my legs. I'm furiously aware that Evan sleeps soundly through all this chaos. As if his part in the whole situation was simply sperm donor—one and done. The rage I feel for my "partner" is indescribable. He has to go to work tomorrow so he can't get up with Peyton, of course. He needs his beauty sleep.

I sigh, loudly, knowing he can't hear me or the baby with his noise-cancelling earbuds, concert-strength, but he can feel the bed moving as I purposefully bounce a couple times on my side.

It hurts my back but I don't care. It's only fair. He talked me into this whole motherhood-will-be-great-for-you situation. I yank my long blonde hair into a topknot, grab my bathrobe from the foot of the bed and prepare for battle.

Across the hall, Peyton has worked up to quite a crescendo. It's an impressively loud sound for such a tiny little girl. I open the nursery door.

"Mommy is here, baby," I say, but she doesn't seem to care. I grab her bottle out of the cooler and paste a weary smile on my face. Peyton stops crying as I approach, and I suppose that's a good sign. I pick her up out of the crib, back spasming with the effort, and cuddle her. I give her the bottle and she begins slurping immediately. This is a bad habit we've created, Peyton and I. I know it's wrong to accommodate these middle-of-the-night feeding requests. But what else can I do? I'm not going to just let her scream.

"When do you think you'll sleep through the night?" I ask her gently.

She doesn't answer, of course, just continues drinking the formula.

"Ok, well, good talk," I say, leaning over the crib and kissing her on the forehead. The fuzzy blonde hairs on her head are so soft, and I'm struck again by how her eyes are miniature versions of mine. Green and sparkling.

"See you whenever you decide you need me. Can you try to sleep past six a.m.? Please?"

She slurps, ignoring me. I often find myself wondering, while awake for these nocturnal feeds, who took care of me at the beginning, who brought me my milk in the middle of the night? Did anyone care, or did I just cry myself to sleep? I was in the foster system, alone and tiny. I don't like to think about it, but the thoughts push into my consciousness every night regardless.

I stretch and reach over to touch my toes. My back aches for several reasons, not just the baby. I took a huge, life-altering fall in Paris five years ago when I was on my one-year wedding anniversary with my now estranged husband. The fall broke my back and resulted in years of rehab. And when I decided to have the baby, the extra strain of carrying her to term and giving birth stirred up the old injuries, I'm afraid. My back aches now from life as a mom.

I'm too young to feel this old, this exhausted, this stuck. I need to make a change. I've needed to for a long time. I wasn't cut out to be a mom, and I promised myself I would never have a serious relationship again, would certainly never get married again. I broke my own rules, well, one of them. Evan and I are not married despite his frequent proposals once I learned I was pregnant. The pregnancy was a mistake, to be honest. I'd forgotten to take my birth control, a stupid oversight uncharacteristic of me. I'm quite cautious normally. And when I say no, I usually mean no. I think of my own mother, the birth mother I never knew because she gave me up, handed me off shortly after I arrived in this world. I know the feeling of rejection, the meaning of no, deeply, in my core.

I couldn't do that to Peyton, not once she was real. Not once I saw her on the ultrasound and began to imagine her in the world. I don't know how my mom did it, had me and then let me go. I can't say no to my baby.

But I can do that to Evan. It's past time for him to go.

I hurry back across the hallway toward my bedroom. As I do, I wonder how long it will take him to pack up and get out. Because I'm not playing house with him anymore. As I slide under the covers, once again annoyed by his blissful slumber, I think of Evan's mother Marian, a pushy woman with her bright red hair and too much perfume. She's much more formidable than her son—but, I reassure myself, she doesn't have any claim on Peyton. She's much too busy with her bridge group to make time for Peyton, though she calls herself the baby's favorite grandma.

That's an easy achievement. She's the only one the baby's got. And, well, once I evict Evan, she'll soon drift away. I'll be sure of it. It'll be me and my baby against the world.

There's just one problem. I love my job as creative director at Evan's event company. It gives me a purpose, and I can work as little or as much as I desire. And we do have the big Malibu gala coming up, where all the celebrities who have second and third homes here will show up to be feted and photographed.

Maybe I'll keep Evan around until after that event. We'll finish on a high note, so to speak. Maybe he'll even let me keep my position at his event company because I've done such a great job. We can be friends, without benefits, going forward. Partners at work, but nothing more. Back to how it used to be.

As I drift to sleep, I think about the glittering event, and I realize I'll need to find a sitter soon if I want to attend anything, ever. I'll put that on my list, but at the same time I find myself wondering how you ever find someone you can trust. How do parents do this?

I've never felt so trapped in my life, not even with my soon-to-be ex-husband, Paul. I didn't feel trapped then, because I had a plan. And it worked. Now he's in prison and I'm enjoying spending his fortune just as fast as I can. I've become quite adept at that, to tell you the truth. So now, I find myself in a gilded cage of my own creation. It's a gorgeous home, a couple of miles and a world away from the mansion Paul and I shared when we moved here from Florida four years ago.

I need a plan for my life without Evan. I've taken charge of things before, with Paul and before him, and I can do it again. It will be fun, and freeing.

Truth is I'm terrified of cutting the cord with Evan. I'm not in love with him, but I love him. We used to have fun. We used to laugh. We created together—sparkling events and, well, the child in the nursery across the hall. But our relationship, such as it is, needs to end. Evan and I started as friends, and we used to have so much fun together. Ever since it turned romantic it also turned complicated, all stress, fights and disappointment. Peyton has, I'm afraid, brought out the worst in us as a couple. I know he knows it, too. I expect him to show up, to participate, to do at least half of the child-rearing duties. But he doesn't. It's like he's back in the 1950s and just wants a good photo with the baby every now and again. It's infuriating. He's absolutely no help.

And I'm beginning to suspect he's having an affair with someone in the office. His long hours, his lack of communication, his complete lack of interest in sex—although, truth be told, that is a relief. But it makes me suspicious. If I find proof, he's out.

But who will help me? I was alone for so much of my life, I don't want to be all alone again. Am I the perfect mother? No. But I know from experience I am better than nothing.

FIVE

LIZZIE

I'm just about to open my car door when Mr. Johnson grabs my arm, spinning me around so we're facing each other.

"How dare you," he says. "You called my wife! You little bitch. She says she's on her way home now. This is not what we hired you for."

"Neither is this," I say, pointing at his towel. "I told you I would call her. Let go of me." He drops my arm.

"You're going to ruin everything. You've got a good gig here, we all do," he says. "It's just a little party. You need to lighten up."

And that's when I know for certain that I must leave this place. He doesn't see anything wrong with inviting me to get naked and swim with him and these women. Nothing at all. He also doesn't seem to care that his wife is locked away in the bedroom most days, drowning her sorrows with Chardonnay.

As we stand on the driveway, I'm almost amused to see a parade of women, in different levels of dress and undress, scampering out the front door. I'm sure they're leaving a wet trail of pool water in their wake. I'm also sure I'm going to be expected to clean it up. I will refuse.

"You know what? Here's what I know to be true. There's right. And there's wrong. And this is wrong. And you're a parent? A dad. To four kids. So this is more than wrong," I say and yank the door to the car open. I don't have anywhere to go, but I'll hop inside and lock the door if he tries to grab me again. "You should be ashamed of yourself."

But he's not, he never will be. I happen to know from personal experience a parent like Mr. Johnson. I called him Dad, but I shouldn't have. I was a prop to him, a smiling cherub they brought out at the right time to show their friends he wasn't a self-centered monster. My mom was an angel, a stay-at-home mom who loved to cook, bake and take care of us. She was a ray of sunshine every day, while my dad was the dark force that would appear in the evening to douse the sun. I don't blame my mom, no, she was blinded by love for my dad, and was weak when it came to having her own voice, even when it mattered. My dad was the one who controlled everything, from beginning to end. He only agreed to have kids for a reason, because it was expected, not out of kindness to Mom and her dreams of being a parent. My dad looked at us like accessories, annoying little mouths to feed. But my baby sister Sally, when she came along, was a dream come true for me and my mom—an angel sent to ease the nightmare of living with my dad. I loved her like she was my own. She was such a perfect, sweet, beautiful baby. I miss my baby sister with an ache that I know can only be soothed, someday, by a baby of my own. That's my dream at least.

For a time, we seemed like the perfect family: big house, happy girls, perfect mother and wife. But we all know the perfect marriage is the perfect illusion, and wealth is relative, although we were considered rich in our town. But, as I found out, all of that can disappear in the blink of an eye.

Yes, I know this world, this life, not of course of Malibu-level wealth, but enough that I can relate. To the kids. To the

Johnson kids. What will happen to them with parents like these? I suppose they'll get by, like I did. I guess they get what they need from me in a way. I'm dependable, although the older they become, the more I realize I am not suited for teenagers. I mean, really, who is? But they'll be fine, just like I was.

Like I try to be.

Like I pretend to be.

I'm going to find a new job, I decide, as Mrs. Johnson pulls into the driveway. She has arrived in time to see the last straggler, a barely dressed woman, shimmy out the front door and slide into a waiting car.

Mrs. Johnson steps out of the car and slams the door. Her face is red with fury as she walks past me.

"Lizzie, go to your room," she says. "I can't believe you called me over. For what? There's nothing going on here."

I turn to look at her. Over her shoulder, I see Mr. Johnson smile.

They deserve each other, but they do not deserve me.

I nod and do as she says, leaving the Johnsons alone in their misery on the driveway. Although I'd love to hear the excuses he makes this time, if she even demands an answer from him, I have more pressing matters. I need to get my résumé together and start reviewing Malibu job postings. It's time. It's past time.

I think about Mr. Johnson wanting to see me naked—ugh—and run up the stairs to my room on the top floor, the attic really. The room is sparse: a single bed with a thin, white comforter, a white dresser of drawers, and bedside table from Ikea bought and assembled by me. And that's it. It is in stark contrast to the lavish and luxurious furnishings found in the rest of the home. It's a room that screams that I'm an afterthought—unimportant and tucked away, out of sight, out of mind.

Once I'm inside, I lock my door. I know he's mostly all bark and no bite, but I also know he's furious I told on him. *And he's walking around imagining me naked*, I remind myself. Once again, *ugh*.

I open my laptop and begin my search. I'm sure there are plenty of families that need my help, I just need to pick the right one this time. One kid, perhaps, that would be easy. Maybe a baby? I love babies. Yes, it's decided. I'm moving on. But to where?

SIX

CECILIA

I wake up the next morning, as always, to Peyton crying. Although this morning, it's not a frantic screech she's emitting, but more of a cooing cry, like a flock of doves has landed in the nursery. It's rather pleasant. I'll take it over the screeches any day. I glance over at Evan. He's still sleeping. I decide I cannot take it another minute.

"Wake up. The baby is awake," I say, shaking his arm. I pull the earplug out of his left ear for good measure.

"Geesh, take it easy. What time is it anyway?" Evan asks, yawning and sitting up.

"It's time to take care of the baby," I say. On cue, Peyton increases her volume over the monitor. She's transformed from a dove into a seagull.

"You have to handle her. I can't. I've got to get ready," Evan says. "The big event, remember?"

I cannot take this anymore. "People work and take care of children all the time, Evan," I say.

"Well, not when they have my kind of job, they don't," he says. His phone vibrates on his bedside table, and he glances at it. I move as quickly as I can with my bad back to the other side of the bed and grab it before he can. The text message is on his lock screen.

> *Can't wait to see you this morning. Last evening was fantastic. Heart emoji.*

"Hey, give me my phone," he shouts.

I feel like I've been punched, even though my intuition told me there must be someone else. "Who's Cassie?"

"What?" he says, stalling. "Cassie. She's... she's a new event manager."

I take a deep breath. "You talked me into having her," I say. It's a familiar refrain for him, I know, but it is the truth. I was contemplating ending the pregnancy. I mean, I'm so glad he did convince me because I love Peyton, she's my whole world, but of course I'm reluctant to tell Evan that at this moment. "And now you're screwing this Cassie tramp? You really have some nerve."

He wipes his eyes, trying to wake up. "I wish I hadn't... It's just that everything changed once the baby arrived. I mean, you barely want to touch me."

"What? Of course, everything changed once she arrived. That's what babies do," I say. "So is it the baby's fault you screwed her then? Do you wish you hadn't talked me into having a baby? And you're so selfish that it's all about you, right? That's why you hired someone to screw? Is that it?"

"No! Nothing... never mind." He looks away.

Peyton's screeches are sustained now, and on the verge of panic. I turn the monitor down but allow her to be my chorus.

"You're the worst, you know that? You wanted to have a baby with me, but then you don't want to spend any time with her because you're too important. The 1950s are calling and they want you back," I say. Sure, I know his business, I'm part of it. It's weekend hours, long hours. Event companies don't take days off, I get it. But when you own one, and you have a baby with a woman you supposedly love, well, you take the time. Or you don't, because you choose not to. "Having an affair with some young employee is just classic and clichéd, Evan. How dare you."

"You just don't understand what work means. You're spoiled," he says, any trace of regret gone and his face now turning red with anger. "This is the biggest event of the year for my company. I wish you would remember that. As for Cassie, it's nothing. It's just that I was lonely, you rejected me, I don't know... I was stupid. It won't happen again."

I look at him, and I really see him. And I do not like what I see. Not any longer. It's all over now, he's made certain of that. He seems to believe a simple apology is all it will take to get back into my good graces. His mother spoiled him growing up, gave him everything he ever wanted, he's admitted as much. It's about time this mommy's boy finds out that's not how the real world works. He needs to grow up and take responsibility for his actions. He talks a big game about being the perfect partner, but he doesn't know how it works. He doesn't know how to show up when the going gets tough. Instead, he turns to someone else. I will never forget this betrayal.

Peyton's cries disrupt my train of thought. She is all that matters. I throw his phone at him, before hurrying out the door and rushing to my baby's cribside. "It's ok. Mommy's here. I'm all you need."

After she calms down, I take a deep breath. I need to confront Evan. I need to end this charade. I walk across the hall and back into our bedroom. He's in the same spot, of course. Heaven forbid he actually get out of bed and come to me, to Peyton. To his family. My rage is on fire.

"Oh, you know what, Evan, I do remember you have the big event tonight. As you might recall, I'm the creative director who came up with this year's event theme, which everyone loves," I say. I cradle Peyton in my arms and take another deep breath. It's time. "You love to use work as an excuse to avoid the tough parts of a relationship. Go handle your big important event, Evan Dorsey. That's your true love, events and creating experiences that don't last. You're the best at it. Your mom ruined you. Telling you someday you'd be someone's Prince Charming. As if."

"Leave my mom out of this," he says. "I took care of you after you came home from Paris. I was there for you."

Such a momma's boy. I should have kept him as a friend, kept my heart safe. "You were there for me until I agreed to be more than friends. Then something flipped," I say. "Once we were a couple, you started taking me for granted. And once I got pregnant, well, it's as if you weren't attracted to me anymore. Reality set in as my stomach grew."

"That's not true," he says, but he knows it is. He looks away, suddenly transfixed by something in the corner of our bedroom.

"You can't handle the tough stuff in a relationship, Evan," I say. "Instead, you bail. And then you find someone else. Where it's less complicated, less messy. Relationships are messy, especially once a baby is involved. That's the truth. Oh, and tell Cassie hi for me. Things will be much simpler for the two of you now. No more sneaking around. Isn't that nice? Or was that part of the fun, Prince Charming?"

"Look, you need to calm down. You're tired," he says, rubbing sleep out of his own eyes.

"You're right. I am tired. Of you. How long have you been with her?" I remain standing by the bed, rocking Peyton back and forth in my arms.

"Only a couple of months. It's nothing, really," he says. "She means nothing to me. You're the love of my life."

I can tell he's lying. "Sure, whatever. I was the love of your life in your imagination, but then I turned into a mother. Go handle your event. And don't come back, do you understand? We're over."

"What? You don't mean that." Evan appears to be very awake now as he jumps up. We glare at each other over the bed. A bed we used to make love in, but not anymore. Those days seem so distant now. I guess now I know why he stopped trying. Cassie.

"I mean it. Clear out your things. We're over."

"We're not. You need me. You love me. We're a team," Evan argues. "You're my dream girl."

I'm much more than that. "I am the mother of your child. But it doesn't matter. Face it, Evan, we were always supposed to stay friends and coworkers. And I love working with you, so we'll still have that."

Evan stares at me, then shakes his head incredulously. "You can't break up with me and still work for me. If we're over, we're over."

"Fine. Fire me," I say. And then, before I can change my mind, I hurry out of the room and across the hall to the nursery, a nursery filled with the best furniture and accessories money can buy. All picked out and paid for by me. It's such a special room. Despite being back in her beautiful nursery, Peyton is fussy, no doubt sensing the tension between us, but I pat her little back and she begins to calm down.

"Mommy's here, and I always will be. Daddy is a cheater and absolutely worthless when it comes to you. It's going to be ok, though. Everything is. We've got each other, and that's all we need," I say. And I hope I'm right.

After a diaper change and a bottle, Peyton is a different, happy baby, and I carry her downstairs. I'm feeling good, too, resolved, and relieved. Evan comes into the kitchen, two large suitcases trailing behind him. I don't want to talk about this, I just want him to leave.

"I'll have to come back, for the rest of my things," he says. He's trying to act tough, defiant, but he looks more guilty.

"Fine," I say. "Text me and we'll figure something out."

I cannot believe I let him talk me into all of this. First trying things out as a couple, then him moving in with me, to help me recover. As if. I smile at my little princess in her playpen. I am so happy she's here, even though she was an accident.

"Why? There's nothing with Cassie. I only want you and Peyton—please, I'll take care of her all weekend, I'll get up in the night when she cries. Just give me another chance? You can paint again. That would make you happy, right?" he asks. He looks pathetic. Is he trying to cry? The whites of his blue eyes have turned red, so I guess those are real tears. The stubbly beard I used to find attractive now looks contrived. I don't know why I let this relationship go on so long. I was needy, and that's not me. My ex, Paul, pushed me into this situation. But I've had enough.

"You're right, I do need to paint again, but first, I'm going to take care of my baby. Alone, as usual. And it's fine. Because I don't love you, not like I need to. Because you never touch me anymore, because you like the idea of us more than the reality of me and Peyton. I'm exhausted and you do nothing for me, or her," I say, pointing at the baby. Incredibly, as I'm pouring my heart out to him, he gets distracted by his phone. Of course.

"Oh, is that Cassie texting again?" I say sarcastically. I never even suspected another woman until a couple days ago, but I should have. Always. "Even while we're breaking up, you're on the phone to somebody else. You weren't even in the room when your daughter was delivered after twelve hours of labor. You can't handle real life."

"I got there, just after," he says, slipping his phone in his pocket. "I had stuff... well, never mind."

"You aren't here for us. You know it's true. Now get out."

Evan pushes his hand through his hair, clearly a bit

stunned. "Wow. You really think that? What about her? She needs a dad."

"Peyton barely has a dad. You're too focused on your stupid events, and, it turns out, Cassie. Peyton doesn't need you for anything. I'm the only one she needs. Goodbye, Evan," I say. I stifle a yawn.

"But she's my baby, I'm her dad," he argues.

I shrug. "You don't act like one. We don't need you." It seems as if he has only just realized he hasn't been very present for the first time. Doesn't matter. I've erased his role in my mind. He appears to be in shock, mouth open, gaping. Not attractive.

"What about my mom? She's going to expect to see Peyton," he says. "She deserves to see her only granddaughter."

Of course he brings up his mom. "No, she doesn't. It's not like Marian's been around that much anyway. Peyton won't remember her, or you," I say. I know that sounds mean, but it is a fact. We're moving on, even though I suppose it might be convenient for Marian to babysit. I wonder if Marian knows about Cassie?

"You know, you've turned into *him*," Evan says, his blue eyes flashing with anger now.

"Don't be ridiculous," I say. "Are you referring to Paul? I'm nothing like him."

He shakes his head. "Selfish, only thinking about yourself, isn't that how you described Paul? Vindictive, too, I might add." He's grabbed onto the handles of both suitcases now. "You'll end up just like him, alone."

"Please, spare me the theatrics. You're the cheater, Evan. You're the one who isn't able to cope with the responsibilities of a long-term partner and daughter. As you'll recall, Paul is in prison. He tried to kill me," I say. "I'm nothing like him." I stand up and point to the door. "Just go, Evan. Like I said earlier, we're over. Go cry on your mommy's shoulder."

Evan takes a deep breath, starts to say something else, but shakes his head and walks away, the suitcases trailing behind him. I follow him to the front door. He yanks it open and rolls his suitcases out. I do feel a moment of sadness, and a bit of fear. What if I did the wrong thing out of pure exhaustion? No, I need to trust myself.

Evan stares at me, one last time, from the driveway. Can he see the truth in my eyes, finally?

"We have a daughter together. We'll never be over," he calls, opening his car door.

"I have a daughter. And it turns out you have a lover. We are over," I call back from the front step. When he gets inside his car, I walk back inside the house, slam the door closed, lock it, and turn on the alarm.

My heart beats quickly in my chest as a stabbing pain shoots down my legs from my back. I double over until the pain subsides. I know this is the right decision, for me and for Peyton, but I can't help feeling incredibly alone. First Paul betrays me, tries to kill me, and still hasn't signed the divorce papers. And now Evan betrays me and acts as if he'll always be in my life. Our lives. He won't be.

I'm startled by a knock on the door. Oh my god, he is relentless. I disable the alarm and pull open the door.

"I said goodbye. Forever," I say, before noticing the man at the front door is not Evan.

"Hello, Mrs. Strom?" the man says. He keeps a professional demeanor even though I notice his lip twitch in amusement. "I'm a delivery driver from your law firm. I have this for you. From your husband."

I take a deep breath. "Is it the divorce papers? Did he finally sign?"

"I don't know, ma'am, but your attorney, Mr. Baxter, says the letter is a step in the right direction and thought you should see it. Have a good day!"

He hands me a manila envelope and walks away. I'd recognize the writing anywhere. My heart beats faster as I hurry back inside, shutting and locking the front door behind me. *I need to change the locks*, I remind myself. A guy like Evan probably isn't the revenge type. But Paul definitely is.

I walk back into the large, open kitchen—white countertops, white cabinets, white everywhere—and then on into the family room just beyond, where Peyton is still happily occupied in her playpen. I have the fancy designer playpen set up so she has a great view of the backyard and the pool through the sliding glass windows, and a view of me in the kitchen, of course.

I take a deep breath and tell myself to calm down. His writing alone has my hands shaking. The envelope isn't addressed, it just has my name written on the front. I rip it open, filled with hope that he has finally agreed to sign the divorce papers. I haven't heard from him since he went to prison, and I don't want to. All I want is a divorce. But Paul may have other ideas.

My dearest, darling Cecilia,

Surprise! I found you! Actually, I haven't but this letter should make its way to you via my attorneys and yours, who because of your insistence on this silly divorce, are an expensive courier system, and nothing more. Where do I even begin? Our story, it's so complex, so full of misunderstandings but also so full of love, don't you agree? As part of my efforts to change my ways, my prison counselor suggested I write to you and apologize for my actions. And I do. But as you well know, my darling, it takes two to tango as they say. And we certainly did tango in Paris. I still remember the love in your bright green eyes, oh, and the tears, too. That last evening together was, well, memorable to say the least. But let's leave that in the past, shall we? I will serve my time for my burst of aggression and then, I will come to you, as you know I will. We have so much more to do together, and so much more money to spend together. You are taking good care of my fortune, aren't you, darling? Do be sure of that. While I agreed to share it with you as part of our little pact to keep me from a harsher prison sentence, I did not agree for you to have it all.

Please write back to me when you have a moment. I'd welcome an update on all things, Cecilia Strom. What's new, my gorgeous wife? Oh, and I do know you'd like the divorce papers signed, and that, in fact, you may have opened this letter expecting to find those documents enclosed. They aren't. I've inserted some blank sheets of paper to give this envelope some girth. So you wouldn't miss it.

I miss you, my gorgeous, sneaky wife. I know you miss me, too.

All my love,

Paul

SEVEN

LIZZIE

I watch her as she waits in line to order a coffee at the super-trendy, celebrity-luring new spot in town. Like me, everybody comes here for coffee, and to be seen. Today I happen to have little Jimmy with me, but often I'm here just taking it all in by myself. I think of Mr. Johnson's unbelievable behavior yesterday and look down at Jimmy standing next to me, innocent and adorable. I hope he doesn't become his dad someday.

"You want your usual, right?" I ask him, referring to a sugary frozen mess of a drink that amps him up, one that his mom wouldn't allow, but also makes him happy. He wanted to hang out today, and I agreed. I called him in sick, even though he isn't.

"Yes, please!" he says.

"Good manners," I say, smiling at him.

"Hey, look, it's Kimmie," Jimmy says, pointing at his oldest sister.

"It is," I say, watching as the designer-clad oldest Johnson drapes an arm around her friend as they place an order, oblivious to everyone and everything around her.

"She's skipping school, too," he says, eyes big. He's easily impressed, this one.

"She should be at school. She shouldn't be here," I say. "Hold our place in line."

I walk over to the counter where Kimmie and her friend, who is dressed in head-to-toe bright yellow Chanel to match Kimmie's hot-pink Chanel, are giggling and chatting like teenaged Barbie dolls waiting for their order. I notice, as I make my way over, that Kimmie is paying for both drinks. Of course she is. She already has a platinum card. I tap her on the shoulder, and she spins around, blonde curls flying.

"What?" she says, blinking at me. "Why are you here?"

"I could ask the same question," I say. I hope she doesn't notice her little brother standing in line. I would lose the moral high ground in a flash. "Aren't you supposed to be in school?"

"We're going back as soon as we get our drinks," she says. The hand on hip adds a dramatic flair. "Not that it's any of your business."

I turn to her friend. "Hi, I'm Lizzie, Kimmie's nanny. And you are?"

The girl has incredibly large breasts and lips that appear enhanced, two puffy pillows. *Why?* "I'm Ali. Nice to meet you."

Kimmie rolls her eyes. "Can you leave us alone now?"

"How did you guys get here?" I ask.

"Ali drove us. She just got her license, and that new G Wagon out there is hers," Kimmie says, beaming. "She's like my big sister, sort of a sorority. For high school. You wouldn't understand."

I would, not that she'd believe that. "Well, I hope you two don't get busted. Don't fake my signature on anything."

Kimmie smiles. "Would I do that?"

I smile back. "You would. But don't. Nice to meet you, Ali."

Kimmie's drinks appear and the two of them give me the once-over and saunter out of the coffee shop, not even noticing

Jimmy. Fortunately, and not surprisingly. Kimmie is all about Kimmie.

I walk back over to Jimmy. "Sorry about that. Thanks for holding our spot."

"No problem. Did Kimmie call in sick, too?" he asks.

"Something like that," I say. "But remember, you weren't here. You didn't see anything."

He nods solemnly. "Of course. Mommy will be napping by the time I get home anyway."

Yes, her usual day-drinking followed by napping as soon as the kids arrive home from school. "Maybe she'll be awake today. But remember, you have to keep our secret."

He nods seriously. "Promise. But she *will* be asleep. She always is."

I go back to watching the woman with the baby. She must know this is the trendiest spot, yet she looks terrible, nothing like the put-together, high-fashion model she appeared to be before she had the baby. I almost don't recognize her anymore. I've been coming here for over a year, and so I know all the regulars now. If this is what having a kid does to you, well, maybe I need to rethink my ambition. But I suppose you just need to know how to handle them. My mom was a pro, she was a nurturer by nature, and I like to think the apple doesn't fall far from the tree. Babies love me, little kids do, too. Maybe it's because they sense I have so much love left to give, love I didn't have a chance to give to Sally once she was gone. I take a deep breath. I miss Sally, and my mom. *My perfect mom.*

I shake my head, push away those thoughts and focus on her. Seeing her as disheveled as she is, I guess makes me feel better about myself in a small way. I'm what you would call overlookable—wearing an almost threadbare t-shirt and jeans—and with the way she's dressed now, in faded jeans, a white t-shirt and oversized dark sunglasses, her hair messily tied up on top of her head, for once she is overlookable, too.

Who am I kidding? She still looks like a million bucks, and I'm still what most people would describe as a plain Jane: thin, stringy brown hair, brown eyes, and a slightly too large nose. I wear large black glasses, not because I need them, but because I think they make me more interesting. Still, as usual, no one notices me. Everyone notices her, even now, when she's so run-down, she still makes a buzz ripple through the coffee shop. People are trying to figure out if she's famous, if she's an actress, if they should ask for an autograph, or a date. We've both been here at the same time before, many times in fact, but nobody notices me, especially not someone like her.

And then the hip vibe and the laughter and chatting are shattered as the baby starts to cry in the stroller. I watch her face flush. She bends down awkwardly and stiffly, her hand to her lower back, and picks up the baby, who cries even harder. She was so close to ordering her coffee, but now, she'll need to step outside, lose her place in line, miss her caffeine hit.

Jimmy puts his hands over his ears. "Ow! It's so loud."

I smile at him. "You were once like that." I take his hand and hurry to her side, pushing through the crowd.

"Can I help you?" I ask. I am smiling my sweetest smile, and I'm sure I look very trustworthy with Jimmy's grubby hand in mine. "Maybe I could place your order for you while you settle the baby?"

"Babies are too loud," Jimmy chimes in.

"I do need help, thank you," she says, her face still flushed with embarrassment as she nods at Jimmy and then locks eyes with me. Her eyes flash with panic.

"I get it. I'm a nanny. I've seen it before. Jimmy here has two sisters and a brother. One time I took them to the beach, when I'd just started working for the family, and they all four scattered like sand crabs. I couldn't keep track of them all. It was crazy. Eventually, I learned how to keep the kids in sight and organized. You learn as you go, and I've had a lot of experience by now. Anyway, like I said, I get it. What can I order for you?" I ask with another patient smile.

"An iced venti caffè americano, extra shot, please." She hands me a credit card with a shaking hand and hurries out the door. "Please, get yourself and your little boy something on me, too."

She's trusting, I like that in a person, especially a gorgeous person who has everything. Who just gives their credit card to a stranger though? I could just walk out the door with it. She's not thinking clearly. I guess she's desperate.

But I do as promised. I order and wait for her drink, and ours, hoping I got the complicated order right and thinking about my future.

"Drinks ready for Lizzie," a voice says, breaking me out of my thoughts.

"Yay," Jimmy says, grabbing the frothy pink sugar creation with a big smile.

"Come on. We need to take the lady her drink," I say. I grab the drink and hurry outside. She's sitting on a picnic table bench, the baby obviously settled and back in the stroller. The baby blinks her beautiful green eyes and gives me a crooked smile as her binky falls out of her mouth. My baby sister had a smile just like hers. I reach into the stroller and put the binky back in her mouth. She's adorable.

"Here you go," I say, handing the woman her drink and the credit card.

"You're a lifesaver. Thank you. You too, little guy." She smiles at Jimmy. She takes a sip of her drink and closes her eyes.

Wait. I want to keep this conversation going. "I'm Lizzie, by the way," I say. "Happy to help. It's sort of what I do."

She opens her eyes and gives me a tired smile before looking at the baby in the stroller.

"Yep, I'm a helper. Oh, well, officially I'm a nanny. We take care of people," I say. It's true. We help the moms, sometimes more than the kids. Child-rearing isn't easy. Jimmy has found a stick and is having a sword fight with the picnic table as we talk.

"That's nice. I'm Cecilia," she says, and sighs as if a conversation with me is the worst thing she could imagine. "Do you nanny here in Malibu?" she asks.

"Yep. The Johnsons. Jimmy is the youngest. They live on Fernwood," I say. "Rambling house, Mercedes out front. Been there a couple years."

She shrugs. "I live on Fernwood, too. I must admit though, I haven't made an effort to meet the neighbors, especially since she came along."

I look at the little girl now asleep again in the stroller, perfect pink cheeks, soft blonde hair. A beautiful baby. She looks just like her mom.

"Understandable. I'd spend all my time with her, too. She's adorable," I say. "What's her name?"

"Peyton," she says with a smile. She seems to be enjoying our conversation a bit more.

"Lovely," I say. "She looks just like you. A little mini me. You're so lucky."

Her eyes fill with tears. *Oh no, I've upset her*. "I'm sorry. I didn't mean to make you cry."

She dabs at her eyes with a tissue. "No, it's not you. It's, well, my partner and I broke up. I kicked him out. He was cheating on me."

"Oh my gosh. And you have a baby!" I say.

"Why do men have to be such jerks?" Cecilia laughs wryly and sniffs. "I mean it. Why?"

I laugh, too, happy to see the tears have almost dried up. "You know, I was just wondering the same thing. I don't think they can help themselves sometimes," I say, and think about Mr. Johnson, and the dad in the family before them—how he'd take photos of me without my permission, how he'd try to get me to watch TV with him in his study after the kids went to bed. Creepy. "It's upsetting, really."

"It is," she says. "Who needs them?"

"Agree," I say, and clink my coffee cup against hers in solidarity. I check my watch. It's almost time to pick up the oldest boy and take him to the dentist. Ugh. My life. I glance at Jimmy, still fighting the picnic table. "Jimmy, it's time to go!"

I smile as he runs to me, giving me a big hug. "Ok, Lizzie. Where to next?" He is hopping up and down, raring to go. That drink does it every time. I think it's cute.

"You'll see, buddy, but you'll need to leave your stick here," I say.

"But it's my pirate sword," he says with a pout.

"Leave it, please," I say to him before turning to Cecilia. "It was so nice to talk to you. We have to go, but if you need me, need help with the baby, please reach out. I can give you my number?"

"Sure." Cecilia hands me her phone and I add myself as a contact.

"I put Nanny Lizzie in as my name so you can find me," I say, handing her phone back.

"Thanks, um... but I'm sure you're completely busy and happy with the Johnsons?" she says quietly.

I drop my voice so Jimmy can't overhear the conversation. "I'm busy, but I'm not exactly happy. I'm ready to move on." I don't want to be too pushy, but I do want another baby to take care of. "I adore Jimmy, but he's getting so big and soon he won't need me. Your little girl is such a darling and I just love babies. I'm super experienced with them. I've taken care of dozens of them." A bit of an exaggeration, but she seems like she needs reassurance. I *do* love babies.

"Wow, well, good on you," she says. She takes another sip of her iced coffee drink and watches me with growing interest. She's managed to put on some red lipstick today, and it leaves a mark on the side of the coffee cup, the ghost of a kiss. "I find this stage kind of hard, to be honest," she continues. "I don't know what Peyton wants most of the time. And she cries all the time and wakes me up at all hours of the night. I need a good night's sleep. I'm exhausted. I have this back injury... and I'm in so much pain, and, well, if I'm honest, I'm also really sad." She looks down at the ground and kicks a piece of gravel, likely embarrassed she's confessed her feelings.

I'm surprised by her admission. Most moms don't admit to the baby blues to strangers, but I am a sympathetic sponge. Full-on empath, that's me. Sort of.

"I bet you're sad and exhausted, that's normal. Every mom I've worked for felt the exact same way. You aren't alone," I say. *But you do look terribly sleep-deprived*, I don't say. I check my watch again. Now I'm going to be late. "Well, you've got my number."

"Thanks again for grabbing the coffee," she says. She gives us a dazzling smile and a little wave. "Bye, Jimmy."

"Bye," Jimmy says, still amped up from his drink. His brow is damp with sweat and his pants are dusty from crawling under the picnic table. "What's our next adventure, Lizzie?"

"The dentist," I say. "For your brother. He'll be waiting for us at school in the office. Likely upset because we're late."

"Ugh," he says.

"Come on, if you're good, I'll take you someplace special for lunch," I say.

"Ok," he says. "I like sick days. At least sick days like this when I'm not really sick."

"Me, too," I say grabbing his hand as we reach the parking lot.

As we walk away, I know she's watching me, and watching how I am with Jimmy. I bend down and give his sweaty forehead a little kiss. *You need me, Cecilia. You know it. I know it.* I unlock the door to the ridiculous minivan but remember to force a confident smile on my face despite my unfashionable ride. Someone like Cecilia would understand that the nanny transports the children in the car provided to her. But it should be sleek, and safe. A Volvo perhaps. Yes, that's what Cecilia would provide for her nanny, I imagine.

I pull out of the parking lot and head toward the middle school. Johnny is a sixth grader who thinks he's the coolest kid in school. He also thinks he's far too cool for me, and far too old for a nanny. He will tell his mom that I was late unless I figure out a way to bribe him.

I park in the drop-off only spot in front of the school and Jimmy and I trot inside to the office. Johnny sees me and smiles before crossing his arms over his chest, remembering he's angry. He does his best imitation of a pout but he's too happy to get out of school to hold the look for long. I sign the form to release him to my care as he joins me and Jimmy.

"You're late," he says. His once sandy blond hair is turning darker with age, and his once easy demeanor has hardened into mistrust. I don't know what he knows about his dad's activities, but it must be in the atmosphere in the home. I feel sorry for him, I do. This is why babies are so much easier.

"Sorry. Traffic," I say, patting the top of his head. "Come on. If we hurry, we won't keep the dentist waiting."

"Can we go get a burrito after? I won't tell anyone you were late if we can go to lunch," Johnny says. He's a deal maker, like his dad.

He's lucky I like burritos, too. "Sure. Sounds like a good idea to me."

"Me too," Jimmy says.

"Yay," Johnny says, sliding into the backseat. "It will be our secret."

It's interesting, really. To keep this secret, all it takes is a burrito. If only all of life were that simple.

I think about Cecilia, the desperation in her eyes, the

exhaustion. And that precious little baby girl who just wants a schedule and a reliable caregiver. It's what all babies want but this generation, well, we tend to be a bit too self-absorbed to realize such things. It's so easy to see the problem when you're not the one in the middle of the chaos. They need me, Cecilia and her baby, and it's almost as if I need them, too. If she calls and says she wants my help, I will jump at the chance. Mrs. Johnson better not try to enforce the employment contract. Hopefully, she'll let me move on graciously, but if not, well, I'll tell her I know about her secret day-drinking issue. I'll tell her she's an addict, and an unfit mom. But who am I to judge?

Do what you'd like, Mrs. Johnson, but if you try to get in my way, or stop me from getting what I want, you'll be surprised how tough Nanny Lizzie can be.

Thank you so much for coming by today. You have no idea what it meant to me. You are my first visitor since I've been locked away in this godforsaken place. I enjoyed all your stories, and I hope you enjoyed mine. Please do, if you find the time, come back again. We have so much more to talk about. You know where to find me. It's not like I'm going anywhere, not anytime soon. Although, we both know I'm trying.

Have a great day,

Paul

EIGHT

CECILIA

Well, that was embarrassing and awkward. Now that Peyton has settled down in her stroller, a top-of-the-line model that cost a fortune, I think back on how stressed out and at the end of my rope I was when she started to cry inside the coffee shop. *I need to learn how to better handle the baby in public*, I decide. Other moms do it every day. What is wrong with me? Her meltdowns don't have to become mine. But somehow, they always do. But I will fix this. That's my new mantra.

I'd left the house in a fury after reading Paul's creepy note and realizing he hadn't signed the divorce papers and that I'm likely going to have to go to court to force the matter. I needed coffee, since I'm out of coffee and mostly everything else because I forgot to place my grocery order for delivery. I'm forgetting everything lately. So I figured, why not go on an excursion with Peyton? And, luckily, she fell asleep as soon as we drove out of the driveway. I was feeling confident and calm. But it didn't last.

When we arrived home, I realized I had left the front door wide open. My heart pounded with fear. I parked the car in the driveway and locked Peyton inside. I raced up the front walkway and searched the entire house quickly, making sure no one had made their way inside. Convinced it was safe, I carried Peyton in and shut and locked the door, turning on the alarm, my heart racing and my body covered in sweat.

How could I be so forgetful, so careless? A combination of sleep deprivation and constant pain are taking their toll. I remember to take a pain pill as I smile at Peyton now gurgling in her baby swing. She's behaving perfectly, a tiny angel, unlike my estranged, in-prison, soon-to-be ex-husband.

Paul also upended my day. He doesn't know about Peyton, of course, although he suspected Evan and I had an attraction and was threatened by him during our marriage, long before our tragic anniversary trip to Paris. Evan and I did have a strong bond for a bit, I'll admit it, but if I'm being honest, he was just someone to talk to, someone who wasn't Paul. A good friend who should never have become a lover. I pick up the letter again. My *dearest, darling*. He only wants the money, and control, I know that. I suppose he thinks that keeping us legally married means I'm tethered to him.

The doorbell rings and Peyton starts to cry. Of course. I have a sign up at the gate and the front door begging people not to ring the doorbell, but no one reads it or cares. I pick up the crying baby and grab a pacifier from the counter and stick it in her mouth. It works, thank goodness. *She is a good baby*, I remind myself. I reach the front door and see who is standing on the porch. Now I know this is the worst day ever. It's Evan's mother, Marian Dorsey. Her red hair looks fiery in the bright sunshine and her bright red lipstick completes the look. I brace myself for the inferno.

"Hello, Marian," I say, opening the door. "It's not a good time."

"What does that even mean?" She pushes past me into the

house. "We need to talk, young lady. I'm missing my bridge game to talk to you."

Ugh. I hate it when people *young lady* me. I'm a 35-year-old woman with a baby—young is in the rearview mirror and lady never really fit, anyway. I follow Marian to my kitchen where she proceeds to plop her oversized designer purse on my kitchen counter before walking to the refrigerator and helping herself to an iced tea. Peyton needs a bottle, so I grab one from the refrigerator door. We all have what we need for battle, I suppose.

"Ooh, let me give her the bottle, please," Marian says, scurrying over to Peyton and picking her up in her arms. Peyton doesn't put up a fuss as Marian settles herself at the kitchen table. I reluctantly hand her the bottle and Peyton begins to gulp down her formula.

I take a moment to stare out at the sparkling ocean and draw in a deep breath. For a moment, I imagine walking away, walking out the back door, crossing the pool area and leaving through the back gate. But I can't. This is my home. My choices.

"What is there to talk about, Marian?" I ask. I notice I'm drumming my fingers on the kitchen counter and stop. "It's been a long day and it's only the early afternoon."

"Yes, you do look unhinged. You kicked my son out this morning, I understand?" she says. Her red lips form a deep frown. Everything about her demeanor is lined and sagging, like an angry elephant with a sunburn.

"You understand correctly. We are over, but I wish him well," I say. I notice a catch in my throat. I will miss him, as a friend. "Evan and I had a good relationship, but it wasn't meant to last. And he has his flourishing company to tend to, which, I might add, grew with my help. And not to mention the new facility and commercial kitchen I bought for him. So, he's all set. I just couldn't take his laziness toward me and the baby, his lack of attention. All he cares about is the company, and his cell phone. This morning, his noise-cancelling earphones, well, they were the last straw. He completely tuned the baby out. Unacceptable. You know that as well as I do."

"My son is busy working hard to provide for you girls. He loves you both. Sure, he's distracted, most men are, and romance is tough with a baby around," she says and places Peyton over her shoulder. I reluctantly hand her a burp towel. "That's what us women are for. We hold down the home front. It's our job."

"No, parenting is a shared job. At least it should be," I say. "And it wasn't only work distracting him. Ask him about Cassie, the new event manager at the office."

Her eyes narrow. She didn't know about Cassie, it appears. "Look, I know how much Evan loves you, and you and I both know boys will be boys. Having a baby is tough, and I agree he should be helping more and I'm sorry about that. I raised him better," she says. "I'll talk to him, dear."

Now it's my turn to frown. "I'm afraid there is nothing left to talk about. Evan can't handle the reality of a committed relationship, you know, for better or for worse? That's a fact. Maybe you shouldn't have told him he was perfect and a prince the whole time he was growing up. Who knows? You need to go. I don't need you butting in. Go meet Cassie, maybe she'll give you a grandkid someday. I've made my decision."

"And the baby?" she asks. "When will I get to see my granddaughter?"

I smile. "You hardly see her anyway." I take Peyton from her, walk away and place her in her playpen. I don't want her around all this negative energy.

"Yes I do, as much as you'll let me. You're the problem. Not me. Not my son. You need to let me see her more. I demand it." Marian's voice rises. "I love her. I *will* be in her life."

I move back over to the kitchen island where she sits and stare at her with the disgust I feel. I take a deep breath and keep my voice quiet and calm, for Peyton's sake.

"You love the idea of her. You've barely seen her since she

was born. You're busy, I get it. But whatever you do all day seems to be far more important than Peyton." The nerve of her acting like she's the grandma of the year.

"You don't know me. You've never given me a chance. You're all stuck-up and hoity-toity—*you're* the one who acts like some kind of princess," she says. "God knows I've tried to be here for you, and Evan and sweet little Pey Pey."

"Don't call her that," I say. "I hate that nickname."

"Fine. Whatever you want, just let me see my granddaughter," she says.

I look at her. "Perhaps we can work something out. Evan will owe a ton of child support," I say. "He hasn't paid for anything."

"That's because you're filthy rich, because you stole your husband's money," Marian says, eyes narrowing. "But anyway, yes, of course, my son needs to contribute to his daughter's welfare. I'm sure he has."

"Not true," I say, staring at her. "Peyton needs her nap. And I need some peace. You need to get out of here. We're done."

"Why don't we come to an agreement? I could watch Pey Pey, I mean the baby, twice a week, for free," she says softly, a snake in the grass.

"Don't most grandparents watch their granddaughters for free?" I say, shaking my head.

"No, not all," she says. "My friend Jane Applebaum charges her daughter-in-law twenty dollars an hour. Money doesn't grow on trees for all of us, dear."

"And you'd do it out of the kindness of your heart?" I ask.

"Yes, I would." She looks at her hands. "And for Evan, my wonderful son. It's his baby, too."

She's exhausting me, and I don't believe her. I stand up. "You need to leave. The baby and I need a nap."

Marian stands slowly, shakes her head. "It's a shame. You

look terrible. You've really let yourself go. Have you even painted anything since she arrived? Done anything productive? If you would have taken care of yourself, he'd have no need to go elsewhere. Any woman knows this. Have you gained weight? And your hair. It's so dull. No wonder it got so hard for you and Evan. It's clear you need help and here I am. Don't bite the hand that feeds you. We can make this work. I can be here for you and little Peyton."

"Get out," I say, between clenched teeth. "You've never been here for me or the baby, and I don't want you here now. Get out, and don't come back ever again." I point toward the foyer and the front door beyond.

"It's sad, Cecilia, all you don't know, all you'll never know about being a proper parent to a child. Good luck. And I know you'll be calling me because you need help. Just look at you," she says as she walks out of the kitchen. I will not see her out, but I'm relieved when she finally slams the front door. The sound startles Peyton and she begins to cry. Of course.

"It's ok, baby." I hurry over to the playpen.

When I bend and reach forward to pick her up, I feel a stab, like a knife, in my lower back. The pain is excruciating. Peyton is wailing, I'm crying now, too. Instead of picking her up, I climb into the playpen and lie down next to her on my back, my knees bent to try to relieve the pulsing pain in my lower spine. Peyton settles for the moment, a little stunned to have me invading her space.

"Hi, baby," I say through the tears. "Isn't this fun?" Another searing pain shoots through me, starting from my sacrum that hasn't fully healed, and likely never will. I'll never forget those hours of excruciating pain, laboring alone, Evan somewhere on his phone. I thought I was going to die.

I smile at Peyton. "But you are worth all this pain. I'll try to be a better mom, I will," I say. Was it yesterday morning I left the front door open by accident? Or maybe it was this morning? Time is blurring together, I realize, as a chill runs down my spine alongside the pain. For Peyton's sake, I cannot be this way. Distracted, exhausted. She needs me alert, attentive, careful. She needs protecting, my tiny one. What she doesn't need is a parent who leaves the door wide open by accident. I wonder what else I've done wrong?

I need help, I do. I thought I could do it on my own. I was doing it anyway with Evan here. But now I know I can't do it, at least not right now. I have all the money in the world, but I don't have the strength to do this by myself, I realize that now. I pull out my phone and search my contacts. There she is. Lizzie, the nanny, the woman who helped me at the coffee shop. I text her:

Hi. It's Cecilia from the coffee shop. Would you be available this evening for a chat about maybe working here?

I push send and hope for the best. She seems trustworthy and earnest and kind, she was great with the little boy she was taking care of. She has experience with babies, unlike me. A family on my own street trusts her with their kids.

She texts back.

I'll come by around 8 p.m. The kids will be in bed by then. See you then!

I'm so relieved, despite the pain in my back, and the fact I don't know her, and the nagging warning signs going off somewhere in the back of my brain telling me not to trust anyone ever again. I guess, if I'm honest, Evan's disregard for me and Peyton hurts more than I let on. It was sad and frustrating all at the same time. It was as if once he had me, and I had Peyton, he could go back to his life as it was. That's just not how it works.

I stare up at the cheerful mobile hanging over us as we lay

side by side in the playpen. Only a couple more hours until help arrives. The stars, rainbows, the sun, the moon seem to tell me everything is going to be ok. I'd like to believe that, that I'm making the right decisions, that we're better off without Evan, and hiring a nanny is a good idea. I guess we'll see.

NINE

LIZZIE

The burrito bribe worked, at least so far, as little Jimmy—as I think of him—hasn't said a word to his mom about our pretend sick day or my tardy pick-up of his brother. I knew Johnny wouldn't because he's getting to the age that he doesn't tell anyone anything, especially his mom. That little issue averted, I finish cleaning the dishes and start the dishwasher. I've made my famous—well, not *really* famous but it's a hit around here—lasagna for dinner tonight. The kids all like the meal as long as I have plenty of parmesan cheese available.

Mrs. Johnson walks by me as she heads to the family room to say hello to the kids. She looks a little disheveled, for sure, but she's humming to herself as she passes. She's clearly had a lot to drink today, likely in an effort to erase the unsightly memories of all the naked women in her swimming pool. Whatever works, I guess. I'm surprised she's not napping.

"Smells great," she says. "Which makes a change. Usually whatever you make isn't very appealing."

That's not true. I'm a great cook, just like my mom was. I ignore her usual insult. "Thanks. I'll be going out about seven thirty tonight, but I won't be late," I say.

She stops at the doorway and turns to face me. "Do you have a date?" She has a weird smile on her face, likely due to her wine stash. But I have to hand it to her, at least she's up and out of her bedroom and appears almost maternal. I watch as she hugs Jimmy and asks Kimmie about homework. Mr. Johnson is nowhere to be seen—likely off on some important business trip where he can go to finish his pool party.

"No," I say. "I just need to run some errands." The way she's still looking at me makes my face flush. One of her diamonds, either in her ears or on her fingers or skinny wrists, flashes at me. Mr. Johnson makes up for his regular absences and dalliances with an avalanche of sparkling and expensive jewelry. He's going to need to bring a doozy back when he gets out of the doghouse for the naked pool party. I've noticed her wearing everything she's got these days. She is dripping in diamonds. I doubt Mr. Johnson has even noticed.

"I think you're lying," she says, still smiling. "And I also think you should up your game, if you know what I mean."

I swallow. I am lying, but not about a date. I am going to get a new job. I am. Tonight.

"No, I'm not, but what do you mean?" I say.

"I mean how about some makeup, and an outfit that helps you stand out? One of Kimmie's dresses would fit you, I bet. Want to go grab one?" she says. "You need to make a good first impression on men. Trust me."

"It's not a date," I say. I sound defensive and lame, even to myself. "But really, it's just a friend I'm meeting. *She* doesn't care what I wear."

She smiles that weird smile again. "Well, ok, don't be gone too long and don't do anything I wouldn't do." She walks away, humming again.

I almost confront her, right then and there. I almost tell her I know what she's doing every day in her bedroom, how much Chardonnay she drinks, but I don't. I shake my head and busy myself setting the table for five—the Johnsons told me when I was hired that a good nanny never dines with the family—and once everything is perfect, I head up to my room to change, but run into Kimmie on the way up the stairs.

"Oh, there you are, Lizzie," Kimmie says, her voice oozing with something like disdain. "Um... you didn't say anything to Mom about my little coffee run, did you?" She drums her long, well-manicured fingernails on the wall.

"I told you I wouldn't. And Kimmie, I cleaned your room because your dad was having guests over, but it won't happen again," I say, and begin walking up the next flight of stairs to the attic.

"Um, that's your job," she says, hands on hips. "You're supposed to take care of us, and our rooms are part of that care. We both know that." She has the nerve to wink at me.

"Kimmie, you're thirteen years old. At your age, I was taking care of everything by myself. You can, and will, handle your room, at least as long as I'm here," I say. *Which, hopefully, isn't for much longer*. It feels good to stand up to her for a change.

"Oh, Lizzie, stop the cray cray talk," she says. "You know your role, and I know mine.' She pauses, mind already elsewhere. 'I wonder what kind of car Daddy is going to get me for my sixteenth birthday. You know, it's only a few years away."

I take a deep breath. "I'm sure he'll get you whatever you want," I say. For a minute, I have an image of a car smashing into a tree, a baby crying, tires screeching, the thud of impact. But then it's gone.

"What's wrong with you?" Kimmie is looking at me with something almost like concern.

I realize I'm shaking, and I grab onto the stair railing. "Nothing. I'm fine. See you later." I start up the stairs. I know she's watching me, calculating just how far she can push me without any repercussions. In this household, she has all the power. We both know it.

There's this thing about rich people, I've figured out. I came from a family with money, I mean maybe not this kind of wealth, but still I have perspective. Rich people, at least rich people like the Johnsons, don't see me as a person in a way. I am simply a cog in the machine, a servant like their housekeeper and the gardeners, the pool cleaner and the fountain cleaning people. We move in and around their home, but they don't see us at all. Meanwhile, those of us who have had to suffer because of them, we see them clearly, everything they have too much of, everything their life of luxury affords them. Everything that we also should have.

"Hey, Lizzie?"

I turn around, just about to reach the sanctuary of my room. But no. "Hi, Kathie. What's up?"

"It's just that I kinda need a ride to Jody's house. For studying. My mom said you'd take me," she says. She's wearing what I, likely, should be wearing if I were to go on a date. A minidress, sparkly and tight, that I helped her pick out at the Chanel store at the mall. It's crazy she'd wear that to a friend's house to study.

"You aren't dressed for studying," I say.

I watch her cheeks flush. She isn't as jaded as Kimmie—I can still get through to her a little.

"Oh, you mean this little thing," she says, pointing to her dress. "Truth is... there may be a couple boys coming over, too."

"Hmm," I say. "Well, Jody lives just around the corner. So, walk over and if you need a ride back, you can call me. It's a great day for a little exercise."

"No. I don't want to walk," she says. "Mom said you'd take me."

"Your mom was wrong. And she knows I have a date," I say. "Have a good study session." And with that, I turn and continue up the stairs.

"I can't believe you said no," Kathie yells at me. "You aren't allowed to say no. I'm telling Mom."

Please do, I think, but I don't say it. I don't care anymore. I think about the fact she's wearing a designer dress to "study". And she's only 11. It's ridiculous. The kids have play clothes that cost more than any outfit I own. I know because I take them shopping at the finest boutiques. They have to buy these things to keep up with their classmates. They must look the part of the spoiled rich kid, all four of them, because that is who they were destined to become. It's who they are, unfortunately, despite whatever I've done to try to ground them, to make them realize most of the world doesn't live like they do. It's a hard lesson to teach, because, like I said, even the kids don't really see me. Jimmy does, I suppose, but not for much longer. Babies and toddlers see you when you're a nanny, but then they grow up.

I flip on the light in my room and look around. I suppose it's pretty nice here. The Johnsons added air conditioning when I first arrived, and if I bend over and look out the window in the eaves, I can see the coastline and the beautiful ocean sparkling on the horizon. As much as I dislike most things about the Johnsons, I've loved living in this simple, sparse room, I really have. But it's time to go.

I change into the hippest clothes I own—jeans, a black t-shirt, ankle boots. I dress this way because I hope Cecilia sees me as a contemporary. I feel like we could be friends, she and I. I'm only a few years younger than her if I had to guess. I take a final look in the mirror and realize I should put on some makeup. Here, I never wear any because nobody would notice. For some reason, I think Cecilia will appreciate it, expect it even. I rummage around in my bathroom drawer and find my mascara and some lipstick. Better. I try to decide whether to bring my studious glasses to Cecilia's and realize, yes, I was wearing them when we met so I should stay in studious mode. I look at my plain face. I need more makeup. I won't wear them when I exit the house, though, because they all now believe I'm going on a date. It's a good thing Mr. Johnson is gone. He'd think I dressed for him.

Mrs. Johnson has every type of makeup you can imagine, an assortment of all the best high-end brands. Makeup is intimate, I know, and personal, but so are one's children, right? I sneak down the back stairs—yes, there are back stairs for the servants like me—and listen for the chatter in the family room. I can hear Mrs. Johnson uncorking a bottle of wine and the sound of her pouring herself a big glass. They are all still there, talking about their days. How wholesome, how unusual and how fortunate for me. I have just enough time. The timer will ring on the lasagna in 10 minutes.

I hustle back up the stairs and down the hall to the primary suite. It's huge and lavish, and what you'd expect, with a grand ocean view and two distinct en suites and closets: his and hers. I veer into hers and quickly find what I need. Foundation, we have the same pale skin tone, and I follow that with some blush and a matte powder. My hand shakes a bit, worried about being caught, but also with the thrill of doing something like this. I'm a rule follower at heart, and this, what I'm doing right now, breaks all the rules. I don't touch her eye makeup or lipstick, that wouldn't be right. I put everything away where I found it and jog out of the room.

I make it downstairs to the kitchen just as the timer goes off.

"Dinner is ready!" I call toward the family room.

Jimmy is the first to appear. "I'm starving!"

"You're not. You had a big lunch. I watched you, remember?" I say quietly so Mrs. Johnson doesn't overhear. "But I made your favorite dish, so have as much as you'd like."

"You look different," he says.

"I'm going out tonight," I say and turn away to cut the lasagna.

"Mom, Lizzie looks different," he says as Mrs. Johnson appraises me. She's still in a Chardonnay daze, fortunately.

She smiles, the creepy smile again that makes me happy I borrowed a little blush. "Lizzie has a date, Jimmy," she says. "See how she's all dressed up. She is trying her best to impress a boy. I'm not sure it's working, but I'm glad she's tried a bit."

I shake my head but don't say anything.

"I'll do the dishes when I get home. See you all in the morning," I say.

"Have fun on your date," Mrs. Johnson calls as I hurry out the door.

I walk past the minivan, glad I don't need to drive to Cecilia's house. It's surprising Cecilia doesn't recognize the Johnsons or me. She lives in the house next door, after all...

TEN

CECILIA

The first thing I notice is that it's dark outside and inside my house. My heart pounds. Where is the baby? And then I feel her, next to me, still sleeping, her tiny little body pressed against me. I have no idea how long we've been like this, in the playpen, sound asleep. I reach for my phone and realize it's almost 8 p.m. There is a text from Lizzie, the nanny.

I don't want to ring the doorbell, as instructed. But I am here whenever you are ready to talk!

Right. I'm interviewing a nanny tonight. I try to roll onto my side, but the pain forces me to roll back onto my back. I'm going to need help to stand. I try to work out what to do. I hope the front door is unlocked. I cannot remember locking it after Marian left, even though I should have. I reply to Lizzie.

Hello! Could you please let yourself in? Unfortunately, my back went out and I'm stuck in the playpen with the baby.

An immediate response.

Of course, OMG! I'm coming.

I hear the swoosh of the front door opening and feel both relief and a spike of fear. What if Evan had tried to come back, or his mother? I really need to be more careful. I have to protect Peyton now. It's all up to me.

"I'm here," Lizzie says in a quiet voice. "Where are you?"

I text because I don't want to startle the baby by calling out to her.

Walk through the foyer to the kitchen and then left toward the family room. You can turn on lights as you go.

And the next thing I know, she's standing looking down at us with a sweet smile on her face. She looks more put together than I remember from the coffee shop, but it could just be my perspective here on the floor. Her large black glasses make her look as if she's closely examining the baby and me.

"How long have you been like this?" she asks.

I shrug. "I'm not sure." I spin the ruby ring on my finger out of frustration. It's the only thing that doesn't hurt to move.

"You should have told me to come sooner. This is like an emergency," she says.

"Not really, we napped," I say. *Thank goodness*, I don't say.

Peyton stirs and opens her eyes. She looks surprised to see the stranger hovering over us, but she doesn't cry.

"Hi, baby. Look how good you were for your mommy," Lizzie says in the perky voice people use with babies. "How about if I take her and get her freshened up? Are you ok like that for a few more minutes?"

I hadn't even noticed the dirty diaper smell. "Sure, ok."

"And then I'll come help you up," she says.

"Yes, great, sounds like a plan," I say, relieved she's here, nervous to move because I know how much it will hurt. But it's better with help. "Thank you."

Lizzie bends over and scoops Peyton up in her arms, my precious little one dressed all in tiny pink sweatshirt and leggings. My little girl doesn't fuss, and it seems she's interested in this new person appearing in her life. Or, at least, I hope she is. "Of course. We'll be right back. I'm assuming the nursery is upstairs?"

"Yes," I answer and then panic shoots through me. A stranger has my baby and I'm stuck here on the floor. If I hear the door open, I'll have to dial 911. Oh my god, what have I done? *Calm down*, I tell myself. This is an experienced nanny. I saw how lovely she was with the little boy in the coffee shop, how she let him play but also kept him in sight. She cared about him, I could tell. Everything is fine. Still, I can't help yelling, "How's it going?"

"I found the nursery. It's beautiful," she yells back from upstairs. It is beautiful, I agree, and I even painted the artwork on the walls. It was the last piece of art I created before she was born, and I haven't painted anything since.

"Thanks!" I call back.

"We'll be down in a minute," she says. "She's such a good baby. Such a beautiful baby, too."

She *is* a beautiful baby. I need to remember that, and not the constant tears. So far, rather annoyingly, Peyton hasn't cried with Lizzie. She always cries, or at the very least fusses about being changed, but this one time, with a stranger, she isn't crying. Is she alright?

"Here we are, all fresh and ready for a bottle," Lizzie says, interrupting my thoughts and sweeping into the room with Peyton and a reassuring smile. I put down my phone in relief as I watch Lizzie find a bottle in the refrigerator and settle Peyton in her DockATot. "Do we heat it up a bit before serving?"

"Um, yes, sometimes," I answer, although I usually don't

because I'm trying to fill her mouth as soon as possible to stop the screaming.

Peyton stays quiet watching Lizzie run hot water over the bottle, she stays quiet as Lizzie tests a drop on her wrist, and she coos when Lizzie brings the bottle to her. What a blessing. Peyton will be happy and well taken care of by Lizzie, it seems. I feel relief wash over me, but, actually, what am I going to do with the extra time? It's been so long since I've had any. First thing, I think to myself grimly: *get back into rehab for my back.*

And before I know it, Lizzie is standing by the playpen. "Let's get you out of there! Does it hurt to move?"

"Yes, but if you'll give me your hands I'll lean on you. I can do it," I say. The stabbing pain almost makes me drop back down to my knees but with Lizzie's help I'm out of the playpen and I make it to the couch where I collapse. "I'm going to need a doctor. I'll call first thing in the morning."

I dread reaching out to the team who put me back together after the fall, but the way I'm feeling, I don't have any alternatives. I suffered from what doctors called a thoracic and complete injury of the spine. Those words don't really do it justice. I broke my sacrum, the triangle-shaped bone at the end of the spine, between the lumbar spine and the tailbone. There are four types of spinal cord injuries, I learned, and I suffered sacral and lumbar. Which is lucky in the long run, because the higher in the spinal column an injury occurs, the more dysfunction it causes.

When I finally got to in the hospital in France, the pain was excruciating in my neck, head and back. I had numbness and tingling in my left hand. My right hand was swollen because I also broke my right arm bracing for impact, so they told me. I had a fractured right hip, broken ribs, too many to count, and a punctured right lung. It's strange, though. As I fell, I remember letting go, almost giving up and feeling calm as I floated through time and space, until I smacked into the awning and landed on the balcony that saved my life. So all in all, it could have been much worse. I should not have put my body through the burden of carrying a baby and the horrible delivery, I realize that now. But I have Peyton, and she's worth it. Although she deserves a strong, healthy mom.

I remember I pay for a concierge doctor so that I can reach out at any time, day or night. I pull up his number.

He answers on the first ring, as he should since I pay him thousands of dollars a year for this type of response. I explain my situation and he's happy to phone in a prescription for muscle relaxants and pain pills and tells me to start taking them tonight.

But I have a baby. I can't knock myself out, even if I could drive to the pharmacy to pick up the pills.

"I can't take anything, Doctor. My mistake in asking. I have a baby here at home," I say. "I'm the sole caretaker." I flash a look at Lizzie. She smiles at me sympathetically.

"You need to get someone to help you. Tell your partner he's on duty," he says.

"My partner is no longer in my life," I say.

Lizzie's watching me from where she stands feeding Peyton. "I can stay overnight, if you'd like?" she whispers. "I can go pick up your prescriptions then run by and pick up some of my things from the Johnsons and come right back."

"One minute, please, Doctor," I say, taking the phone away from my ear. "Don't they need you?" I ask Lizzie.

"They can handle one night without me, don't worry," she says.

I could really use help. I need Lizzie. "I wonder, would you ever consider leaving them? Taking a new job?" I ask, forgetting about the doctor on the other end of the phone for a moment.

Lizzie smiles and it lights up her whole face. For a moment, she doesn't look so plain. "Sure, I'd consider it. But first, let's get you those drugs." She points to the phone.

"Right. Ok, Doctor," I say into the phone. "Please call in the prescriptions. I guess I might well have someone to help me. Thank you."

I hang up with relief, but also a bit of trepidation. Lizzie smiles at me.

"Do you have any references?" I ask. I realize this is a bit late in the conversation, given that she is holding my baby.

"Just the Johnsons, I'm afraid, but I'd feel funny asking them since, well, you'd be taking me from them," she says with a shrug.

"How long have you been with them?" I ask.

"Two years, it will be three this fall," she says. "I'm surprised you haven't met Mrs. Johnson out and about."

"I moved to this street because we all have spacious lots, and houses built for maximum privacy. I don't want to see my neighbors," I admit. "I don't really go out and about. Since I got out of the hospital, and came home to Malibu, first I focused on recovery while helping Evan, my partner, build his event company. And then, well, I got pregnant with Peyton, and since she was born, it's been all about her. We're just homebodies."

"Nothing wrong with that if you can do it," she says.

"You'll need to give them proper notice, right? Two weeks or something?" I ask.

"No, actually, the Johnsons and I have an agreement that if I find something else, I can take it right away," she says. "The fact is, they just don't need me anymore, not like they used to when the kids were young. Like this precious one."

"You're sure?" I would imagine any contract for domestic help would include some sort of notice. Mine will. "I'll need to run a background check, of course, and we'll sign an official employment contract." I don't really know how to do that but I'll figure it out. It's times like these that I wish I had friends in the community, or a friend anywhere. I know I should likely call a nanny agency, go through a long process of interviews. But

Lizzie is here. She's experienced. She likes Peyton, and Peyton likes her. I'm going to do this.

"Yes. Positive. I'm so excited," she says.

"Ok, well, how about a trial period so we can all get to know each other?" I say. "I'll have my attorney draw up a proper employment agreement in the next few weeks, with your terms. And I'll have him run a background check, of course. Would that work? And if you like it here, you can give the Johnsons a proper notice. For now, tonight, if you're able to go to the pharmacy I'd be forever grateful."

"Of course. Um, do you want me to take her with me?" Lizzie asks.

I'm not ready for her to take my baby anywhere, not yet. "No, thank you. Maybe if you just burp her and put her back in the playpen? I'll be right here on the couch with her. We should be ok. Then you can just hurry and grab everything."

"Sounds good!" she says, seemingly unfazed by my lack of trust. "I'll be back just as soon as I can. Call me if you need anything. I can come back and help."

As she leaves the house, I tell myself that this is great. Everything is fine. I need to heal again from whatever the stress of the day has done to my back. And Peyton seems to like Lizzie already, so I'll trust my baby's judgement, drug myself to sleep to dull the pain and maybe have a nightmare-free night, and hope Lizzie and my baby are happy and here when I wake up.

My attorney will make sure everything is legitimate with Lizzie, but I'm going to trust my instincts. I live by trusting my instincts, I survive by staying cautious and one step ahead.

She's worked for the Johnsons, whoever they are, for four years. That's saying something, right?

I pull out my phone and type a text to my attorney, Jim, requesting his help with the new nanny contract and a background check.

He texts back.

Cecilia! So good to hear from you and I'm delighted you're getting help. You've been through so much, my dear. Please do send me the young woman's full name and last known employment. I'll get right back to you. Good next step. How are you feeling?

How am I feeling? Like there might be a light at the end of the tunnel, if Lizzie checks out.

Better, Jim. As long as you approve of her. I'll get the info to you tonight.

Good. Do take care of yourself, dear. I'll draft up an employment contract. This is the right step for you.

I smile. It is. He's right.

The days are so much longer without a visit from you. It's as if the sun doesn't shine unless you're here with me. I do hope I'm not overstepping, but I did want to tell you how much you, and your stories, brighten my dreary days.

Come back soon. Please.

Very truly,

Paul

ELEVEN

LIZZIE

As I hurry back to the Johnsons' house on the quiet dark street the two households share, I pinch myself. I've done it. I've almost manifested a new job, a job that wasn't even a job until I planted the seed. I can't believe it. Cecilia wants a trial period, but as far as I'm concerned, it's official. I'll become indispensable in no time. Watch me.

And Cecilia is having me "name my terms". Ha! There are a lot of terms I can think of naming. I need to make a list and get it all written down for her to give to her attorney. I'll ask for weekends off, and a paid vacation once a year. I'll ask for double what I'm making at the Johnsons and settle for a little less if she pushes back. This is going to be so great. I love babies, and Peyton and I will have so much fun together. Poor little thing just needs reliable care and confident love. And that's what I'm going to provide. And she's *so* cute. I smile just thinking about her sweet little face.

I've arrived at the Johnsons. On the driveway standing next to the annoying white minivan I debate whether to go inside and grab my things or head straight to the pharmacy. I don't want to wake any of the younger kids, and I don't want any questions about my date from Mrs. Johnson. So, I climb into the car and start the short drive to gather Cecilia's prescriptions. I can always sleep in these clothes and go grab my things in the morning.

Quitting is going to be harder than I thought, I realize. I have a tiny pang of nostalgia gnawing at my insides, a little sadness over leaving Jimmy in particular. But I'll be right next door. He can come over and I'll make him lasagna. It will all be fine. No more lurking Mr. Johnson to worry about, and no more of Mrs. Johnson's ups and downs, or the spoiled-beyond-reason girls, or the grumpy and sneering Johnny. And they'll find a replacement nanny, somebody who enjoys preteens and teenagers. That is not me, not by a long shot. Give me a baby, somebody who doesn't talk back, who doesn't pry, who doesn't question where you're going and why you're dressed up.

The fuel light pops on. I hate going to gas stations. It's a weird fear from childhood. My father hated pumping gas. As a teen he'd had to work at a gas station to help support his family. He detested that job and everything about his childhood with a dark fury. How far he'd come from it seemed to evaporate the minute he started pumping. Like the gas station itself was going to suck him back into his miserable past. Every gas station visit with my dad was filled with toxic stress. I feel it right now, bubbling up from my memories of him.

But then I remind myself: as of tonight, this minivan isn't mine. After this run to the pharmacy, I'll park it and be finished with it. The new nanny can fill it up with gas and then enjoy herself toting the Johnson kids around town. I'll make one of my terms access to an electric car, something fancy and safe, for Peyton and me. I'm sure Cecilia will agree. She might even have an extra car just sitting around. It seems like she's richer than the Johnsons, just from the size of her house, and a few other things I've noticed, like the way her whole house is accessorized perfectly, like a glossy magazine crew was just inside doing a photo shoot. Coffee table books displayed just so, interesting items like a huge crystal on the bookshelf. It's rich people stuff. And the way she dresses, too, the cashmere sweaters she trots around town in, the clothes Peyton wears, the nursery decorated for a French princess. Yes, Cecilia is loaded.

I pull into the drugstore parking lot, the eerie lighting casting long shadows as I hurry into the store. Cecilia gave me her credit card. It feels fun to have something without a limit in my pocket. If I needed to, or wanted to, I could buy anything in the store. Not that I would, of course. I pick up the prescriptions and walk down an aisle with toothbrushes and toothpaste. I need one of each, and a nightshirt. I dream of a shopping spree as I find myself in the makeup section. *I need everything, just one of everything*. Face wash and face cream. Foundation and blush. I eye all of it, but leave it on the display. I shouldn't push my luck. I'm sure Cecilia will understand the toothbrush and nightshirt I've added to the basket. I wonder if I should text and ask her but decide not to bother her. If she wants to, she can deduct the cost from my first paycheck. I don't think she will, though, she needs me too much tonight. She probably won't even remember once the pills from the doctor kick in.

The cashier rings everything up quickly. "Thank you, Ms. Strom."

I don't correct him because that's what it says on the credit card. I smile and say, "Thank you. Have a great evening."

This is what it's like when you have one of these no-limit credit cards. People respect you just because of that. It doesn't seem right, but it's the way of the world.

I make it back to Cecilia's and park the minivan in the driveway. I'll go see how she and the baby are doing, get them settled. I have already decided my plan of action. I'll wake up at my usual time, drive back to the Johnsons', pack my bags, make the kids breakfast, drop them at school and be finished. I'll leave Mrs. Johnson my resignation letter on the kitchen island.

Should be a clean break. No need for any further drama, especially if she's been drinking.

I use the keys Cecilia told me to retrieve from her purse along with the credit card I used to pay and I unlock the front door. I am careful to lock it again behind me. It's a safe community, but you can just never be too cautious. Cecilia emphasized locked doors before I left to run the errand. I make my way down the hallway, quietly, in case Peyton is asleep. As I walk through the kitchen, though, I realize the baby is awake, laying in the playpen, batting at toys and grabbing her toes.

"Thank goodness you're back! I feel like she's about to get fussy again," Cecilia says from the couch, unable to move.

"I've got her," I say, as Peyton executes a rollover. "Good girl! How would you like a bottle?"

I pick up the baby and carry her to the kitchen to find a glass of water for Cecilia. I place Peyton in her highchair while I get Cecilia's things together. She needs to take her pills. And then we all need to turn in for the evening. I'm excited. This home smells like baby lotion, strawberries and expensive candles. The smell of luxury.

"Here is your first round of pills, and some water," I say, carrying everything on a tray over to Cecilia.

"Thank you. And you'll be here, overnight, right? I know it's a big favor to ask." She grimaces as she reaches for the water and the pills.

"Yes, I'll sleep upstairs, I can sleep in the nursery, if you'd like," I say.

"I really can't tell you how much I appreciate this. The guest room is just at the end of the hall. You can sleep there. Take the monitor from my room, across the hall from the nursery, so you can hear her cry," Cecilia says. "It's plugged in on my bedside table."

"Ok, sounds good," I say. "Can I get you anything else?" I navigate my way into the kitchen again with Peyton in my arms.

"I'm fine. Thank you. Just need the pain pills to kick in," Cecilia says. "There are bottles in the fridge. And she's started trying solid foods, but tonight just a bottle will be good."

I open the fridge and find the bottle. After a couple wrong turns, I find the microwave hiding in a cupboard and warm the formula up. I can't wait to change Peyton into a cute sleeping outfit. I'm sure there are loads of choices upstairs.

I carry Peyton and her bottle over to Cecilia. "Ok, you just rest. Call me if you need anything, I'll have my phone on," I say. "Peyton, kiss Mommy good night." I hold Peyton so she hovers over Cecilia and their faces touch. So sweet.

"Night, baby," Cecilia says. Her voice has softened, the pills are starting to take effect. "Oh, Lizzie, can you please set the alarm? The code is 5432."

"Yes, I'll do it on our way upstairs. And don't worry, I've got this. I do have to leave for a bit in the morning, to take the other kids to school and to quit. I hope you don't mind," I say. "I'll make it fast."

"Of course," she says. "My doctor is coming in the morning, too, so he can help me if need be."

"See, everything is working out as it should. Get some rest," I say. "Peyton says 'feel better, Mommy'."

Cecilia blows a kiss in our direction before sighing in pain. Perhaps the pills haven't quite started working yet. Meanwhile, I'm giddy to see what the guest room looks like. I know the thread count of the sheets is going to be over-the-top, the furnishings exquisite.

From the Johnsons' backyard I watched the high-end decorator standing in Cecilia's driveway shortly after she purchased the home. She directed a dozen or so staff members to unload two large trucks full of furniture and accessories. As they carried the items inside, I got a glimpse of the style—warm contemporary—and I approved. Cecilia had hired the best of the best out of Beverly Hills, I found out. Who knows how much it all cost, but I imagine a fortune. The house is like an art museum, all white walls, light wood floors and stunning furniture everywhere. As I walk down the hallway to the guest room, my feet sinking into the plush carpet, I have a feeling I'm never going to want to leave.

And I'm right. I open the door to an oasis of tan and white, fabrics and textures that work together to create a stunning effect. I feel like I've stepped into a luxury hotel room. I sit down on the bed and feed Peyton, rocking her softly in my arms. Designer pillows in subtle patterns of tan and white adorn the bed, which is a contemporary style, light wood. Across the room, a matching dresser anchors the other wall while large windows will provide a spectacular view in the morning. This isn't an attic, not at all. This is a room meant to envelop a visitor in comfort, impress them with all the things that money can buy.

Once Peyton's finished the bottle, I prop her over my shoulder to burp her. I carry Peyton across the room and examine the artwork on the wall, a framed oil painting of the coastline, adding the only pop of color to the otherwise tan and white room. I'm sure it was painted by someone important, of course it was.

I decide to get Peyton ready for bed before I explore the rest of the suite. Just the thought of the bathroom has me smiling. It's like I've finally arrived.

TWELVE

CECILIA

I wake up from a fitful, uncomfortable sleep and I don't know where I am, what time it is. Where's the baby? I try to sit up, but searing pain pierces my spine. I take a breath and remember I'm on the couch, pain pills within reach. And then I also remember —the baby is upstairs asleep in her crib, with her nanny watching over her. Her nanny. Thank goodness for the encounter at the coffee shop that led to this. I can't believe Lizzie was next door all this time! I'll admit, I haven't done a good job of getting to know any of my neighbors, and really it's not Peyton's fault. After the accident in Paris, after I moved to this house, I just have kept to myself. My life consisted of work with Evan, mostly designing invitations and event branding from home. And then Peyton arrived. But it's tough on my own, as I've already discovered. I don't know what I would have done without Lizzie arriving to help us when she did tonight.

I reach for the pill bottles without moving my back, open the lids and pop the pills in my mouth. I notice the ruby ring on my left hand sparkling in the dim light. I bought it to celebrate Peyton's birth. I reach for the glass of water and notice that Lizzie has even been thoughtful enough to leave a straw. I take a sip and swallow the pills, waiting for the pain to subside. I know what's caused this backslide, so to speak. It was all the stress of the baby, the disappointment in Evan as a partner, Paul's menacing letter and lack of compliance with the divorce, and the final straw, Evan's mother coming by to harass me. What a day! But this is just a temporary setback. I'll be fine again in no time.

And I'm going to take my life back. I'm going to start painting again, painting the subject matter I'd like to paint, and I'll find a gallery that will carry my work. And I'll start working out with a trainer—Marian's comments stung with a hint of the truth. Oh, and I'll make an appointment with the financial planner, finally, and get a good assessment of how much I have left to spend and how much I should be saving—I am a mother now, after all, and I need to be responsible.

An uncomfortable thought nags at me now. Peyton was so happy with Lizzie, I realize. Happier than she ever has been with me. Maybe it's because I'm not a natural, was never meant to have a kid. Maybe she senses that every time I hold her, every time I feed her. Perhaps I don't comfort her, I just worry her. Poor baby. I love her with all my heart, and even if I'm not a natural, I will learn.

My eyelids feel heavy again as the pills kick in. Everything is fine, everything is awesome. I hear footsteps, I think, in the kitchen, but I'm too tired to move.

THIRTEEN

LIZZIE

Peyton makes a cooing sound as I feed her and wraps her tiny hand around my pinky. We've bonded already, which is great. I hate to leave her to go next door and quit, but I know I have to.

I slept so well last night. I've never experienced a bed with so many soft pillows, and blankets and the sheets—oh my. From the bed, I have a full view of the sparkling ocean, as predicted. There is a walk-in closet, a huge bathroom with a bathtub and all types of fancy buttons to push to turn it into a spa experience.

I cannot wait to move in for good.

"Ok, baby, it's time to get dressed and go see your mommy," I say. After I get the baby changed, I put on my clothes from the previous night and run a brush through my hair. I realize while I don't look great, I don't look horrible either. Today is the beginning of the rest of my life.

The doorbell rings as I'm carrying Peyton downstairs. The glass window reveals a rather handsome-looking man. I assume it's the doctor coming to take care of Cecilia. I open the door.

"Hello. Are you Cecilia's doctor?" I ask.

"Yes," he says with a warm smile. He has a dimple, and it's cute. He's cute. "May I come in? I'm Doctor Jay."

"I'm Lizzie, the new nanny," I say. I kiss the baby on the head. "I'm sure you know Peyton?" I step aside and he walks through the door. I make a note to lock it behind him.

"Actually, I don't," he says, tickling her under the chin. "She's such a cutie. Cecilia stopped her rehab with me when she became pregnant. Her obgyn doctor wanted to take over her care, considering it a high-risk pregnancy. We both worried about the toll pregnancy and childbirth would take on her after her injuries, but she made it through. Until now."

"Sure," I say. "I wasn't aware of all of that. She's in the family room. This way."

Cecilia is where I left her last night, asleep on the couch. She must have taken more pills at some point because the caps are off the bottles and the water is half gone.

I put Peyton in her playpen and turn back to Jay. "Would you like coffee? I can make you a cup before I go. I need to run a couple errands. Cecilia said you wouldn't mind keeping an eye on the baby?" I say. "I'll be back as soon as I can."

"Uh, um, sure, I'll take a coffee. The thing is, I don't really have much experience with babies." Jay looks a bit stunned. His dimple has disappeared. "I do have other patients to see."

"You'll be fine. Cecilia trusts you, and she needs you," I say. I'd already noticed the coffee maker on the counter the previous evening, and find the pods in the drawer below it. I have to open a few cupboard doors before finding a coffee mug, but I finally do. I make Jay a quick Nespresso and carry it over to him.

"I'm not going to be gone long. I just need to run some kids to school," I say. "My old job."

Cecilia stirs on the couch.

"Look, she's waking up," I say. "Hi Cecilia, good morning."

"Morning," she mumbles.

"Hey, I'll be right back – just heading out to drive the Johnsons to school for the last time," I say.

Cecilia nods and starts to sit up. It's clear she's still in a lot of pain. The doctor hurries to her side. They'll be fine watching Peyton.

"I'll be right back," I say.

"We're good," the doctor says. He's wrapping a blood pressure cuff around Cecilia's arm.

"And remember to keep an eye on Peyton," I say with a smile. He sure is cute when he's flustered.

"I will," he says. "But maybe give me your number, in case I need you?"

When he says that my cheeks feel hot for some reason. *Focus*, I tell myself. I write my number on a magazine cover and hand it to him. "You'll be fine, and I'll be back within an hour." *I hope*.

"Thanks, Lizzie," Cecilia says. "You're a lifesaver."

"Peyton is in her playpen, happy as can be, and I'll be back just as soon as I can," I say. After this, I'll never leave her side.

I watch as Cecilia struggles to sit up. "Do you need me to stay?" I ask, concerned.

"No, I'm fine, we'll be fine, go ahead," she says.

I grab my purse and the minivan keys and hurry to the door. As I'm closing it behind me, I hear Peyton begin to cry. It breaks my heart but I can't stay or I'll be late to take the kids to school. I'm just backing out of the driveway when I spot a man in the rearview mirror. He's cute, blond with fashionable facial hair. I stop and roll down my window. I realize I might have seen a photo or two of him on bookshelves in Cecilia's house. And from spying on the people who live next door, of course.

"Can I help you?" I ask, surreptitiously fluffing my hair out.

"Oh, well, I'm Cecilia's partner... well, ex-partner, I guess. I wanted to go grab some things, check on Peyton, that sort of thing," he says. "I'm Evan. Evan Dorsey. Who are you?"

"I'm Lizzie, the new nanny," I say. He is *really* cute. I don't think I would have kicked him out of my bed.

"I can't believe she'd hire a nanny so quickly." He looks at me suspiciously with squinted eyes.

"Well, it's on a trial basis. I need to quit my other job today. I've been a professional nanny in Malibu for quite some time." I smile. He might be cute but he shouldn't be so judgmental. He doesn't even know me.

"Well, that's great, I guess. But how did you two meet?" he asks, still unsure of the idea of me and his baby.

"I really have to go, but we met at a coffee shop. I love babies, and I know I can be of help here. Ok?" I say.

"Did you give her references? Do you have experience? I mean, I can't trust just anyone with my precious little girl." He stares at me, tilting his head.

"Of course. And Cecilia's attorney drew up my contract. Apparently I passed the background check. I knew I would but it's scary when someone says they're doing that." I laugh, trying to give the impression of being lighthearted and talkative. "Anyway, what you see is what you get with me. I'm so excited to be here." I hope I'm not overdoing it. But then he smiles and I feel my shoulders drop from my ears.

"Ok. Well, I guess it's good she found some help," he says. "What's your name again?"

"Lizzie. Lizzie Lamont," I say. "Nice to meet you."

"I'll be around a lot, Lizzie. Peyton is my daughter and I love her very much," he says.

"Good to know," I say, and I believe him. "Look, I need to go. I'm quitting my other family today."

"Oh, well, yes, get going, you've got important things to do," Evan says with a smile. "I'll just be on my way, too."

"Ok, bye," I say.

I find myself hoping that Evan comes around, a lot. But I

remind myself to focus. I need to finish with the Johnsons. I drive next door, walk into the house and up the back stairs. I glance down the second-floor landing, stunned by the silence. The kids all seem to be in their rooms, but surely they should be getting dressed by now? I hope Mrs. Johnson remembered to wake them up. I head down the hall opening the first door. "Good morning, sunshine! It's time to wake up! And we're running late!"

"Ugh," Kathie says. I'm not sure if that's directed at me or the situation.

"You still have time to look gorgeous," I say knowing she really doesn't, and that somehow makes me happy. She should just bounce out of bed, looking like a teenager, instead of spending so much time trying to look like a grown-up. It's sad, really.

Kimmie's room is next. I open the door. She's standing in the middle of the room glaring at me.

"I set an alarm. You really should knock first. And you still haven't seen my purse, right?" she asks.

"Glad you're awake. And nope, I haven't," I say, hurrying from the room.

I knock on Johnny's door. "Time to get up!" I open the door as he sits up. Clearly he'd still been sound asleep. I soften. He looks like a little boy even if his attitude has become all teenager. Although he certainly smells like a teenage boy. His room, too, is a disaster of dirty clothes and midnight snack debris. There's even a pizza box with a half-eaten pepperoni pizza tossed on the floor.

"Hey, I'll make you breakfast, but you need to hurry."

"Why didn't you wake me up at the right time?" he asks.

"Your mom was on duty last night. I was out. Sorry," I say.

He shakes his head. We both know she's never really on duty. I head to the last room and slip inside. I creep over to

Jimmy's bed and rub his back, whispering, "It's time to get up. And we're a little late, but don't worry. I'll pick out your clothes."

"Ok," he says, rubbing sleep from his eyes. "Thank you."

"You're welcome, kiddo." I smile. He really is the best. I'm going to miss him.

At the end of the hall, I knock on the door of the master suite. "Mrs. Johnson, it's time to wake up!" I hope that works.

I sprint up the stairs to my attic room and grab my suitcase from under the bed. It only takes a couple minutes to pack my things. I take one last look around at what has been my home for the past few years and then smile. *Good riddance.* I roll the suitcase behind me down the back stairs, noting the sounds of the kids getting ready for school. I tuck my suitcase away outside the front door, behind a huge potted plant, and hurry to the kitchen to make egg sandwiches to go. If I get them out the door in the next 20 minutes, they'll be on time.

Jimmy appears first. His hair is still a mess from sleep but wearing the outfit I picked out for him. "My mom's not awake yet, Lizzie."

That's odd. She does usually join us for breakfast and inspects the outfits they've selected. "Why don't you go jump on her? That would be fun!"

"Ok," he says, and he's off.

I finish making four sandwiches, load them into environmentally friendly totes complete with environmentally friendly aluminum water bottles, and wait by the front door. The kids bound down the stairs and take a breakfast tote on the way to the minivan. Mrs. Johnson finally appears. She looks horrible. Like she's been crying for hours. Something is happening here,. either with Mrs. Johnson herself or with somebody else in the family. She looks even more miserable than usual.

"I need to take them to school," I say. "Are you ok?"

"I'll be fine, go," she says. "But I do need to speak with you."

"Yes, sure, I'll be back after drop-off." Whatever she has to say, whatever she's upset about now, will not change my mind. I've made my decision. Mr. Johnson's leering eyes pop into my mind and I shake my head to get rid of the image.

The kids all sit in their designated seats as we head to school. Kimmie in the front seat, since she's the oldest. Today she's thrown together quite a chic look—a designer sweater, blue jeans and her favorite Chanel purse.

I check the rearview mirror. Kimmie, sitting behind me, is busy eating her egg sandwich. We lock eyes.

"Are you sure you didn't find my Prada purse yet? I swear someone took it," she says.

"I didn't," I say. Of course, I didn't look either. "But if you keep your room tidier, it'll be easier to find things you've misplaced."

"I didn't misplace it." She glares at me.

I roll my eyes.

"I have practice after school," Johnny says. "I'll get a ride home with Tom's mom."

"Sounds good," I say. He'll find out I'm gone last, it seems.

We reach the drop-off for the middle school and high school, and the three kids slide out the door as I chirp, "Have a great day!" It's just me and Jimmy for the drive to the elementary school.

"I don't really want to go to school today," he says. "Can I skip it again? Please?"

I smile and catch his eyes in the rearview mirror. "Sorry, sport. You skipped yesterday, remember? We can't do it all the time."

"Fine," he says, a big frown on his face. My heart drops.

I hate disappointing him, and when he realizes I'm gone when he gets home from school, he's going to be so sad. I pull up to the curb. "Jimmy, you know I really love you. I do. You're my favorite. And no matter what, you can always call me. Ok?"

"Ok," he says with a shrug. "Bye!"

"Bye," I say, pushing the button to close the van door after he gets out. And just like that, my life is starting anew. I drive back to the Johnsons' and park the minivan one last time.

I walk back into the house and head to the laundry room where I hang the minivan keys on the hook. I note the pile of laundry to be done and smile because I'm not going to be the one doing it. I make my way to the kitchen and find Mrs. Johnson there, drinking coffee, still looking terrible, eyes puffy and swollen from crying. I think about asking her what's wrong, but I don't have time and I'm about to make things worse for her by quitting. I take a deep breath.

"Kids are all dropped off," I say to break the ice. "Oh, and Johnny's getting a ride home from practice with Tom's mom."

"Good, great," she says. "There's a pile of laundry in the locker room. Not sure why it piled up so fast, but you need to get all of that done today. I hate the look of it."

"Yes, laundry is never-ending with four kids," I say, not that she's ever done a load. "Um, look, Mrs. Johnson, I want to thank you for the opportunity to work here. I learned a lot, but, um, I've been offered another job. It's time for me to move on." A pang of regret passes through me when I see the look of sadness in her eyes. But the look turns to ice.

"You aren't quitting, you can't," Mrs. Johnson says, shaking her head, eyes flashing with anger. "You're under contract through next spring."

"Look, you and I both know the kids don't need a nanny anymore. They need a taxi service, and that's not what I want to do," I say. "They've outgrown me and that's a good thing."

"But what about me?" she says. "I need you. You're the only way I get any time for myself. And you're wrong about the kids. They need you, too. Jimmy loves you. I see the connection you two have. It will break his little heart if you leave."

"I do love him," I say, my voice breaking a bit. "And I'll keep in touch with him. I promise. But it's time for me to move on. It's the right thing to do. I don't feel comfortable around Mr. Johnson, not anymore, not after what happened."

She drops her head and stares at her hands. "He's gone, I told you."

"He'll be back," I say. "You know it and so do I."

She's silent for a moment, but then she says, "Still, I'm not letting you break your contract."

"You have to. Your husband invited me to his latest orgy. I don't feel safe here. It's best you let me go quietly without getting the cops involved," I say firmly.

"You wouldn't!" She looks at me, wide-eyed with panic. "What am I going to do?"

I shrug. She never was nice to me, so it's hard to feel anything for her situation. She's created her life, all of it.

I watch as she walks across the kitchen, pulls out her purse and writes a check. She hands it to me with something like hate in her eyes.

"Get out of here," she says. "I knew you were trouble. You act all plain Jane with your big glasses and stick-straight hair, but underneath, there's more going on, isn't there? You aren't what you seem, not at all. The way you lead my husband on, flirting with him. It's all your fault he behaves the way he does."

"That's ridiculous. I didn't do that," I say. She doesn't even see me, has no idea who I am besides being her servant. I start backing away from her. "I only ever tried to help you by taking care of the kids. And I did a good job. Jimmy loves me."

"He does. But the girls think you're weird so they'll be relieved, and Johnny, well... who knows what he thinks? Well, thanks a lot for all of this help, and good luck. You'll fail again, of course you will."

As I reach the front door, I hear shattering glass. She must have thrown something. I quicken my pace, rush out the door, grab my suitcase and head for the street. I suppose I've just created an enemy, an enemy who lives next door.

But I don't care. It's time to help myself for a change. And I will help myself to plenty going forward, believe me.

FOURTEEN

LIZZIE

Three weeks later

I have packed a picnic for Peyton and I, and we are headed to the private beach, complete with a coveted key to open the metal gate that keeps anybody who doesn't live in one of these fabulous houses from going to the beach here. I pause to take a selfie with Peyton, the gate prominent in the background. This is perfect.

Even the Johnsons didn't have a key to Little Dume, although the kids often snuck in with all their friends whenever they wanted to. Peyton coos in her carrier as I walk down the winding path. Once we reach the ocean, I notice we have the place to ourselves, except for a couple of surfers in the water. It's a perfect day, as it often is in Malibu, and I take a deep breath.

This is what life is supposed to be like for me, I've decided. I spread out the picnic blanket, bright blue on the tan-colored sand. I place a playmat on top of the blanket for Peyton, and she giggles as I lift her onto it so she's on her stomach.

"Isn't this perfection, baby?" I ask her as I snap another

selfie of the two of us. Her adorable pink sunhat is the perfect frame for her beautiful face.

I sit down beside her, kick off my sandals and wiggle my toes in the warm sand. It's still early morning, so the temperature is perfect, the summer heat hasn't kicked in yet. A surfer runs past us, his board under his arm, but he stops and smiles at us.

"She's such a cute baby," he says with a grin.

"Thank you," I answer. She truly is stunning. "Would you mind taking a photo of us?"

"Of course." He drops his board and reaches for my phone. I make sure Peyton and I snuggle as he snaps the photos.

He hands my phone back. "Thank you so much," I say. "Enjoy the waves."

"I will. You take care of that little one." He gives us another grin and then jogs away.

Oh, I will. I smile at Peyton. Suddenly, the back of my neck tingles. I glance around with a weird feeling someone is watching us, but there is nobody in sight.

"Baby, how about getting your little toes wet at the edge of the water?" I ask. She seems fine with the idea, her little hands flapping in joy. I carry her down to the edge of the water and make sure the waves are calm before bending and dipping her little feet in the cold water.

"Isn't that fun?" I say, splashing the water on her little legs as she giggles. I'm so happy she loves the beach. I stand up, with Peyton on my hip, and look around. For I second, I think I catch a glimpse of something, someone on the dune above us, but when I look again there's nothing there.

"Let's get you back to the blanket and dry you off," I say to Peyton.

As I'm settling her on the blanket and drying her tiny toes, I see him.

Behind us, up on the dune, is a man. He steps behind a tree

when I look up at him, but I know he's there. I twist back around to Peyton, and then quickly turn and look behind me again. He's still there. And he's staring at us. He's wearing a dark green t-shirt and jeans. His hair is blond, but from this distance I don't recognize him. I look toward the ocean, hoping I can call out to my new friendly surfer buddy if necessary, but he's way out offshore waiting for his break.

A chill runs down my spine. I can't make out his features from this distance, but Cecilia has enemies, of that I'm already certain. She's a security freak. Over-the-top. The Johnsons have four kids and hardly lock their doors at all. Point Dume is a safe neighborhood, but Cecilia has alarm system, deadbolts, windows locked shut.

Cecilia thinks danger lurks everywhere, I can tell. I didn't ask her permission to bring Peyton here, because she was still asleep when we left. Shoot, maybe she doesn't want the baby down here despite the fact she showed me where the beach key was. And now she's made me paranoid, too. I look over my shoulder again, and he's gone. But where did he go?

Another chill runs down my spine despite the warm, beautiful day.

I need to take Peyton home.

"Ok, baby, I know it's a short visit but we'll be back, I promise," I say, forcing a smile on my face as I hurry to clean up our picnic spread, the sand still warm and welcoming under my feet despite my sense of urgency.

Peyton fusses a bit and I give her a binky which she sucks on gladly. My heart pounds in my chest and I make sure to check my phone is in my back pocket. I wonder if this man followed us to the beach. But maybe I'm overthinking and he's just a random guy. Who knows? I make a point to hum a cheerful tune as we walk toward the gate. Everything is fine if I'm humming.

I reach the gate and don't see the man anywhere. I place

Peyton in her stroller and look down the street. There's no one out and about, and no sight of the man lurking. But how can I know for sure where he went?

I run the block back to Cecilia's house pushing the jogging stroller and my heart doesn't stop racing until we are safely inside, the alarm on. Maybe I was just imagining things, but I'm also sure next time I take the baby to the beach, I'll get Cecilia's permission first.

"Ok, baby, let's go take a swim in the beautiful, safe swimming pool in your own backyard," I say. I've already taken some adorable photos of us in the pool, and even though I'd wanted to take more photographs of her and us on the beach, I didn't have the chance. I glance around the beautiful backyard, completely fenced, with only a small metal access gate in the far corner of the yard. I know that's locked tight. We're safe in the backyard.

Maybe I'm being paranoid, but for now the pool will do.

FIFTEEN

CECILIA

It's another beautiful day in paradise. The sun shines brightly, and the sky is a vibrant shade of blue. I'm peeking out the kitchen window and watching Lizzie and Peyton splashing in the swimming pool. The baby is in a floating rubber duck, laughing and patting the water, with an adorable pink sunhat and pink sunglasses completing the baby model look. I walk over to the refrigerator and pick one of the fresh-pressed juices Lizzie has made. There's green juice, a ginger and turmeric and orange juice blend, and a fresh strawberry and lime concoction. They're all equally good. This morning I choose a green juice, unscrew the lid and enjoy.

I'm so glad everything is working out with Lizzie. When my attorney Jim called me last week and told me everything was in order and there were no red flags on Lizzie's background check, I was beyond happy.

"So you feel comfortable drawing up an employment contract for her?" I asked, grinning into the phone.

"I do. The only person who wouldn't provide a positive reference was a Mrs. Johnson who lives next door to you. Apparently, she isn't pleased that Lizzie left abruptly," Jim said.

"Lizzie told me Mr. Johnson was hitting on her," I said. "I believe her."

"So do I," Jim said. "I think it holds up, and Mrs. Johnson seemed unwell on the phone."

It's tough being a mom, I thought. "Ok, well, get the contract sent over as soon as you can," I said.

"You'll have it today," Jim said.

And I did. After I printed it, I'd left it on the kitchen table for Lizzie to find when she set the table for dinner.

She'd clapped her hands with joy when she found it. "We're official?"

"We are," I said, smiling, and I handed her a pen. "As long as the terms are to your liking?"

I watched as she read it over, grinning ear to ear. "More than generous. Thank you."

When she signed, I felt such gratitude. This was going to work out better than I'd dreamed, I just knew it.

Now, as I watch the happy scene in front of me, I realize I never even thought to take the baby into the swimming pool. Every day was a struggle. I was literally in a daze, barely functioning, until Lizzie appeared. And then there was that first night, the night my back went out and she stayed and took care of Peyton when I could barely move. Uncharacteristically, I trusted her immediately, her confident warmth with my baby softening my usually cynical view of people. And there was something more. She'd literally saved Peyton's life that night. If she hadn't been there, if I couldn't care for Peyton, couldn't even lift her out of the playpen, I shudder to think what would have happened. I would have had to call Evan, I suppose, but I don't want him back in my life. Since that terrible night, everything is getting better. And it's all thanks to Lizzie. In fact, everything is going so well, I find myself knocking on wood, so I don't jinx myself.

I go to the front door and make sure it's locked. It is, but when I look out the half-window of the door, I spot Evan leaning against my car, hands shoved in his jean pockets. He looks contrite, but who knows?

I open the door. "Go away," I yell.

"I need to get my things, the rest of them, but more importantly, we need to talk. I miss you. I miss Peyton," he says.

"You should have thought about that before you fucked Cassie," I say. "I've had the nanny box up your things. They're in the garage. I'll open the door." I turn to walk back inside.

"Wait, please. I need to see Peyton," he says. I hear him walking toward me, gravel crunching under his shoes.

"Again, you should have considered that before you cheated. You should have also considered helping as soon as she was born," I say, and in one quick move, I make it inside the house and lock the door.

I hurry down the hallway to the door to the garage, push the button to open the garage, and then rush back inside, locking the door. *Goodbye, Evan. I'm finished with you. We both are.* I watch through the laundry room window as Evan carries boxes to his car. When he's finished, he turns to look at me. I wave goodbye. He shakes his head, but he slips into his truck and drives away.

A wave of tiredness washes over me as I walk outside to join Peyton and Lizzie in the sunshine of the backyard, but my heart fills with something that feels like joy and contentment. My back is feeling better again—of course, it might never fully heal, but the flare-up seems to have subsided. My life is happy and it's all thanks to Lizzie. Not only is Peyton now on a schedule, and doesn't even cry very much at all anymore, but I am, too.

We start each morning with a homemade breakfast at the kitchen table, with Lizzie serving eggs and bacon and freshly squeezed orange juice, or one of her signature juices she prepares for us daily. She's replaced my coffee machine with a French press, and I love the taste. This morning, she surprised me with fresh strawberries from the farmer's market, the sweetest strawberries I've ever tasted. Beside me, Peyton sits in her highchair happily cooing as Lizzie feeds her breakfast. Some sort of homemade mash—she's started introducing solids, the old-fashioned way.

After breakfast, I'll head to my studio and paint for a while. It's remarkable what a little time pursuing my passion has done for my overall well-being. Once I've tired of painting, I'll join Lizzie and Peyton in the family room, or outside by the pool, and do my rehab stretching routine for my back, and play with the baby, too. She loves to join me on my yoga mat, I've discovered, and Lizzie takes cute pictures of us face to face on our bellies or lying side by side on our backs.

Lizzie takes this time to handle all the dishes and laundry, or makes the grocery order, or sorts any of the other details that make the household run smoothly now. When it's time for lunch, Lizzie does it again, creating a picnic to eat outside in the garden somedays, or a lovely spread inside in the kitchen. She's even found my tablecloths and linens, and there are always fresh flowers in a vase in the center of the table. She has taken to setting the table as if I'm a guest. It's really much more than I ever expected it could be. I'm happier than I can ever remember being in my life. I don't know how to thank her, beyond the generous salary and the constant thank yous and letting her drive my BMW, which I know she loves. Nothing seems enough to repay her for regaining my peace of mind.

"She loves the water," Lizzie says as I join them. I'm so lucky I have a pool guy who comes and cleans the pool once a week, balances the pH and makes it look perfect. Paradise that I should take advantage of more often. With my baby girl.

I'm wearing shorts and my softest white t-shirt. I've washed and curled my hair, and I even had time to do my makeup, including applying my favorite red lipstick. I sit on the side of the pool, dangling my legs in the warm water, and I must admit, this is the good life. Despite the fact we just saw each other, Evan sends a text that lights up my phone. It's a daily thing with him, ever since I kicked him out three weeks ago. He wants to make a time when he can stop by, to talk, to get things figured out. He's sorry, so he says. But who needs him? Not me. Not anymore. He had a chance to step up, and he backed away.

I realize Lizzie is watching me. I smile. "She obviously gets her love of the water from me," I say. "I used to come out here and swim and lay out in the sun when I was pregnant with her. The doctor wanted me to do gentle exercise, like swimming. But then, once she was born, I sort of lost myself." I pause. "But you already know that."

"I hear that's normal. My last family, the Johnsons, well, the mom was a mess, even with me there to help," Lizzie says. "It was very sad. But you are doing so much better."

"I feel like myself again. I'm even having fun painting, and I wake up with a smile on my face every morning. Peyton is thriving, too, because of you," I say. "And speaking of fun, I was thinking we should do a little shopping today."

"We just went yesterday, but I'm not going to say no to that." Lizzie laughs. "As long as you promise not to buy me anything. You've spent too much on me."

"Nonsense. You need chic work clothes, you need to look the part of Peyton's stylish nanny," I say. I think about how she arrived to start working for me with a tiny beat-up suitcase holding all her belongings. And she walked to the house from next door. She didn't even own a car. So the first thing I did, once Dr. Jay cleared me to start driving again, was take Lizzie shopping.

I found it sad that Lizzie had so few belongings when she first moved in with us. She wore the same outfit every three days. Day one, a rather threadbare t-shirt and jeans. Day two, a floral blouse and navy pants. Day three, a simple dress with blue and white stripes that looked one size too big for her. Of course, I didn't notice that at first, I was in too much pain, too sleep-deprived. But eventually, after the first week, I started to come back to myself. Back to life. And when I suggested a shopping spree to Lizzie last week, she'd jumped at the chance.

"It will be so good to get you out of the house," she said, holding Peyton up and smiling at her. "Yes, let's do it. Where do you want to go? What do you need?"

As I'd climbed into my car, I was grinning from ear to ear. I didn't need anything. "You'll see."

We had so much fun that first time clothes shopping, just the three of us. At 5 months, Peyton charms everyone she meets. The salesperson at the store thought Lizzie and I were best friends, when really it had only been a couple of weeks since we'd met. We'd already fallen into an easy, comfortable routine with Peyton, and a friendship of sorts with each other.

I smile at the memory as Lizzie splashes some water, delighting Peyton.

"I guess I could use a new bathing suit," Lizzie says. "This one is from who knows when or where. I can buy it myself, though. You're giving me a generous salary."

I did notice the one she's wearing is a bit see-through in places. "I was going to mention that. We'll find you an amazing new bathing suit," I say. "I insist. It's my treat."

"You know, I don't want to take advantage of your generosity. I'll save up and buy my own suit," she says. "I've never been able to save up, not until this job with you. Parents always try to pay as little as they can for childcare. It's ridiculous given it's their most precious possession, their kids. It's so strange. The people before the Johnsons, they were filthy rich but they made me fill out a timesheet every day, and keep a record of everything I did. They'd fine me, too, if I didn't get a long list of chores done each day even while I was taking care of their two kids. But now I'm here with you two, and it's so much better."

"I'm so glad. That sounds horrible," I say. "I'm sorry people haven't treated you well."

"I'm sorry people haven't treated you well, either," she says.

I chuckle. "Yes, well, in my case, it's been men. Who needs them?"

"You know, in my case, it's been men, too," she says, but she wades further into the pool, pushing Peyton on her inflatable before I can ask her more. Maybe she'll tell me about it someday.

I look at Lizzie and see a younger version of who I used to be, before I had all of this. Lizzie's had a tough go of it for a long time now, a sad story I can sort of relate to when she started sharing. She's five years younger than me, and she grew up in a wonderful family, she says. But then, her parents both died in a tragic accident when she was 10, and she's been on her own ever since. I don't know what's harder, never having anything and being on your own from the minute you can remember, like me, or having it all and then losing it in a split second. I think perhaps Lizzie's story is worse. I never knew what I was missing.

"Save your money. It's my pleasure to buy you a new bathing suit," I say. "You know, before I had all of this, before I met Paul, the man I thought was my Prince Charming, I was poor. I grew up with nothing, and nobody really, just another kid who was part of the foster care system."

"I never would have imagined that. You seem like you've always been rich," she says. "You seem so at ease with all the stuff that comes with money, the house, the cars, the jewelry, the outfits. You're a natural."

"No, quite the opposite. I learned how to live like this, look like this," I say. Paul helped, but I don't need to give him any credit. Anything he taught me about fitting into high society was only for the purpose of making himself look better. People are only there to reflect him, that's all. It took me too long to figure that out.

"You've done a great job. Fooled me," she says.

"Thanks," I say. "Sometimes I still feel like an imposter, like this could all be snatched away at any moment. But we'll get you looking your best, too. It feels good. Boosts confidence and all that."

"I can't afford to look like you," she says with a wry laugh. "I have a pretty good idea how much all those clothes and accessories cost. I had to take the Johnson girls to all those fancy boutiques and designer stores. I'd often look at what I was spending on a ten-year-old girl and realize it was more than my salary for a month in one outfit."

"You know, there are ways to look good on a budget. I'll teach you how to do it as long as you stick with me," I say.

"Oh, I plan to. Like glue," she says and gently pushes Peyton and her floatie toward me.

I grab the baby's little hand and kiss the top, making her giggle. "Then first things first. I did a little closet cleaning this morning and pulled some things that will look beautiful on you if you're interested. I mean, they are hand-me-downs, but not more than a season old. I think we are the same size in just about everything."

Lizzie stops splashing and turns to look at me, swirling Peyton's duck next to her. "I really cannot believe how kind you're being. I just don't know what to say."

"You know, it feels great to be able to share with you. I've had a tough go of it these past few years, despite all the money," I say. "My husband, the one who had all the money, who I thought was my dream come true, turned out to be a nightmare."

"I was going to ask you about him," Lizzie says. "But I didn't want to pry."

"It's not like it's a secret. We made international news," I say. "People couldn't get enough of the romantic Parisian evening gone so wrong." A chill rolls down my spine as I remember again the moment my husband shoved me from a rooftop bar. I'll never forget the feeling of free-falling through the dark sky, waiting for impact, waiting to die.

"Do you want to tell me about it? If it's too hard, you don't have to," Lizzie says carefully. She and the baby are so happy, so innocent.

I used to be that way. Happy. Carefree. And yet, the fact is, if you pick the wrong partner, all of that can be taken away from you in the blink of an eye. I guess she should learn that lesson, too. I decide to tell her the horrific truth.

"My husband accosted me in Paris during our wedding anniversary trip. He grabbed me and threw me off the rooftop of our hotel, tried to kill me," I say. It still seems surreal.

"Oh my gosh. Why?" Lizzie eyes widen. "Wait. Peyton's father tried to kill you? He threw you off the top of a hotel? That's horrible... terrifying, unbelievable!"

"Exactly. I'm lucky to be alive. That's why my back is messed up," I say. "Thankfully no, he is not Peyton's father, thank god. That's another story. She doesn't have a father. Well, that's not true, his name is Evan, but he faded away as soon as she was born. He just did. Focused on work, and his phone, twenty-four-seven. It was so infuriating, and then he found a young woman at the office to spend time with," I say.

"I'm so sorry. He must be kicking himself that he messed things up with you and Peyton," she says.

"He is. He wants to come back, but I won't let him," I say. "And if he tries to make any contact with you, please tell me. Anyway, back to Paul, the awning of an apartment next to the hotel broke my fall and saved me because I landed on their outdoor patio. But I still fractured my pelvis, and broke my sacrum and my right arm in two places. Paul was arrested shortly after the fall and eventually sentenced to prison under a domestic violence statute. My lawyer pushed for attempted murder, but I just wanted it all to end. It was quite the story."

"Wow. Where is he now?" Lizzie asks.

"Still in prison, here in the States," I say. "But I don't know how long he'll be in for. I worry every day that they'll let him out. Even though I had a prolonged hospital stay in Paris, and months of recovery time back here in the States, obviously I'll carry the emotional scars for life. Not to mention the physical ones. Anyway, now you know why my back went out the day we met. And he may know where I live. He got the letter to me via the attorney. But I wouldn't put it past him to pay off the courier to give him scoop about me. He's relentless." A shudder rolls down my spine. I wonder if I've shared too much.

"I'll say." Lizzie shakes her head. "I can't believe you went through all of this. Just wow." Peyton fusses in her floatie, getting tired of pool time. "I'm going to go change her and feed her and then we can do whatever you'd like."

"Sure, that sounds great," I say. "Thanks for listening to me. You can tell me anything about your life, too, you know? I'm all ears."

Lizzie smiles. "Me? I'm boring. I told you, I grew up rich, even had my own nanny, folks died suddenly, and then I was poor and alone. But it's ok, I'm a survivor and I'm finally finding my way. Thanks to you and Peyton."

"We're all helping each other," I say. "And you're a natural with Peyton." They climb out of the pool, and Lizzie grabs a big white towel and wraps it around both of them, tickling Peyton in the process. I love the sound of her laughter. Lizzie looks over at me and smiles.

"We'll be ready in half an hour. Maybe we can pick up another cute swimsuit for Peyton, too. She's a water bug."

"Sure," I say.

I watch as they make their way through the garden to the house. My backyard is gorgeous, expertly landscaped and meticulously cared for. There's a fountain gurgling in the rose garden, and just beyond is the area where I grow herbs and vegetables. I need to be out here more often. Lizzie has even given me my yard back. I look to the far corner of the yard at the metal gate that leads to the state park across the street. It's locked tight, I've checked. I take a deep breath. I'm starting to feel more at home in my home.

I reach the door to the house and my stomach drops. The ruby ring I bought myself to celebrate my baby girl's birth isn't on my left-hand ring finger. It's always there. I never take it off. Where could it be? I hurry inside before Lizzie can make it out of the kitchen.

"What's wrong?" she asks.

"My ring, my Peyton ring, it's gone," I say, holding up my left hand.

"The ring with the red stones?" Lizzie asks. "I'm sure it's somewhere. When do you last remember having it on?"

I try to remember when but all I know is it's always on my finger, but now it isn't. "I don't know." I can feel myself panicking.

"Here, take Peyton for a minute, let me look around," she says. "Maybe go back outside and walk in the garden. It's going to be fine. Promise."

I did what she suggested and carried Peyton out to show her the orange tree. We watched a bee pollinating a flower and I began to relax. It was just a ring, after all. Sure, it was special, but not so important that I need to have a panic attack.

"You're my biggest gift," I say to Peyton.

"Guess what?" Lizzie says, arriving in the garden with a big grin on her face. She's holding her hand in the air and the ring glints on her left ring finger. "I found it!"

"Oh my gosh, thank you," I say. *All is well. Everything is just fine.* "Where was it?"

"In a little dish in the kitchen, up on the shelf," she says. I watch as she slips the ring off her finger and hands it to me.

And then I remember, I tucked it away up there when I was washing the dishes. "Silly me. I can't believe I didn't remember where I put it. Thank you so much," I say. I guess memory loss is another sign of being overwhelmed. But I'm getting better.

"No problem. Are we still on for shopping?" she asks, taking the baby from my arms.

"Absolutely," I say.

We both hear the doorbell ring. I worry who it could be.

"Do you want me to get that?" she asks.

"I'll come, too." We both head into the house and to the front door. And that's when I see it's Evan, staring through the glass window of the door. He's looking right at me.

"Let me in, Cecilia," he says.

I turn to Lizzie. "Please take Peyton upstairs to the nursery, get her changed. Stay there until I tell you to come out."

"Sure." Lizzie casts a quick glance outside at Evan and then at me before hurrying up the stairs.

I take a deep breath, open the door and step outside, pulling it shut behind me. "We're over. What are you doing here again?"

"I need to see Peyton," he says. "She's mine, too. I know she misses me."

"She doesn't," I say. "Remember how you never spent any time with her, or me, since her birth? That means you aren't bonded. It's your fault."

"Please," he asks. "I can do better. I, um... I'll fire Cassie."

"Don't. It doesn't matter anymore," I say.

"That's the thing. I couldn't handle work and you and the baby, so I focused on the job, and then she was there, and comforting, and she liked talking to me. She listened, and... ugh, I know it was wrong," he says. "It was so wrong. But I'll do better."

The thing is, dear Evan, I like my life much better now that you're out of it.

In a quick move, I duck inside, slam the door closed and lock it behind me. The locks have been changed, so there is no way for him to follow me. I smile through the glass window and wave goodbye. Again.

"I'm not giving up," he yells at the door between us.

I shrug and walk away. He'll leave, for now. But I am certain he will appear again, unfortunately.

Later, as we shop for bathing suits for Lizzie and Peyton, with Peyton asleep in her stroller, the saleswoman asks if we're sisters. I take a closer look at Lizzie, her threadbare jeans, simple white t-shirt. She's wearing a pink Prada bag, a gift from her last family, she told me, but otherwise, she's pretty plain. If she changed her hair color, dyed it blonde like mine, and learned how to apply makeup, well, she could look the part, could be my little sister. I wonder what it would feel like to have a sister who looks up to you, who actually loves you. Better yet, I suppose, it could be nice to have a real, true friend. I've never had a best friend. Maybe Lizzie could be that for me? I'll suggest a makeover for Lizzie, my treat. That could be fun.

And I know one thing she needs to do right away. She needs to wear contacts instead of those big glasses. I smile slowly with a realization. Yes, I like it. I will transform her.

"I'm only the nanny," Lizzie says to the woman before ducking into the dressing room.

"She's more than that," I say. "She's a lifesaver."

SIXTEEN

LIZZIE

As I stand in the dressing room of the glamorous boutique bathing suit store, I smile. Cecilia called me a lifesaver. Wonder what I should call her? I also wonder how many bathing suits I am allowed to buy. I've tried on three, and they all fit and are flattering, which is so fun. I push open the curtain and model the fourth one—a bright red one-piece—for my adoring audience comprised of Cecilia and the saleslady. Both ooh and ahhh again. I flush but I'm enjoying the attention, and I must admit, my body does look great these days. I've been working out, just like Cecilia taught me.

It started once Cecilia's back felt better. I'd be playing with Peyton, and Cecilia would pop in and tell me she'd be in the gym working out. I'd assumed that meant she was driving someplace, but no, she has a whole bunch of stuff in a special room just for her. Peyton and I followed her to the gym a couple of days later.

"Have you ever worked out?" Cecilia asked when we walked through the door. She was lying on a padded mat lifting pretty pink weights up in the air. The whole gym was sleek with a lot of black machines and chrome, but her weight set was the color of the rainbow.

Have I ever worked out? No. Have I always worked? Yes. "Um, no, not really," I answered.

"Next nap time, want me to show you a few things? I think you'd enjoy it," she'd said. I'd shrugged and agreed, so now during Peyton's afternoon nap, I go to the gym and do a little workout. Even after only three weeks, I can already see the difference in my body.

"It's going to be tough to pick one of these," I say, twirling around for fun.

"Who said anything about picking one? How about picking two?" Cecilia says. "I insist."

The saleslady beams. "How nice of you, Mrs. Strom."

That comment makes Cecilia frown. "How do you know my name?"

"Oh, well, I recognize you from the media coverage," she says. "I'm so glad to see you looking so well and happy. And you're dating Evan Dorsey now, right?"

I bet this notoriety drives her nuts. "Well, Cecilia is finished with that chapter of her life, if you don't mind," I cut in, "and she's not dating anyone. No need for any more gossip, right?" I wink at Cecilia and hope she doesn't mind me stepping in.

"Of course, no, I won't say another word. Shouldn't have brought it up. Me and my big mouth." The saleslady looks horrified, clearly worried she's about to lose a sale. "Shall I ring up the two suits, along with the two for the baby?"

"Yes, please," Cecilia says. The joy has floated out of her voice, though. No wonder she has been such a homebody these past few weeks since I've been working for her. She is sort of famous. I bet she hates being known as the victim.

"Thanks so much," I say.

"Thanks for sticking up for me," Cecilia whispers as the

saleslady busies herself with wrapping the suits up. "It used to be worse, the stares and the whispers. It's not as bad with time. People used to ask me how I made my husband so angry, like it was my fault. It was horrible. But people will forget eventually. And you didn't know anything about what happened, so that's a good sign."

"I'm so sorry you had to go through all of that. I'm going to get dressed and then we can go wherever you'd like to go," I say. I slip into the dressing room.

"I have a fun idea if you're game," she says from the other side of the curtain. "I'd like to give you a makeover. Hair, makeup and we've already been working on the wardrobe. Oh, and contacts. Have you tried wearing those? What do you think?"

I look at myself in the mirror. I thought I was looking pretty good, but I guess not. Hmm, well, Cecilia knows what she's talking about, I'm sure of that. I remind myself to be grateful. This is like a fairy tale, really it is. Despite the fact I don't need contacts, or these glasses, I need to act excited. "Are you serious?"

"I texted my hairstylist and he can fit you in this afternoon, and we'll get an appointment at the mall for a makeover with my makeup artist," she says. "The optician is just down the way, too."

I hear Peyton moving around in her stroller and hurry to dress before she begins to cry. I slide the curtain back and I'm amazed to see Cecilia holding Peyton, and Peyton is smiling at her mom, instead of crying like she usually does.

"Wow, look at you two," I say. Peyton notices me and waves her arm in my direction. Cecilia hands me the baby.

"I don't want to press my luck, but I think she likes me a little better these days," she says.

"She *loves* you," I say as we walk to the front of the store. Cecilia has so little confidence in her parenting skills. It's a shame, but it's also why she needs me.

The saleslady is out of small talk and hands Cecilia a gold shopping bag with pink tissue paper. "Here you are. You can just tap your card there."

Cecilia taps the credit card, the one I'm quite familiar with by now since she pulls it out for everything from the grocery order to clothes for Peyton, but the machine makes a loud noise. *Declined.*

"That's weird," Cecilia says. "I don't have a limit."

"You can try again?" the saleslady suggests.

It doesn't work. I don't know if Cecilia has another card. I hope so because I love the bathing suits.

"Do you have another card?" the saleslady asks.

Cecilia's cheeks have flushed. She isn't used to being denied or declined, that's for sure. She takes another card out of her wallet, taps, and it works. I relax, happy that the crisis is averted and so excited for my new things.

I notice Cecilia still looks worried as we walk out of the boutique, though. "Are you ok?"

"No. That's never supposed to happen. I need to meet my financial advisor, make sure everything is going well. I keep putting that off," she says. "I've been terrible about checking my online banking apps."

"Um, you should do that," I say. I'm getting used to the spending sprees we've been on the last couple weeks, and if I'm honest I really don't want them to end. She said she's loaded, so I'm sure it was just a glitch. But I'll make sure she schedules that meeting. It's in everybody's best interest.

"I need to take this call. Can you excuse me?" Cecilia looks flustered as she walks away, heading toward the other end of the shopping center. I decide Peyton and I will walk in the other direction to give her privacy, despite the fact I'm dying to know who's calling to make her look so concerned.

I reach into the shopping bag and show Peyton the colorful bathing suits one by one, like show and tell. She giggles and coos as I pull each one out of the bag dramatically. It's like a peek-a-boo game, and she loves it. The suits are all so fancy, so soft and made by designers I've never heard of, but now I'll memorize their names. The price tags taunt me, even though I checked them out as I was trying them on and knew I wasn't the one paying the bill. Each one is more than $400. Even the tiny one-pieces for Peyton are exquisite. And more than $500 for the two of them. She'll outgrow them in the blink of an eye. As for me, I'll have these bathing suits for the rest of my life.

I can't wait to toss the one I was wearing today away. It's from high school. It's embarrassing how long I've kept it around. It's a reminder of where I came from, how far away I've gotten from that place, those people. Sure, when I was the rich girl everybody wanted to be my friend, but after the accident, everything changed. I fight to suppress the feelings bubbling up inside, the anger that drives so many of my actions. I take a deep breath.

I'm ready to let it go. If only they could see me now.

SEVENTEEN

CECILIA

I'm walking fast on the sidewalk of the outdoor mall, dodging other shoppers like it's a video game, as if I could outrun the person on the other end of the call. But I can't.

"I don't understand how I could have spent so much already," I say again.

"I don't either, Mrs. Strom," Charles Reed, my financial advisor and banker says. I imagine his dark black glasses and his furrowed brow. "But you have, and it must stop. I've been asking you to come in for more than a year now."

"I was busy. I had a baby," I say.

"And that's another problem. You need to be saving for your daughter's future, too," he says. "I'm not sure you can pay your credit card bill this month without liquidating an investment."

I stop and put my hand over my face. How could I have done this? I'm much smarter than this, much more cautious. I've lost my focus, but I'll get it back under control. I will.

"Did you do something to my card to make it declined?" I ask.

"I put a hold on it. That's why I called. I need you to come see me. We need to sort this out and make a plan," Charles says. "A fool and her money are soon parted, as they say, and I'm afraid without the proper planning this may happen here. It may already be too late. And, eventually, your husband will be released from prison and expect his share. His banker called me the other day to check in. I haven't returned his call."

"I can come by today, if that works." My heart races and my palms are sweaty. I don't think I've spent that much, but I haven't been paying attention. The amount of money in the account seemed so vast, impossible to spend in a lifetime.

"Yes, I'll make the time. Say two this afternoon?" he says. "I'll pull together all the numbers, and we can go from there."

"Thank you," I manage as we hang up. I turn around and start walking back to Lizzie and Peyton. The two of them look so happy, so blissfully unaware that the party might be over. *No, it can't be.* I still have a fortune left, even if I've been careless during my pregnancy and since Peyton was born. I try to imagine what I will do to earn money, but aside from my art, I don't have any skills. I need to start painting again, start selling my art to wealthy collectors. Who am I kidding? I never did have much real success selling my art. I need to be careful and invest my money, not spend it so readily.

I log in to my two different banks, each holds five accounts. The balances are fine, great even. I log in to the bank with Paul's shared account, the one tied to my credit card. Yes, there has been some spending, but it's still a hefty number. I log out of the apps and head toward Lizzie and the baby. I know I should forget about the idea of Lizzie's makeover until I know what my finances look like.

"Hi guys!" I say as brightly as possible. Maybe Charles is being too much of an alarmist. Maybe he's all wrong. Yes, that's likely the case. His fees come from how much time he spends managing the financial matters of our estate, and he needs more billable hours. That's got to be it. It's not, though. I know I'm kidding myself.

"Is everything ok?" Lizzie asks.

"Sure, great, wonderful," I say, looking away. "But I do need to go into LA this afternoon for a meeting. You two will survive without me, I'm sure."

"We'll be great. I think we'll try out our new bathing suits," Lizzie says as we head back to the car.

I find myself wondering if this will be my last shopping trip for a while. I decide I'll take another closer look at all my accounts when I get home, not just the joint account I use most of the time. It's not my only account, not by any means. I'm too careful for that to be the case. Still, the call from Charles was alarming.

We're almost to the car by the time I see him, but it's too late to hide. He's standing by my car, blocking the driver's side with his body, leaning against the car door. It's too late to slip into the car and drive away.

"Cecilia, we need to talk," Evan says as we reach the car. "Hey baby, Daddy's here." But as he smiles at Peyton, she begins to whimper. Evan's face falls.

Peyton turns her face into Lizzie's neck. He's scaring her. I click the doors unlocked.

"Move, Evan," I say.

"No, we need to talk," he says.

"What are you doing here? Are you stalking me?" I ask.

"No, I just want to see Peyton," he says, hands on his hips. "Please?"

"Go away. We are over, remember?" I say. "I'm not sure how much clearer I can be. No second chances. Done. Give my best to Cassie."

Lizzie figures out what's happening and slides Peyton into her car seat in the back and closes the door. She looks at Evan and says, "We're late for a very important appointment, for the baby. We need to get going."

Evan takes another step toward me. I've never considered him to be a menacing man, but right here, right now, I feel fury flowing from him like an erupting volcano. "We need to talk. This isn't fair. It's not just your decision. I miss you, and the baby. Cassie is nothing, really. It's over."

"I don't care, I really don't," I say. "She can have you and your phone obsession and attention disorder. Leave me alone. Stop following us."

"I'm really not stalking you—I just so happened to see you across the parking lot. I'm not leaving town. It's a small place. You can't avoid me. We will keep running into each other, Cecilia. I guarantee it."

Lizzie walks around to my side of the car and stands next to me, arms crossed in front of her. "She said it's over. That means it's over. You can't bully her into a different outcome, Evan."

"Who the hell do you think you are? You aren't part of this," Evan says, fury directed at Lizzie now.

"I'm the nanny, so if it involves Peyton, I'm involved," she says.

"And she's a friend," I say. "Evan, I don't need or want you in my life. I finally have the help I need, that you never provided."

"I was there for you, I'll be there, for both of you," he says, shoving a hand through his blond hair, his blue eyes flashing with anger.

"Leave me alone. And leave the baby alone." I slip inside my car as Lizzie hurries to the other side. Evan stands where I left him in the parking lot, staring at me. I reverse the car and drive away.

"Wow, that was intense." Lizzie exhales audibly. "Are you ok?"

"I'm fine. You know, he used to be fun," I say. "We were

friends when I was first married to Paul and new to Malibu. Evan helped throw all our parties when Paul was trying to social climb his way into Hollywood. We used to laugh and talk every day. And then, after what happened in Paris, he was by my side all through rehab, and so I thought that was love. He took care of me. But I see now it was just to pin me down—and I'm sure my money played no small part in that."

"It stinks when people change. I think money makes people change," Lizzie says.

"It's hard to manage, to be honest. A blessing and a curse," I say as we pull into the driveway of my mansion. "This place also drains funds. I know, because I pay all the bills. But I'll get this under control, I will."

"I know you will," Lizzie says with more certainty than I feel. She drops her voice as we glide into the driveaway. "So, he's Peyton's dad? I guess I can see that. She has your eyes and hair, your cheeks, but she has his more reddish skin tone and that cute dimple in her chin, like him. He probably is a lot more handsome when he's not furious."

"He's cute, I suppose, and unfortunately, yes, he's furious at me, but he should be mad at himself. He is her biological dad, but he's not on the birth certificate. He was MIA when the hospital had me fill it out, so too bad. By the time she was born, he and I had been fighting for months. We were over, but just tried to make it work because of the baby. That never works, I've learned. So he turned to another woman named Cassie. Such a cliché, really."

"I'm sorry you had to see him today," Lizzie says. I watch as she unfastens Peyton from the car seat, and somehow the baby sleeps through the extraction.

"Thanks for sticking up for me," I say.

"That's what friends are for." She smiles at me. "I think you scared him off. He could tell you were serious."

I feel better as we walk inside, me carrying the new bathing suits while Lizzie carries the baby. I turn off the alarm and hold the door open for Lizzie, making sure it's locked behind us.

I need to be careful. Evan is angry. I don't know what he's capable of doing.

"I hope he'll leave me alone, but let's remember to always lock the doors, day and night, like I've told you since the day we met," I say. "Just to be safe."

EIGHTEEN

LIZZIE

So much drama, is all I can think when Cecilia finally leaves for her meeting in LA with one of her many lawyers. I mean, she has an attorney named Jim who did my contract, and then another one who is working on her finances, and who knows how many others. I guess money brings more people into your life. Meanwhile, I'm exhausted by the encounter with Evan. I bet she must be, too. I mean, the guy is cute, hot to be honest, and I feel bad for him, but she is clearly over him. He needs to move on. He blew it. She needed someone, and he wasn't there. I get it. It's like she needed me, and I appeared. That's sort of how it worked. Why would she need Evan now when she has me?

While Peyton naps I decide to tackle some housekeeping and laundry. Compared to washing clothes for four kids, a baby is easy. Tiny clothing items, although when I read the tags on some of them, designer brands of course, with a lot suggesting dry cleaning or handwashing. I'm not going to do that. She's going to outgrow these items before I could get them to the cleaner and back. If I ruin an outfit or two, who cares? We can always buy more cute things.

I putter around in the nursery tidying up. The cleaning crew comes every Thursday and gets the house in great shape, top to bottom, so all I need to do is keep things picked up. Once again, I remind myself how lucky I am. I walk down the hall to my luxurious guest suite, Lizzie's Suite, as Cecilia calls it now. I've placed my new swimsuits on the bed so I can admire them and decide which one to wear in the pool this afternoon with Peyton. Such fabulous choices.

It's funny, when I think about it, what I'd be doing over at the Johnsons right now versus here at Cecilia's during the early afternoon. The houses are so spread apart on this road I can't even see the house from here, but in my mind I see the scene clearly. There, I'd be folding mountains of laundry, fixing an afternoon snack for the spoiled ones and figuring out what I would be making for dinner that night. At 3 p.m., I would rush to the minivan and begin school pick-ups. By the end of the day, I'd be exhausted and invariably a bit angry. Mrs. Johnson was typically napping, sleeping off her day-drinking. Even if she wasn't asleep, she hardly lifted a finger to help. *Good riddance.* I guess I learned from my time there, as one does in every bad situation. I hear you learn more from the bad than the good in life. I'm not sure, though. I think it's time to learn from the good, the uber wealthy. It's my time to shine.

I swoop down the grand staircase and head to the kitchen to make a batch of smoothies. Cecilia lets me select groceries to have delivered twice a week, the finest produce from the best farmer's market in Santa Monica, seafood from the best fish-monger, meats direct from the cattle ranch, everything is organic, and the best, and expensive, I'm sure. Peyton's food is handmade, just for her, beautiful glass jars with handwritten labels. Solid food is a new development since she's just turning 6 months old. We're just starting to work our way through the selection of fruits, vegetables, yogurts and meats. All formulated to give little Peyton all the vitamins and minerals she'll need for a bright future, an extraordinary future.

I wonder if she's going to turn out to be spoiled by too much stuff, too much ease, too much of everything? I think of Kimmie and Kathie and hope not. Cecilia seems relatively normal, although she can be a bit pretentious at times. It's likely because she grew up poor. She doesn't take all of this for granted, at least I hope she doesn't. As far as I can tell, Cecilia says the money is a blessing. All I know is that we've just been busy spending it. And that's fine with me.

I finish making my smoothie, a beautiful pink concoction made with the sweetest strawberries I've ever tasted. As I sip it I'm flipping through a glossy magazine—I like to keep up on all things home- and lifestyle-oriented. This magazine explains how to make cleaning supplies from scratch—organic and healthy for your home and family. I flip the page and discover all the latest beauty products to make your husband happy to be home when you greet him after a long day at the office. I'd like to be a wealthy, pampered traditional housewife someday. It's true. It's my dream. That's why I'd been so excited about Cecilia's offer of a makeover and disappointed when it seemed to be forgotten about. I realize now that I need it, desperately. I hope she'll remember what she promised me, even though she had to cancel my hair appointment to speak to her advisor.

I wonder what all of this is about, although I know she'll share the details with me when she returns. We've become like sisters, confidantes. Upstairs in the nursery, Peyton stirs in the crib, a precursor to fully waking up. I'm ready for her and can't wait to see her in her new little yellow polka dot bathing suit. It matches mine. We're going to look so cute. The photos are going to be adorable. I mean, with this setting of Cecilia's house and a cute baby, I can imagine this whole life as mine. A baby. A home. What I've always dreamed of. Nannies can have a little fun sometimes, too. I smile when I think about my social media channels. I have so much content now that I work for Cecilia and Peyton.

People see me, the young, beautiful woman with an adorable baby smiling in the sunshine, here, there and everywhere fabulous.

I think about my own mom as always, my role model, and my precious little sister Sally. They would be so proud of me, so proud of where I am, what I've become. I try to push the memory away, but it comes at me fast, unwelcomed. Mom, Sally and me in the kitchen of our home. Sun streamed through the kitchen windows and Sally giggled in her highchair. We'd been making cookies from scratch and flour covered the counter and puffed in the air as Mom kneaded the dough. If I could have pictured the perfect day, this would be it.

But then he came home from work—well, from the bar he frequented after work.

"Go to your room! Now! And take that screaming baby with you," he bellowed at me as soon as he entered the kitchen. When I hesitated, he lunged at me. "Now!"

I grabbed Sally, who by now was wailing in terror, and hesitated by the doorway. "Mom?" I wanted to grab her, too, to protect her from what I knew would happen next.

But she shook her head. "Take care of the baby, Lizzie! Go!"

And so I did what she asked, because I loved her, but I'll never forget the sound of his fist hitting her face. Not ever.

I realize I've been lost in thought as I hear Peyton on the monitor. She's awake now.

I hurry upstairs and into the nursery. Peyton grins at me and holds out her arms. Such a good baby. I wonder what Cecilia would think of throwing a half-birthday party for Peyton. I could make things so cute, and we could invite some people—does Cecilia even know any people? Well, it could just be the three of us, but we could make it seem fun and exclusive via the photos. I think a party could be just the thing for all of us.

"Do you want to have a half-birthday party, Peyton?" I ask her.

She smiles. She's in. I see a little white tooth about to emerge from her bottom gum. Poor baby hasn't complained at all. I will freeze a couple toys for her to chew on and buy some Orajel with the next grocery order.

The doorbell rings as I'm finishing putting on my bathing suit. We look adorable in our yellow polka dots, if I do say so myself. Sure my bikini is tiny, but I'm rocking it. I run to Cecilia's room and borrow one of her many plush robes so I don't answer the door in only a bathing suit. But then again, should I even answer the door? What if it's that Evan guy? Although I realize I wouldn't mind him seeing me dressed like this...

I hurry down the stairs with Peyton on my hip and see a woman standing on the stoop. Red hair, kind of looks like a stereotypical nosey neighbor kind of person to me. I assume she's harmless.

I open the door. "Can I help you?"

"Hi, Peyton! It's Grandma!" the woman says. She's talking too loudly, and the baby is scared. She starts to cry. "I came to give you a present. Your half-birthday is coming up soon, I just know it!" The woman is trying to get inside.

I don't know who this woman is, but I do know Peyton doesn't like her. And she isn't even sure when Peyton's half-birthday is.

"Look, um, I don't know you so I can't let you in," I say. And then I realize who she looks like. Evan, if Evan had bright red hair, which, lucky for him, he doesn't. I know for sure this is Marian. Cecilia warned me about her. I'm not to let her near the baby. "Cecilia's not here, so you'll have to come back later."

I try to close the door, but the woman jams her foot in the

way. "Take this for my granddaughter. When she stops crying, give it to her," the woman says. "Who are you anyway?"

"I'm Lizzie, the nanny," I answer, taking the small bag from her. I'm tempted to tell this woman to leave us alone, but I know that's really Cecilia's job.

"Why are you dressed like her? You aren't her mom," Marian says, hands on hips, looking us up and down, the expression in her eyes inscrutable.

"Well, Peyton doesn't even know who you are," I say. "So it's none of your business."

Oops. I couldn't help it. I shove the door closed and lock it. I turn and walk away, confident she can't get in. Peyton and I have an important photo shoot to get to in the pool. I saunter down the hallway, baby on my hip, knowing that woman is watching me from outside. *Enjoy the view.*

NINETEEN

CECILIA

Charles stares across his desk at me with a look of sheer disappointment, manila folders spread out in front of him. Just looking at all this paper makes me exhausted.

"Where do you want to start, Mrs. Strom?" he asks. "I have a lot of different categories that document your overspending, your recklessness." He points to the folders. "We have beauty, shopping, taxes, cars and homes, parties and travel, real estate. I suggest tackling the big ones first."

Ugh. This is not fun. "Sure, talk about whatever you'd like, but everything I've done is done. Spent. I think we should look to the future. Maybe you could help me make a plan for that. Isn't that part of your job? I think a lot of this is your fault, to be honest."

"Don't be ridiculous, Mrs. Strom. I've been trying to reach you for months," he says. Then he coughs and regains control of himself. He's supposed to be the professional here.

"Watch your tone, Mr. Reed," I say. "I haven't done anything wrong, I just didn't pay attention."

"Yes, of course, I'm sorry. We should do that, make a budget for you, if there is anything left," he says. *Doom and gloom.*

"Also, do you know when Mr. Strom is scheduled to be released?"

"He has a few more years," I say. "I know they will notify me, the *victim*," I emphasize that word, "when he is about to be released. I hope it's years from now. He was sentenced for ten years, and he's only served four and a half. There's plenty of time."

"It may be prudent, to protect yourself. You should carve out some of the remaining money to go to him upon release. Keep the peace," he says.

"He tried to kill me," I remind him.

"He's paying the price now. I'm sure he's learned a lesson," he says. He picks up a file. "Taxes. Looks as if you forgot to pay state and federal last year, correct? So they'll be coming after you, with fines. It looks like that's more than $260,000 in unpaid state taxes, and triple that in federal."

Numbers, numbers, numbers. I'm an artist. I cannot be held responsible for this. My running joke was that I don't do math in public. But it's not funny anymore. "Paul used to handle all of this stuff."

"Well, he can't right now, so you need to hire someone. Here's a tax accountant. I can call him today and get him started on this."

"Ok," I say. He's looking at me like you'd look at a strange animal, one you just can't believe exists in the wild.

"Real estate," he says, picking up another folder. "You've purchased considerable assets, all cash, for an event business. A building, a fleet of vans, a commercial kitchen, and so much more. Why?"

"I used to work for my ex's company but I don't anymore," I say. "It's fine. I wish them well."

"Millions of dollars spent there," he says, shaking his head. "With nothing to show for it."

"Can we move on?" I ask. I fold my arms across my chest and stare at him. All problems, no solutions.

"You sold the home you and Paul owned, for a loss, and then purchased a larger, more expensive home two streets down, and you had the interior completely redone by this Beverly Hills designer. You paid cash, for everything," he says. "They must have loved you as a client."

"They did. My house is exquisite." I stand up and walk to the window of his office, stare down at the snarled-up traffic below. "Look, I don't need to go through each of your folders. Let's focus on the future."

"If you continue to spend this way, you won't have a future, at least not a financial one," he says. He stands and begins pacing back and forth behind his desk.

"I come from nothing, so you're not scaring me," I say. He is, but I'm not going to show it.

"Let's make sure you don't return to that state," he says.

"Agreed." I sigh.

"And you've been on several shopping sprees to high-end boutiques." He looks at me questioningly.

Well, that was for me and Lizzie, and the baby. It's fine. "Yes, it's been nice to be out and about. I've been depressed since the baby was born," I say. *I think it was since she was conceived*, I don't say.

"I understand you've been through a lot, and I'm sorry," he says. "Does the child's father help? Pay child support? Surely, with your finances spiraling like they are, you would want to collect money however you can?"

"No, she doesn't have a father," I say. I married Paul, suffered his arrogance, survived a near-fatal fall. I refuse to be beholden to anyone. I won't be. And neither will my daughter. We will live on Paul's money, my money, and that's all. It will be plenty. "Tell me what my budget should be per month, and I'll try to stick to it. Would that work?"

"It would be for everything. Dining, shopping, travel, house maintenance and services, gas, groceries. Everything," he emphasizes and scribbles a number on a piece of paper and hands it to me.

"You're kidding," I say. "I can't live on that amount. I live in Malibu."

"Maybe you shouldn't," he says.

"I'm not moving," I say, although in the back of my mind I'm starting to wonder if I should. Just escape from everyone and everything, me and Peyton.

"I'll provide the monthly allowance on the first day of each month," he says. "I will work with the accountant to clear up all the debt owed to the government. But, Mrs. Strom, you must do your part. Have you made any investments? Anything that can be liquidated?"

"I've bought art and sculpture, mostly for the catering business and my home. Oh, and antiques," I say.

"Those are not good investments, typically," he says. "Stocks, bonds, that sort of thing, that's what I'm talking about."

And then it sinks in—what I've done by accident, and because I wasn't keeping track, paying attention. I must do better, for Peyton at least. And I should think seriously about getting a job.

"No, I don't own any of those things," I say.

"You need to liquidate an asset. Think of something, Mrs. Strom, and think fast," he says. "You'll need to have something to offer Mr. Strom when he's released. Something substantial, I imagine."

TWENTY

LIZZIE

I've decided to make dinner for myself and Cecilia, in case she makes it home in time to join us. I've opted to make chicken breasts stuffed with a sharp French cheese and herbs from Cecilia's garden out back, and a kale and shaved Brussels sprout salad from the farmer's market produce in the refrigerator. I sort through the glass jars of baby food and select a yummy jar of homemade goodness for Peyton. This one is mashed potato and turkey. I look at my watch. Whatever Cecilia's doing in LA, it's taking a long time. I hope she's ok, for all our sakes.

It's strange that she has so many enemies lurking around trying to mess with her. It makes me glad I don't have any enemies to speak of. I suppose Mrs. Johnson isn't a fan, but she's nothing. Maybe Cecilia needs some dirt on Evan and his mom. Maybe she already has some and doesn't realize it. Thinking about Evan makes me hope we run into him someday soon. Well, not me and Cecilia, but me and the baby. I bet he'd like that.

My heart skips a beat when I hear the front door opening and the alarm starts to beep, but then I remind myself it's likely Cecilia.

"Welcome home," I call out and hurry to the playpen to pick up Peyton. I'm ready to sprint out the back door if it's not Cecilia.

"Hello, it's nice to be home," she says. I hear her disable and reset the alarm before appearing in the kitchen looking tired. "Smells good in here. I'm starving."

"Great. Dinner is almost ready," I say and hand Peyton over.

I see Cecilia staring at the gift bag on the counter.

"Oh, that's from Evan's mom, who tried to invite herself inside. I kept her out, though," I say. "I didn't give the present to the baby either. I don't know what it is."

"Good," she says and closes her eyes. "I'm going to have to do something to get them to leave me—us—alone."

"I was thinking the same thing," I say. "Do you have anything on them? Any dirt?"

"Why, Lizzie, you're too nice to think that way. But since you asked, no I don't, no, just him messing around with a woman who works for him, and a total lack of support and care for the baby and me," she says. "I hope he just stays away, but I'm not so sure. What is my problem that I make such bad choices?"

Cecilia carries Peyton over to the couch and puts her down before sitting next to her. I watch as she covers her yawn.

"I'm sorry. You'll pick better next time," I say. "I mean, if he keeps bugging you, you could get a restraining order."

"Evan will back down, I'm pretty sure of it. Oh, I'm *so* finished with men." She sighs.

"For now. And those restraining orders don't work anyway, not really," I say. "I mean, that's what I've read." I busy myself with taking the chicken out of the oven and plating up the meal.

I glance over at the two of them on the couch just in time to see Cecilia slump sideways, fortunately falling away in the opposite direction from where the baby is lying. I rush over to them, snapping a photo before grabbing the baby. She's unharmed of course, but what if I hadn't been here?

"Cecilia." I shake her shoulder. "Wake up."

She blinks and sits up slowly. "Did I just fall asleep? Sitting up?"

"Yes," I say. "The baby's fine."

"Oh my god." She jumps up. "I'm sorry, baby. And what were we talking about, Lizzie?"

"Um, restraining orders," I say.

"What do you know about restraining orders?" she asks, following me back into the kitchen. I strap Peyton into the highchair, and she sits down at the table.

"Oh, nothing really. I just read some article where a woman got one against her estranged husband but he just ignored her and came after her one day. With a gun. And she died," I say. The image of my mom's bloody, battered face floods into my mind and I push it away fast. After he killed my mom, my dad grabbed my little sister, placed her into her car seat without strapping her in, and drove into that tree. I like to reimagine things, that they were all in the car. It's cleaner, more simple that way, the idea that they all died together in an accident. But it's not the truth. The truth is even more horrid. I wasn't the one who found her, my baby sister, dead, thrown from the car by the violent crash. But I'd imagined the scene a million times from the news accounts and the few photos released of the scene. The police ruled it a double murder-suicide. I close my eyes and will the images away.

"Wow, ok, well, I don't think that's the case here," she says.

"You never really know someone though, do you?" I say, putting the plate in front of her and sitting down across the table. Peyton is playing with her favorite teething ring and waiting for a spoonful of turkey mash from me. We look like the perfect little family.

"No, I guess you don't. I learned that lesson the hard way," she says with a sigh. "The chicken is great, thank you."

"How did your trip to LA go?" I ask, purposefully changing the subject.

"It was ok," she says, but it doesn't sound like it was. She stifles another yawn. "I need to make a few changes, lifestyle changes, unfortunately."

Uh-oh. "What does that mean? Are you firing me?" I ask.

"No, of course not. You're essential. I still don't feel strong enough to carry Peyton around all day, to take care of her the way she deserves. I need you. And besides, I love having the company. I just need to try to live on a budget," she says.

I bite my lip. I haven't known her that long, but I can't help thinking that budgeting and Cecilia do not go together. I cannot imagine it. She's clearly outgrown the days when she knew how to stretch a dollar, of that I'm certain. "Ok, I can help you," I say. Frugal is my middle name, not that I had a choice.

"I'm still getting my head around all of this. I should have been paying attention, but it just seemed like such a vast amount, you know, an endless supply, or so I thought," she says.

"Mmmm," I say. I thought so, too. That's why I'm so happy to be here. *Darn it.*

"I'm afraid we should return some of the stuff we bought today, as long as the tags are on and all of that," she says.

"Shoot, I removed all the tags, and put the new bathing suits in the delicate wash. Peyton's, too. I hate to think other people tried them on first," I say. "I'm sorry."

"It's ok," she says. "We'll just consider today's purchases our last hurrah." She smiles at Peyton. "Mommy is going to learn how to budget again, like the good old days. Doesn't that sound fun?"

Peyton doesn't answer. She's busy chowing on her turkey mash. She dips her hand into the jar and spreads the goop all over her highchair tray, pleased with herself. "Peyton, no, we don't do that," I say. "Oh, I put all the mail on the credenza in the hallway. There's quite a lot of it," I say. "The mailbox was full."

"Thanks," she says, pushing away from the table and clearing the small amount of food left on her plate into the trash. "That's another thing I forget about. The mail. There's never anything fun in there."

"Well, it does mostly look like bills this time," I say, and then I realize I shouldn't be adding to her worries. The one good thing about moving all the time, and not having a home of your own, is that you don't have to worry about mail. "There are a couple catalogs. Those are fun."

"If you're not on a budget," she says.

I watch her walk away, shoulders rolled forward, and realize I need to do something to cheer her up. Maybe Peyton and I can come up with something. "Oh, hey, Cecilia?"

She stops in the doorway.

"I was thinking I could put together a fun little half-birthday celebration for the baby tomorrow, if it's ok with you?" I ask.

"We can't spend anything," she says.

"I know. We don't need to. I can bake a cake, and we have balloons in the pantry. I'll handle everything with what we have already. Ok?" I clap my hands and Peyton imitates me.

"She looks excited," Cecilia says, and finally smiles.

"It's a big milestone," I say. "It should be documented, and celebrated, at least that's what all the parenting podcasts say."

"Well, if they say it's a must, then sure," Cecilia says. "Let's party. I'm certainly in the mood."

"Oh, and you should try one of the smoothies I made this morning. They taste like dessert," I say. I have such a good recipe going for all of these special smoothies. Just for Cecilia.

"I will, thanks." She heads toward the refrigerator. "And go ahead with the party, but just for the three of us, ok? Simple."

"Of course," I say. As she walks out of the room, I smile at the baby. I'm going to throw a fun party for Peyton, and for me. Cecilia can choose to come or not. It would be better if she didn't, in all honesty. She's sort of a downer since her card was declined. I watch as she drifts out of the room, likely headed upstairs to her bedroom. She's obviously had a long day.

"Don't worry, baby. Your mommy is rich. Look at all she has," I say. "Plenty to go around."

It's so nice to have a new friend, don't you agree? I cannot thank you enough for visiting me. So many people these days are too busy to tend to the people in their lives. Too self-centered to take time to reconnect. But not you. No, you are very special, my dear. You take the time for me, to get to know me, and I want you to know how much I appreciate it. And your stories! Enchanting. Please do come see me again, very soon. I'll have some more stories for you, too!

Very truly,

Paul

TWENTY-ONE

CECILIA

I feel like I'm drowning. It's the only way I can describe it. It's like I'm underwater and operating in slow motion as everyone else is going about life as if nothing has changed. But everything has changed, at least for me and Peyton, although she's too young to understand. At the very end of the meeting, as I was trying to leave, Charles stopped and looked me right in the eye. He told me I should sell my house and move to a smaller, more affordable place to cut down on my expenses and to replenish the funds I've *squandered*— his word—from the joint account.

But I love my house. It's really the only thing that's mine. I feel safe here, and it's the only home Peyton has known. There must be another way. Besides, why should I replenish an account so that my husband who tried to kill me is rich when he's released? Why would I do that? I wouldn't. I won't.

But I do need to save money and cut out the excess.

I pick up the stack of mail and begin thumbing through, sorting things. Most of it is junk and catalogs I should toss without opening. I recognize the electric bill and another utility bill, the pool service, the landscape service, the maid service. I've paid all these people regularly. But I guess I've missed some big ones. Thank goodness I paid for my house using the proceeds of the sale of the house Paul and I owned. As this place cost more than the one we lived in, I paid the shortfall in cash.

My phone pings with a text from an unknown number. I pick it up.

You are a bad mother. You are. Don't think you're not. Everyone knows.

My stomach drops and my hand begins to shake. Who would send me something like this? I call the number but it goes to a generic voicemail. I hang up, unnerved. I check the front door—it's locked, and the alarm is on. I rush upstairs. I wonder if Lizzie feels the same way about me? Is she thinking about leaving, going back to the family she was with before, where things were, I'm sure, much more normal and much calmer? I hope not. But truly, I wouldn't blame her if she wants to walk away from me. Sudden sadness at the thought of that washes over me and I'm surprised to realize my eyes are filled with tears. I will not tell her about this text.

It's from Paul, I know it is, although Evan and Marian have easier access to mobile phones. But my gut tells me it's Paul. Somehow, he's found out about the baby. And he's jealous and vengeful. But at least he's behind bars.

I close my bedroom door and walk to the window seat. I look out at the ocean, but it's black with nightfall, more menacing than comforting. There is no moon tonight and the fog is blowing onto the point in tendrils, like smoke or a swirl of ghosts. I remember reading that the tip of this point was sacred land to the Indigenous people who lived here.

Sometimes I wonder if it is their spirits haunting us here on nights like this.

My thoughts go back to the text. I suppose he's right in a

sense; I was a bad mother, but I'm getting better with Lizzie's help. I take a deep breath and realize I feel a little something else, too. Triumph about having had a baby, my little girl, with another man after not allowing Paul to get me pregnant.

This day has exhausted me, and I feel a little guilty for not helping with Peyton's bedtime routine, but I know Lizzie has it down—heck, she created it—and she knows I'm wiped out. I decide a bath is just what the doctor ordered and walk into my huge en suite to get things ready. I start the water to fill the huge marble tub and look around for my bath salts, usually in an expensive antique dish right here on the edge of the tub.

That's strange. Perhaps the cleaning crew moved it, or somebody broke the dish and didn't want to say anything? I rummage in my closet for another bath solution and find an expensive bath oil I bought during the ill-fated trip to Paris. *C'est la vie,* I think, and pour it into the warm water. I slip into the tub and try to relax. I know that tomorrow is the start of a new day, and I must change my spending ways. I also know I need to deal with Evan and his mom if they continue to come around hassling me. But perhaps they won't.

My bath water has turned cold and it's time to get out of the tub. I reach for my plush white towel and step onto the soft white bathmat. As I walk back into my bedroom, I flip on the fireplace and the gas lights up the room with a warm glow. I take a deep breath, but I cannot shake the dread that's come over me. A thump in the hallway makes me jump. I hurry to the door, open it, and look both ways down the hall. There's no one there. I'm sure Peyton is asleep in the nursery, and Lizzie is in her room. Everything is fine.

I need to be sure the security system is turned on. Lizzie knows how to set it, but I've noticed she sometimes forgets after a long day of caring for Peyton. The same thing has happened to me. I think about when I left the front door wide open and shudder. Tonight, she's remembered. The panel glows red, activated. I drop my shoulders and head back upstairs.

I climb into bed and shiver as a chill rolls down my spine. I think about my letter to Paul, imagine him opening it in his prison cell and then slamming his fist on the cinderblock wall. Who am I kidding. He's not going to care about our divorce or anything else.

He's going to want to murder me again when he realizes what I've spent, what I've done.

TWENTY-TWO

LIZZIE

It hasn't taken me long to get used to all this fancy living. My poor dead mom would be impressed. First, I imitated my mother, I loved everything about her. And then, after what happened, after I lost her, lost both of them, I lost those memories, the comfort of class. But I've learned again. I've remembered. I've refined myself to be a proper lady by watching Cecilia. I've cleaned up my words, learned how to say a proper please and thank you, and I've imitated Cecilia's mannerisms so much that I'm surprised she hasn't noticed.

I flip my hair over my shoulder the same way she does now that it's long enough. I still need the promised makeover, but I'm going to need to tread lightly about that since she's in this feeling poor phase. I tilt my head when I smile, just like she does, and bite my bottom lip when I'm thinking, like her. Getting dressed this morning, I decided to wear all of Cecilia's hand-me-downs: thick brown corduroy pants, a cream cashmere sweater, with cute brown slides, Gucci no less, to complete the look. I'm still using the pharmacy makeup, but I have gotten a lot better at putting it on. Social media tutorials are helpful for so many things, I've discovered.

If you search makeup application for a woman in her twenties, there are hundreds of helpful tips. Or you can search, I don't know, lock-picking and learn a new skill right on the spot. I haven't done that yet, no need of course, but I thought about it a few times when I was with the Johnsons and one of the kids wouldn't come out of his or her room for dinner, the little spoiled brats. Imagine their faces if I simply unlocked the door. Ha!

I hear Peyton babbling over the monitor, so I check my fashionable self in the mirror one last time. I grab another Cecilia hand-me-down, a Louis Vuitton purse, and I look, for once, like I belong in Malibu living this life. It's everything Hollywood movies have portrayed of it here: sunshine, dramatic coastlines, fabulous wealth. I tilt my head and smile at myself one last time and hurry down the hall to Peyton.

I see Cecilia's already arrived. She's holding the baby and talking to her softly, both of them facing the window. For some reason, this makes me mad. But I'll cover that emotion with my new Cecilia-like smile.

"Good morning," I say, chipper as a robin singing first thing in the morning.

"Morning," Cecilia answers, turning around.

I almost freak out. She looks horrible. Dark circles ring her eyes, her lips are pale and dry, her hair is a mess. "Is everything alright? Are you feeling ok?" I ask.

Cecilia sighs. "Sure, it's all great," she says.

I don't believe she believes that.

"Ok, well, if you'd like, I can take the baby, and you can go back to sleep. Sound good?" I say. "Oh, and I made some fresh new smoothies, and there's a quiche, if you're hungry. It's in the fridge." Peyton reaches for me and I grab her.

"Ok, thanks," Cecilia says. "You look nice this morning. Are you going somewhere?"

"Thank you! Well, this entire outfit is from you, so I know I look good. I do have a few errands that Peyton and I were going to tackle, if that's ok," I say. Mostly I just want to go walk around the mall with the baby, see what kind of attention I attract when I look like I belong. I also have an appointment with Cecilia's hairstylist. I should tell her, I suppose.

"I have an appointment with Raul today," I say. "I hope that's ok with you?" I tilt my head and smile. "The baby can come, too. She'll love all the activity of a hair salon."

Cecilia stares at me and bites her lip. "Sure, good, um, he's the best. He's expensive, though."

"I've been saving up for it, you know, from my salary," I say. "Ever since you mentioned a makeover, well, it's all I think about."

"I wish I could pay for it, but as you know, things have changed," she says.

"It's fine. I'm excited to pay and to get it done!" I assure her. And I am. A new hairstyle is the final part of my transformation.

"Ok, enjoy your time. It's a fabulous salon," she says. "Tell him I say hi. And I'll be in soon, I hope."

"Will do," I say. As Cecilia drifts out of the room, I call after her, "Can I help you with anything?"

"Not now, not yet, I need to make a plan. On my own. And I will," she says.

"Ok, don't forget to drink your smoothie," I say. I start to change Peyton, getting her ready for the day. I open her closet and admire the row of fashionable baby clothes, all hanging on tiny hangers, arranged by color and season. I find an outfit in brown and cream so we can complement each other. Once she's dressed, we head downstairs for breakfast. But we eat fast. I am so excited to get out of here and want to be sure to get to my appointment on time.

We have one stop before the hair salon, but it shouldn't take long. I pack up all the things Peyton will need for our outing, check my purse to be sure I have everything I need, and hurry to disarm the alarm system. I glance up the main staircase, but Cecilia is nowhere to be seen.

I hope she gets some rest. I know the stress of the last couple days is getting to her, but she looks really terrible. Haunted almost. If she needs money, she could sell a few things. Heck, everything she owns is worth so much. She has art everywhere, she has clothes—well, I guess she gave me some she could have sold—and jewelry. She never wears the same necklace or ring or bracelet twice, that I can tell. She likely has a whole fortune in jewelry.

She'll be fine. She just needs to get herself together. She's become too soft, too accustomed to doing and spending whatever she wants. She still has plenty, I'm sure of it, she just needs to be more careful.

I walk out to Cecilia's BMW and smile. I love driving this car. But it's not just about me, I remind myself, it's important that Peyton rides in a safe car. I slip her into the car seat in the back, pushing the inevitable horror of memory from my mind. I take a deep breath. My dad drove a Mercedes. It was different, a lifetime ago. I'm no longer that orphan girl, and the monster is gone. I'm here, now, with baby Sally. I close my eyes. No... baby Peyton. I exhale and walk around to the driver's seat, forcing myself to the here and now. I smile at Peyton in the rearview mirror. "Ready for our adventure today, baby?"

Peyton kicks her little legs in response. She's happy, I'm happy. Life is good. I wonder if sometime soon Cecilia will decide I need a car of my own. *Maybe I'll drop some hints about that*, I think, as I start the car.

Everything she's given or bought for me is mine to keep. I deserve these things, I do. It's why I work so hard, it's why I moved to Malibu in the first place. To get these things, to have what I used to have as a child. Comfort, security. The trappings of wealth the people who live around here all take for granted.

But as Cecilia's beginning to learn, it's a mistake to take anything, or anyone, for granted.

"Happy six-month birthday," I call back to Peyton. I can't wait to gather all the party supplies. We have so much to do this morning. As I pull out of Cecilia's driveway, I look to my left and notice two kids standing just outside her gate. It's Jimmy and Johnny. What are they doing here? I roll the window down.

"Hey, what are you two doing? You should be at school," I say, looking at my watch.

"Why did you leave us?" Jimmy says with a pout on his cute little face. His eyes are two oceans as a tear works its way down his cheek.

Oh gosh. I turn off the car and climb out, kneeling to be eye level. "I had to leave because the lady who owns this house needed me. She has a baby. See her in the backseat?" I point to Peyton but realize too late that's likely not what he wanted to hear. I've replaced him. But it's true. "You're a big boy now, both of you are. You don't need me like she does."

"I'm sad," Jimmy says. "I miss you."

"I miss you, too," I tell him.

"My mom's a mess. You need to come back and help us," Johnny says. "She doesn't even wake up in the morning anymore. She locks herself in her bedroom and drinks every day and then she can't wake up. We have to get ready on our own and walk to school. She hired a lady who comes in the afternoon. But she's mean. We don't like her at all. And my dad is still gone. He must've really pissed Mom off this time."

Yes, a naked pool party when you're married does tend to make people angry, for good reason. I realize for these spoiled kids that taking responsibility for themselves must seem like a real hardship. And it is a big change. *At least there's food in the refrigerator and a roof over your head,* I want to tell him. Both are things I had growing up until my dad took it all away, took everyone I loved away, too. It's tough but they need to learn to fend for themselves at some point, and I guess the time is now.

"I'm so sorry, Johnny. I know your mom needs help. Have you talked to your dad?" I ask. "Why don't you guys get in the car, and I'll drive you to school? I'm headed that way. Where are your sisters? Do they need a ride?"

"They got a ride with Kimmie's friend, but there wasn't room for us," Johnny says.

The boys climb into the backseat. Peyton takes one look at them and starts to cry.

"She's annoying," Jimmy says. He shakes his head and glares at Peyton, which makes her cry louder.

"My dad's out of the country for work," Johnny explains over the fuss. "He can't come home for a few weeks, at least that's what he says when I call him. Sometimes I don't think he cares about what's going on here at home."

We lock eyes in the rearview mirror. We both know his dad is a liar, and I really do feel bad about their predicament. But I've moved on. I take a deep breath.

"Peyton, it's ok, baby," I say in my new soft mom voice. I reach back and slip a binky into her mouth, and she settles, still side-eyeing Jimmy. "Boys, you guys are great, and I loved our time together, but I have a new job now, new responsibilities."

I pull up in front of his school and Johnny opens the door. "Yeah, I figured you'd be no help. You always have been all about you from the beginning. I don't know why nobody else sees it. See you after school, Jimmy. I'll come get you and we'll walk home." He slams the door without another word. Well, at least he's taking responsibility for his little brother.

I drive Jimmy down the street to the elementary school and pull into the familiar drop-off zone.

"Bye, Jimmy. Have a great day! I'll visit you soon," I say. But I won't. We both know it. It's best to cut ties cleanly, to make your moves and never look back. When things change, things change forever.

"Bye, Lizzie," Jimmy says sadly as he gets out and closes the door.

I take a deep breath. I tell myself he has it easy, really. They'll eventually hire another nanny and he'll forget all about me. He doesn't know real trauma. The images flood my brain again like an unwanted horror movie.

It was late afternoon, the sun a bright orange in the sky. From the outside, our home looked like all the others on the street. A sprawling two-story house with a graceful front lawn and a swing set in the backyard. Plenty of room to play. So many happy memories. *Before*. I walked inside that afternoon bursting with good news. I'd won the spelling bee and was holding my very first—and only, it would turn out—trophy. I couldn't wait to show my mom. I was in fifth grade. I had so many friends, and a mom I loved dearly. My baby sister was a welcome surprise in my life, not a competitor like Jimmy viewed Peyton.

The house was still, too still.

"Mom?" I called out. I walked in the backdoor and kicked off my shoes, our house rule. "Mom! I won the spelling bee!".

I raced through the house looking for her, but she wasn't in any of her usual spots: the kitchen, the laundry room, reading on the screened-in porch. I began to wonder if she'd gone to a friend's house but told myself she'd leave me a note. My heart thudded in my chest. I knew something was wrong.

"Mom?" I called again. Where was she? Where was Sally? Maybe they were all out at a mommy and me class? Perhaps they were grocery shopping, planning a special dinner, I told myself.

I raced up the stairs and stopped at the top. Time moved in slow motion, as I walked down the hallway to my parents' bedroom. I opened the door slowly and that's when I saw her.

At first, my brain told me she was asleep. She had to be asleep. But then I noticed the blood. Everywhere. Pooling on the thick carpet, splattered on the wall, the pillow. My beautiful mom. The screams were mine as I backed out of the room. I ran down the hall to find Sally, to protect Sally, not knowing it was already too late. He had her.

I remember Peyton in the backseat. "It's ok, baby. I won't let anyone take you!" I take a deep breath. I survived, even though I lost my entire family that horrible day. But I'll always remember my mom telling me that she had the best life with me and Sally. I hear her voice now, as if she's in the car next to me.

Lizzie, my darling girl. Grab your life and don't let anyone take it away from you. Have a baby, or two, or three, and be there for them. Bake cookies, play with them in the backyard on the swing set, take them for picnics. Be there. That's all I hope for you, and Sally, to become happy moms like me. Pick a partner who is kind and loves you. That's the only mistake I made.

A mistake that killed her. I smile at Peyton in the rearview mirror. *I've got this, Mom.* I'm thriving. Well, at least I'm beginning to. I check my watch. There's still time to run the errand before my salon appointment. Despite the surprise appearance of the Johnson boys, everything is fine. I am fine. The horrors of the past don't define me anymore. The fond memories are what I'm going to hold onto. This life, this is what and who I am. And nobody is going to take this away from me.

TWENTY-THREE

CECILIA

I open my eyes and know it's late morning from the brightness of the bedroom. I fell asleep again. I know I should have been out of bed hours ago. I did get a chance to share a moment with Peyton this morning looking out the window and watching the hummingbirds together. I'm falling more in love with little Peyton every moment. She's more of a person now, smiling and giggling. She's not a screaming newborn anymore. And I treasure our time together. We had such a peaceful, loving morning together before Lizzie appeared, all dressed up and in full makeup like she had somewhere important to be. I guess your first proper hair appointment is a big deal, at least it seems to be to her. She'll end up spending more than a week's salary on the appointment with Raul. I hope she realizes that.

I stretch my arms over my head and finally summon the strength to sit up. I look over at my phone on the nightstand, the anonymous text haunting me, as whoever sent it no doubt intended. Who am I kidding? It's Paul, it's always Paul. I should delete it, or report him, but how do I prove it's him? I call the number, and as before, it rolls to a generic voicemail. I block the number, but I know it won't stop him.

I wonder where I put the letter he sent, his first warning to me that he hasn't forgotten about me or the money. I haven't seen it since the day I read it. I'll need to look for that. I wouldn't want Lizzie finding it and reading it, or the cleaners for that matter.

But today's a new day. I walk into the bathroom and stretch, paste a smile on my face and get ready, even imitating Lizzie a bit by applying makeup. It helps me look a little more alive. I stare at my reflection: today I will take charge, or try to. I walk into my closet and use the keypad to unlock the cabinet that contains my jewelry, a special custom-built display studio like you'd see in a jewelry store. It makes it so easy to pick out what to wear for the day since it's all here, sparkling at me. It was a splurge to have it built, but I love it. All the jewelry in here was a gift to myself, from myself, and it all started with the diamond necklace I purchased on our anniversary trip to Paris. Paul refused to buy it for me, considered the piece too gaudy, too showy, and instead bought himself an expensive watch. But I loved the necklace and couldn't stop thinking about it, so I snuck back to the store and purchased it, a bold act of defiance for me back then. I decide to wear it today and put it on. The huge diamond pendant hangs from a substantial gold chain. It's the centerpiece of my jewelry cabinet, and of this part of my life. I was wearing it when Paul tried to kill me, so it's symbolic of survival in that sense, too.

I pick out my watch of the day from an assortment of six treasured beauties and slip it on my wrist. Since Paul made such a big deal about watches, I decided I needed to start my own little collection. This one, an elegant silver face with diamonds and a black leather strap, is classic, or so my jeweler told me. *Wait, something's wrong.* I blink and realize one of my designer watches is missing. How could that be possible? I tell myself to think about the last time I wore it, a Rolex with a sleek gold band and a face encrusted in diamonds—I'm drawn to diamonds, it seems—and can't remember. It had to be before Peyton was born, before my world stopped functioning normally.

I remember a date night with Evan before I was pregnant, when we were basically friends with benefits, no strings attached. The busy days, working parties together and then recapping the events over candlelit dinners at the best restaurants in Southern California. Sure, I could tell he was a helpless romantic, desperate for love but bad at finding it. I think it had something to do with his overbearing mother, if you ask me. We had fun together, though. Food was our love language, that's for sure. I remember this particular night at an intimate restaurant on the coast, just the two of us. We are holding hands and I'm wearing the Rolex.

"Cecilia, you're the most gorgeous, fun and creative woman I've ever known," he'd said that evening, staring into my eyes. "I want to build a life together. I'll be the perfect partner. You deserve it."

I'd smiled. Sure, friends can become lovers, it happens all the time. "Let's take it slow, but yes, you're a great guy," I'd said that night, my Rolex sparkling on my wrist, the champagne we'd ordered making my head a little dizzy. "Let's see where it leads us." That was before I'd become pregnant with Peyton. It's ironic, really, after all his professions of love, after convincing me to keep our baby, that he'd cheat. So much for his undying love for me and our child.

I push the memories away and return to thinking about the jewelry cabinet and my missing watch. Perhaps it had never even been inside this cabinet. I could have misplaced it, I suppose. My life has been crazy since those simple, happy days.

My phone rings and I take the call.

"Cecilia Strom?" a man's voice asks.

"Yes," I answer, but a knot of dread has lodged in my core.

"This is Sam Walter, an associate with your law firm in the

matter of your divorce," he says. "I wanted to let you know we just received word that your husband has been released from prison early due to good behavior. Apparently, he has moved back to his former home of Palm Beach, Florida. That is all the information we have at the moment."

Paul is out of prison. My mind tries to make sense of the news. I close and lock the jewelry cabinet and walk into the bedroom. I take a deep breath and sit at the window seat. I remember the man, Sam, is still on the phone.

"Mrs. Strom, are you alright?" he asks.

"Yes, sorry, just a little stunned," I say.

"Mrs. Strom, I know it's upsetting news. It's understandable that you are thrown off."

How about completely shaken? Like a huge earthquake rolled under my feet. I take a deep breath. "He's written to me from prison, and it seems he doesn't want to sign the divorce papers," I say.

"We can serve him the papers again. We'll find out where he is in Florida," Sam reassures me.

I doubt they'll find him unless he wants to be found. "You know, he had so much more time left on his sentence. How can this happen?"

"An overcrowded prison system, I'm afraid, and credit for good behavior. Shaved a few years off his sentence. He'll remain on parole and they'll keep track of him. And now that he's out, like I said, we can serve him a new round of papers," he says. "I'll try to find an address. You just take care of yourself."

"When was he released, do you know?" I ask, chill after chill rolling down my spine.

"We only just got notified, but it looks like he was released several weeks ago," he says.

"He could be anywhere then." I know Paul. I know what he's capable of doing.

"True," he says. "Although, like I said, he will have to check in with a parole officer."

"He's going to want the money," I say. "Or what's left of it. It's a joint account."

"Well, yes, I'm assuming he'll be drawing funds from it now that he's released. We've agreed to a fifty-fifty split as I recall," he says. "You should check your account."

"Yes, I will. And that's what we agreed to," I say. Sam doesn't need to know that 50 percent of not a lot is what Paul will find. He'll be furious. I open the app. He hasn't made a withdrawal, not yet. Likely, he didn't want me to know he's a free man.

"I'm glad he's headed to Florida. I think distance is protection for you," Sam says. "Were his letters to you threatening in any way?"

"No, in fact, very loving, like he wants to get back together again," I say. "I don't, to be clear. Can you find out if he really is in Florida?"

"I'm going to track him down and I'll be in touch. Stay safe." He hangs up.

I scream in frustration. The breath catches in my throat as I hear rustling outside my bedroom door. I hear a soft voice. I can't quite place it.

"Mrs. Strom? Are you hurt?" a woman's voice asks from outside my bedroom door. "Should I come in?"

Who is in my house? Who heard me screaming? I rush to the door and open it. It's Agnes, of the cleaning crew, her dark brown eyes wide with fear. I forgot today was their cleaning day. Evan lined them up during his still dependable days after I bought the new house, and they've been great ever since. Problem is, I might not be able to afford them any longer.

"I'm so sorry I frightened you, Agnes," I say. I fold my hands together to calm the rage I feel inside. I need to breathe. How can Paul be out on the streets? Who decided that was a good idea? And why did I only find out after the fact?

"Good, ok, I'm glad you are fine," she says. Although from the look in her eyes, she's pitying me, and perhaps a little worried, too. "Where is the precious baby? I didn't see her in the nursery."

"Oh, she's fine. She's with the nanny," I say. At least I have that part of my life under control.

"Ok, good. Um, Mrs. Strom?" I can sense uncertainty from Agnes. "I know Mr. Dorsey really misses you and the baby."

"Well, he should have realized his actions have consequences," I say. I know I'm being grumpy, but she's annoying me.

"A baby does need both parents," she says. "And he wants to come home. He's desperate for your love, you should know that."

"Did Evan tell you to say that?" I ask. *Why is everyone ganging up on me?*

She looks down at her feet. "Yes. But I do know he misses you. When I clean his place, he's so sad. He's living in those tiny apartments just off the highway. He's just moping really."

Great. Now my cleaning woman is a relationship counselor. "Agnes, we're over, Evan and me. He slept with an assistant at his company. I mean it, ok?" I say, softening my tone. I need her. "I know you mean well, but shouldn't you get to work?"

"Yes, ma'am, it's just the baby. Fathers are important," she says.

"Peyton doesn't have a father. She just has me. Do you understand?" I realize I probably look a little angry but that's because I am furious. At her. At Paul. At Evan. At everyone in my life, well, except Lizzie and Peyton, of course. I flip my hair over my shoulder and walk toward my bathroom.

"I understand, ma'am," Agnes says.

I stop in the doorway, remembering I had something to ask

her. Security is the top priority now, especially with Paul out of prison. "Hey, was the alarm on when you arrived this morning?"

Agnes pauses, thinking. Her face falls into a frown. "No, ma'am," she says sounding worried.

"Did you see the nanny?" I ask. "When you arrived, was she still here?"

"No, your car was gone," she says. "Anyway, I'm going to get back to work."

"Great idea," I say and walk into my bathroom and plug in my curling iron. *I am nice, Agnes, perhaps too nice.* I need to assert myself, and I need people to follow the rules. No bringing up Evan in this house again, ever. And I need to remind Lizzie to set the alarm every time she leaves the home. Even if she and the baby are out and about, I'm still here, still vulnerable.

I hear the doorbell ring. Now what? I make my way downstairs. Agnes stands by the front door, arms crossed in front of her.

"It's your mother-in-law," she says with a shrug. "Want me to let her in?"

"I'll handle her."

Agnes scurries away as I disable the alarm and yank open the front door. "What is it, Marian?"

"We need to talk, young lady," she says, trying to push her way past me.

"You can't come in. The cleaners are here. Whatever you have to say, we can discuss right here on the porch," I say.

"Well, fine. You look better, but I still think you're unstable. I've heard that from a lot of people. And I'm worried about Peyton," she says. "I'm not sure you're a fit mom. And then there's Evan. My son is a hopeless romantic and he's put his heart on the line for you, for some unknown reason. So, until you take him back, which you should, I will help with Peyton. Babies are a lot of work."

I chuckle. "That's rich. Evan is a cheater, not a hopeless romantic. And now you're worried about the baby? Suddenly, she's top of mind for you? I wonder why?"

"You need to let my son back into your life," she repeats.

"You just want access to my money," I say. "And you aren't going to enjoy any of it. That's a promise."

"How could you even think that, you spoiled woman?" Her face is bright red now, like her hair. "And that money isn't yours to begin with. You married into it. You maybe don't even deserve it from what I hear."

"Marian, you're a gossip and a terrible person. And you're probably the reason Evan is an untrustworthy partner. I need you to leave," I say with a sigh.

"Not until I see my granddaughter. I need to be sure you're treating her well. I would be within my rights to send child services around," she says.

"You wouldn't dare," I say. "And the baby isn't here. She's out on a playdate."

"Oh, that's perfect. A playdate at six months?" She laughs. "You're so clueless. I demand to see her."

I shake my head. "She isn't here. And even if she was, I wouldn't let you see her."

I step back and quickly shut the door. She tries to follow me but I'm faster than she is. I slide the lock into place. I take a deep breath. I need Evan to sell the building I bought him for his business. After that, I will have nothing more to do with Marian Dorsey. Ever. And neither will Peyton.

I hurry to the alarm system and turn it on. I remind myself Marian is the least of my worries. We need to be extra cautious to stay safe now that Paul's out. I have no doubt he'll make his way to Malibu sometime soon, if he hasn't already arrived.

TWENTY-FOUR

LIZZIE

This has been the most amazing day, and it just keeps getting better. I walk into the salon that looks more like a fancy nightclub with sheer draperies, club music thumping, and a gorgeous young man with a chiseled face and slicked-back hair waiting to greet me. When I'm a proper, traditional wife—my dream—I'll be visiting a salon like this regularly. A woman must always look nice for her man. All that's missing, of course, is my man.

"Welcome to Raul's Place," he says. "I'm Dylan, Raul's assistant. We're so excited to get to work on you, Lizzie."

"Thank you," I say, grinning from ear to ear. I can already feel the sophistication and style oozing toward me. "This will be so fun, baby!" I whisper to Peyton. As I take a "before" selfie of us, she gurgles in agreement.

"Follow me, dear, and we'll get you in a robe. Raul will be out for a consultation shortly, but I can already imagine what he'll do for you," he says. "Cute baby, by the way."

"Thank you." I beam with pride. I'm sort of getting used to people thinking that Peyton is mine. But then I remember that these are Cecilia's friends. Even though she hasn't been here since Peyton was born, she likely told them she was pregnant.

"Thank you. She's a cutie and the best baby," I say. Am I flirting? Maybe.

"She looks a lot like you," he says with a wink. "Good looks run in the family."

"Oh gosh, thank you so much," I say as we reach Raul's consultation station. Fortunately, there's room for a stroller.

"So who referred you to our salon? We're a strictly referral business," he asks.

"Cecilia Strom," I say.

"We love Cecilia. Haven't seen her lately. Tell her she better get back here." He grins. "Wouldn't want her friend to outshine her, would she?"

"There's no danger of that." I feel my cheeks flushing.

"We'll see. I think I will reserve the right to disagree," he says. "Change into this gown and we'll get started."

After three hours of color processing, stripping my old color, adding new and the like, and shampooing, and cutting and blow-drying, all with Dylan helping with Peyton when needed, I'm finished. The hair salon is a celebrity favorite, I know, and little signs are posted everywhere that anything you overhear is private and there are no photos allowed of other clients. I love that there could be someone sitting in the chair next to me spilling genuine celebrity gossip. *Pinch me.*

Peyton naps in her stroller for the time being, so when Raul himself appears for the final reveal I can give him my full attention. Beside him, Dylan grins.

"Darling, it has been a delight working with you," Raul says. "But I wonder if you could lose the glasses? They distract from my art."

I take the glasses off and blink. They still haven't let me see my new hair and I'm dying to spin the chair around. "Better?"

"Much," Raul says. "Do not put those on your face again. I think you don't need them even, right?"

"No, they were a prop, to make me look smart and dependable," I admit.

Dylan laughs and sticks out his hand. "Give them to me!"

"Only if I can finally see what you guys have done," I say and hand the glasses to Dylan. Good riddance, truth be told.

"Lizzie, are you ready to see the new you?" Raul asks with a dramatic flourish.

"I am, beyond ready, yes," I say.

Raul pushes a button, and a curtain rises to reveal a mirror lit by twinkling lights on the edges. I stare at myself and burst into tears.

"What's wrong, dear?" Raul pats my shoulder. "You should be happy."

"Oh, I'm so happy. I look beautiful," I say, touching my now blonde hair, spilling elegantly around my shoulders in soft waves.

"Very beautiful," Dylan says. Our eyes lock for a little too long.

I'm wearing Cecilia's clothes, I've just had my hair done by her hairstylist, and the effect is that suddenly I look like a younger version of my boss. It's uncanny, really. Peyton stirs in her stroller, and I go to her, holding her up and showing her the sparkly mirror. The baby seems to notice my new hair, taking a clump into her fist with a grin.

"I'm glad you're happy, dear," Raul says. "We'll see you in two to three weeks for your next appointment. The color needs constant upkeep." With that, he disappears, no doubt to prepare for his next celebrity client.

"You really do look great," Dylan says. "Would you ever consider going on a date?"

Maybe. But not likely with a person working in a hair salon, even one as fancy as this. I need to find a man who can take care of me in the lifestyle I deserve. Like Cecilia's. But I'll be nice.

"Sure, give me your number. But Dylan, when Raul says come back in three weeks is that, umm, three weeks forever?" I think about the cost associated with that sort of maintenance and bite my lip.

"Here's my number," he says, handing me a thick business card. "And yes, you must. Beauty takes time."

"And money," I say.

"Yes, lots of that," he says. "Speaking of that, I can take your credit card now."

"Is cash ok? I prefer cash," I say.

"Sure, a little unusual around here, but that should work," he says. "Here's an appointment card. I'll see you then, if not sooner."

As I stroll out of the salon with Peyton, I feel different, inside and out. I feel confident, and yes, beautiful. And something deeper—happy. I don't think I've ever been able to properly sustain that feeling, ever. I hope it lasts. It needs to last.

One way to make it last is to avoid Cecilia when she's in the depressed mood she's in over money, I realize. I decide Peyton and I will head to the park, and then take a stroll through the high-end outdoor mall where everyone who is anyone goes to see and be seen to pick up birthday party supplies. Cecilia wants it low budget, but you only turn six months once. As we walk into the park, someone calls my name.

It's Evan.

He's smiling at me, and the baby. Of course, I'm not supposed to let him see Peyton. *But he is her dad*, I say to myself.

I can't help but smile back at him. He's even cuter than the last time I saw him. "Hey."

"There's my baby girl!" he says, walking over to us. "Hey, Peyton. It's Daddy."

Peyton wiggles her arms and smiles.

"You look great, Lizzie," he says.

"Thanks for the compliment, I just got my hair done," I say, picking Peyton up out of the stroller. "Would you like to hold her?"

"More than anything," he says.

I give him a few minutes to play with her and kiss her tiny head. I'm keeping watch for Cecilia, but I know that's ridiculous. I have her car, and she's likely still in bed. But nonetheless, I'm on guard.

"I think we should get going," I say finally.

Evan nods, and I'm surprised to see his blue eyes filling with tears. "I just miss her. So much. I've messed everything up."

I take Peyton from his arms. "Well..." I hesitate. "Maybe we can meet up every now and then, so you can see her?"

"I'd really appreciate that, more than you know," he says. "She's growing so fast. I don't want to miss a minute. So, how can we coordinate this? Any ideas? I don't want to upset Cecilia even though it's clear she's never going to forgive me."

"I think you're right about that. I could give you my number?" I suggest as I put Peyton back in the stroller.

"Yes, perfect," he says, and we exchange texts. "Thank you. I'm so grateful for this, Lizzie."

"No problem. See you." I watch him walk away and then lean over to look at Peyton. "That was your daddy. I wonder if he'll be invited to your birthday tomorrow? If it was up to me, I'd include him, but your mommy needs to make that decision. I don't want to overstep." And then I remember that I still need to grab the cake I ordered and the other supplies to make it special. Cecilia won't even notice the spend. I took it out of our grocery budget.

It's so good to be out and about in town, and with this new haircut and Cecilia's clothes, I sense that men are looking at me differently now. I am ready to be seen, that's for sure, I've never been so ready. A part of me wishes I had Cecilia's credit card with me, with her unlimited budget, but I still have some money left over from the hair salon appointment. I'll be able to pick up a little something for myself.

Looking like this, the salespeople will be flocking to me instead of glaring at me like I'm going to rob the place. Yes, I've had those looks, too. I guess I used to look the part. And to be honest, I played the part all too well.

TWENTY-FIVE

CECILIA

Where is Lizzie? How long can a hair appointment take? Even with Raul's over-the-top production and dramatic reveals, she should be finished and home. I realize, right at this minute as if for the first time, that I miss my baby. I miss her sweet baby smell, her smile, her tiny fingers. Missing her is a good feeling, an appropriate one for a mom to have.

A strong wind rattles the house, swirling dry leaves and other debris across my backyard and likely into the pool. It must be the Santa Ana winds. I hear a door bang open somewhere in the house and the security alarm beeps a warning. I stiffen before hurrying to the pad by the front door, pushing in the code and disabling the system. I'll have to do a search of the house to find out which door wasn't properly shut and locked. *That must be the explanation*, I assure myself.

As I start my tour, I walk into the living room and notice a photo of me and Evan in a sleek silver frame in a prominent position on the bookshelf—a black and white taken at one of our company's events. Evan's in a tux and I'm in a ballgown. We look elegant and happy. That's when I believed he loved me, that I was the one and only for him. Those days are over. I grab the photo and shove it into the cabinet below. I rearrange the books and grab a piece of glimmering quartz from another shelf to fill the space, making it seem like the photo was never there. I call Lizzie.

"Hello, Cecilia! How has your day been? Hope you're feeling better," she says.

"Much better, thanks. I just needed rest, and time to think. I've done both," I say. "Are you almost home? I miss Peyton."

The first floor is secure. I climb the stairs to the second floor and start in the nursery. I find the culprit. One of the double doors that leads to a small balcony off the nursery has blown open.

"Oh my gosh! Hold on a minute." I drop the phone on the changing table and hurry to close the door as another gust of hot, dry and dusty air blows through the room, bringing with it various debris from outside. What a mess.

"What's happening? Are you ok?" I hear Lizzie ask. "Cecilia, answer me!"

I pick up my phone, and as I do I see a piece of paper sticking out from under the changing table, likely blown there by the wind. I do a double take when I realize it's Paul's letter. The one I couldn't find.

"The winds blew the nursery doors open," I say. "You have a mess to clean up, I'm afraid."

"Oh gosh, no problem. I sometimes open the door to get the ocean breeze," she says. "That's my fault. I'm sorry."

"I don't think you're taking me seriously enough when I say all doors and windows must be locked at all times." I know I sound mean, but I'm really annoyed.

"I understand. It won't happen again," she says. "I'll be home in ten minutes."

"Oh, and Lizzie," I say, trying hard to keep the edge out of my voice. "Did you read the letter, the one from my husband?

I've found it here in the nursery under the changing table. Did you put it there?"

"I'm sorry, Cecilia, I don't know what you're talking about," she says.

I wish I'd waited to ask her in person, so I could watch her face. So I could spot a lie if there was one. But why would she lie about this or hide his letter? My situation doesn't have anything to do with her. She's just the nanny. And besides, Lizzie has proven herself to be nothing but trustworthy these past few weeks. I wouldn't have made it through without her. But still, I can't help but feel that the letter was hidden rather than blown there by the wind. A distant alarm bell rings in the back of my mind.

"Ok, well, see you soon. We're celebrating Peyton's birthday, right? I'll unlock the front door for you," I say. I'll be waiting out front for them when they get here. I can't wait to see my baby. Maybe I'll even tell Lizzie to take the night off.

She pulls into the driveway sooner than I expected and my spirits lift. As soon as she parks, I hurry to open the back door. Peyton greets me with a big smile and outstretched arms. It's the best.

"Hi, baby, Mommy missed you," I say, unbuckling her from the car seat.

"I can take her in and get her changed," Lizzie says quickly.

I do a double take when she steps out of the car.

"Wow, nice hair. Totally love the whole look," I say. Oddly she looks a bit like me, but that's likely because everything she's wearing is mine and her hair is now a soft blonde, also like mine. And now that she's not wearing the big glasses, her features do resemble mine. She could be my sister. I'd always wanted a sister, a kind sister—a real sister—and I had begun to think of Lizzie that way, so I cannot understand why I suddenly feel so unsettled by the transformation. Maybe it's nerves from what happened in the house, but it could be something more. It's

Paul's fault I'm so on edge, but Lizzie's appearance, her mirror-like reflection of me, feels wrong. I force a smile.

"You like it? I do, too. Thank you!" she says.

"Where are your glasses?" I ask.

"Oh, the guys at the salon convinced me I'd look better without them, so *voilà*, no glasses." She reaches out her arms. "Come here, Peyton."

"No, it's ok. I'll change her. I'm going to play with her for a bit," I say. "We need some bonding time. Why don't you go clean up the mess in the nursery, and afterward you can take the evening off? You haven't had a break since you started. You look too nice to just sit at home tonight. The baby and I will be fine. You should go out on the town and show off the new you."

"I don't need a break," she says. "Is something wrong?"

"No, not at all," I say. I realize I'm watching her more closely than I normally do. "I just need some time alone with my baby at my house, that's all. Some time when my back's not out and I've had enough sleep. I want us to enjoy some time together." I squeeze Peyton and she giggles as I nuzzle her little neck.

Lizzie takes a deep breath and smiles. I can tell it's fake. "Great, yes, good idea. Here's the diaper bag," she says. "I'll just get that room cleaned up and scoot out for a bit. Can I make dinner at least? And I have a cake and balloons for the birthday celebration."

"Oh right. Well, maybe we can celebrate tomorrow? It's not like Peyton knows today is the day. So you go on, I've got it handled," I say. When I walk away, I feel her watching me. Sure, it's a bit different for me to want to be alone with Peyton, especially since the three of us have been hanging out together nonstop. But I'm on edge, and one thing I know for sure is I will protect my daughter, and I will love my daughter, as best I can.

There are too many strange things happening, too many people who want something from me. I need to keep Peyton close. I need to stay one step ahead. Of all of them. Maybe even Lizzie.

I turn around, remembering something else. "Say, this is weird, but would you have happened to see a Rolex watch lying around anywhere? It's gold with a mother-of-pearl face, and diamonds, lots of diamonds."

"No, but it sounds beautiful," she says. "I don't think I've seen you wear it."

"I haven't in a while, true. But it's missing," I say. "Just like the letter from my husband was and now it turned up. Maybe the Santa Ana winds will stir it up, too."

"Ha, I doubt that, but it would be amazing if the wind delivered expensive watches. Usually all I get from the Santa Ana winds are allergies." Lizzie says coolly. "I'll keep my eyes peeled for your watch. Did you ask the cleaning crew?"

"No, Agnes' team would have told me if they found it," I say. And then I remember another couple of missing items. "Also—and I'm really not trying to accuse you of things—but you wouldn't happen to have my bath salts, would you?"

"No," Lizzie says, and now she sounds a little offended, which makes me feel guilty.

"Ok, no problem," I say.

She looks at me with a sad frown. "I'm going to get started cleaning the nursery."

I nod as she rushes past me into the house. The worrisome thing about all of this is that a lot of strange things are happening at my house, things are disappearing, doors are popping open. I don't know if I'm being paranoid or if I should feel threatened. I now think back to the previous night and how I thought I heard someone in the backyard. But of course, when I opened my curtains to look outside, nobody was there. It was just the winds, of course it was. If it's not Lizzie, and I don't think it is, I don't want to think who it could be.

But what if Paul is behind everything? I ask myself. *Was*

Paul in my backyard last night? My heart skips a beat at the thought.

What if he isn't in Florida and instead has come here, back to Malibu, looking for me and his half of the money? I mean, I did send him away to prison for attempted murder while effectively concealing what I had done to him in return. But he knows the truth. He also knows where to find me, I'm certain of that.

Another gust of wind swirls through the air and I hurry inside with Peyton. I lock the door and reset the system. I'm likely overreacting. There are simple explanations for everything, I'm sure. At least that's what I'm going to believe for now. It's the only way to stay sane. I'll focus on loving Peyton and trust that we're safe.

TWENTY-SIX

LIZZIE

The dust that covers the nursery floor reminds me of the fine sand that seems to appear everywhere after a day at the beach. As I sweep it away, I think about taking Peyton to the beach again. Maybe I could invite Evan to join us there instead of just watching us from the top of the dune? I'm almost positive it was him watching us that day. I smile at that idea. That beach is both uber privileged and super fun. I love exclusive, one-of-a-kind things. It's not that I grew up knowing about these things in the Midwest, not at all. In fact, when I was growing up, it was all about the country club we were members of... until that night when everything changed. But even the country club is nothing compared to what people have here. It took moving out here to help me see just how much other people have, how separate the lucky people are from the real world I grew up in.

The mangled car pops into my head. I didn't see the accident in person, only the photos in the press with scary headlines screaming: *Prominent family, dark secrets*. And: *Murdered his wife and then grabbed his baby and drove into a tree*. And: *No skidmarks: Husband kills wife, baby, himself*.

But I still feel as if I was there, like a part of me died that night with baby Sally. I can practically see my drunken father behind the wheel, guilt-ridden for what he did to my mother —or so they say. He violated the restraining order that day, but of course he didn't care about such things. He just wanted my mom, and if he couldn't have her, nobody could, including her daughters. Why didn't I get home sooner to protect them? If I hadn't stayed late for the spelling bee, I could have been there, too. It's a question that haunts me every day. I shake my head to clear my thoughts. I have a new life now, I have a new baby girl to be there for, and I need to take advantage of everything this situation has to offer. I'll make my mom proud.

Tomorrow, I decide, I'll grab the beach key from Cecilia and head back to Little Dume. This time, I'll let her know we're going so I don't get in trouble, although she never found out last time. I know from all the online celebrity news I follow that it's where the celebrities hang out, where they surf, where they have picnics, and it's where I will frolic with the baby in my new bathing suit with my new hair and fabulous new look. I'll look just like the pampered Malibu mom I dream of becoming. I'll look like a California version of my precious mom. I'll live her life because hers was cut too short.

I've wiped down the windowsills and the dressers, changed the sheets in the crib and basically de-dusted the entire room, walls and floors included. Everything is back to perfection. I head down the hall to my bedroom and hurry into the bathroom to admire my hair. I look fantastic, it's true.

But I spent way too much money on myself today, and there's nowhere affordable I can go round here. There's nobody I really want to call to meet up, nobody I can depend on to pay for my dinner out. I suppose I could call Dylan, but I don't want to lead him on. I'll get all dressed up and gussied up again tomorrow. This look is the new everyday me, after all. As for tonight, this is my idea of the perfect life. I'll just stay in my room. That shouldn't bother Cecilia. It'll be like I'm not even here.

I change into pale yellow cashmere sweats and a sweatshirt —more of Cecilia's hand-me-downs—and turn on the huge TV in my room. I flip through the ridiculous number of channels and settle on the Star Channel to get some more celebrity news. My phone pings with a weather alert. I guess there's a strong wind advisory for tonight. I could have told you that.

I scroll to a streaming channel and pick a movie. A romantic comedy I've always wanted to see. The $15 charge is nothing; I'm sure it would be fine with Cecilia, although I better not push her too far. I worry she might be annoyed that I stayed in. She seems a little angry with me, and accusatory. I decide to find a free movie instead. After the movie, I'll sneak downstairs and make myself a quick dinner. Cecilia and Peyton will be sleeping. This is working out so well.

A gust of wind rattles the house, but we're safe, all tucked in. I focus on the movie until there's a knock on my door.

"Coming," I say after I pause my movie. I slip my bare feet into the softest slippers I've ever owned and float to the door. I hope Cecilia's not mad at me for staying in tonight. Maybe she needs me after all?

"Hey, what's up?" I ask as I open the door to Cecilia and Peyton. "Hi, baby!"

"I guess it's fine that you didn't go out tonight because I actually need you to watch her for a few minutes. But why didn't you go out?" she asks, a curious look on her face.

"I was just so tired from the day, and well, to be honest, I just love it here." I give her a big smile and then remember this isn't a good thing. She wanted the baby all to herself tonight. "Here, let me take Peyton. What's going on? Is everything ok?"

"Evan's here. Outside. He banged on the door and scared Peyton. I told him to stop it. He wants to talk," she says.

"What? Do you want me to call the police? That's creepy." I

force a shudder. Does he really want to get back together with her? I hope not. I have to make her see they need to stay apart. "I mean, I know he wants you back, but he's turning into a stalker. That's the opposite of romantic. You've had enough unstable men in your life. Don't give in to him."

"I know. You're right. I'm going to talk to him, try to make him realize we're over for good, once and for all," Cecilia says, biting her lip. "I need to talk to him, anyway. I've decided I need to sell his office building. It's the only asset I can liquidate quickly."

"Oh. He's not going to like that," I say.

"I know, but it must be done. I'll lock the door behind me and turn on the alarm. I'll have a key to let myself back in," she says. "You guys will be safe."

"Sure, um, ok. Maybe Peyton and I will hang out in your room so we can see the backyard and watch for any sign of trouble?" I say. She's so paranoid. I mean, this guy is the father of her baby—he's not going to do anything. Evan is not the type to resort to violence, that much I know. Because I know that type only too well. In fact, he's more the type who could make someone a wonderful husband, if given the chance. But right now, I need to reassure Cecilia. "I'll keep my phone nearby. I think that's for the best."

"Good idea," she says. She takes a deep breath, her hands ball into fists by her side. "Ok, I can do this. I must do this. It's my only liquid asset, besides this house."

I nod. "You can't sell this house. This is Peyton's home. She deserves to live like this. Good luck. We'll be watching," I say. "Do you mind if I turn on my movie, you know, just to pass the time? I'll watch you and Evan, too, of course."

"Sure. That's a good one, how love is supposed to be." She glances at my TV screen, the actors paused in a passionate embrace. She kisses Peyton on the cheek and hurries away down the hall.

"Ok, baby, let's go relax in your mommy's palatial room. Sound good?"

I'm so excited I practically float down the hall. I mean, as much as the guest room is wonderful, Cecilia's bedroom is the best, of course. I can't wait to explore it all. And this time, I have her permission.

Thank you for the lovely visit. You know, spending time with you gives me hope for the future, it really does. And I'm glad that I could help you, too. All problems are solvable if you just set your mind—and some helpful technology—to it. I'm glad you agree. Some people just don't appreciate what they have, and some people should not have what they've got. They don't nurture it, care for it. But you're different, you are. I can see the lover bursting from you. Do come back and see me if you need any other pointers. I'm here, at least for the time being. I'm smiling because of your visit, and that says something when I'm stuck in a place like this. Do take care, and come back soon.

Very truly yours,

Paul

TWENTY-SEVEN

CECILIA

I spot him waiting for me on the driveway, leaning against my car. The Santa Ana winds make the air electric, like any moment a fire could burst to life. The Woolsey Fire in 2018 destroyed hundreds of homes in Malibu, including here on Point Dume, and the memory of those dark days lives on in the collective memory of the town. Even though Paul and I hadn't moved here yet, we'd hear about it often.

I'm on edge for several reasons, though, not just the winds. I walk over to where he stands.

"Hey Evan, crazy winds tonight," I say. I'm trying to be nice, reasonable, talking about the weather. Hopefully it'll mean he'll be nice, too. It's a win-win, I hope.

"Cecilia, I am trying to accept the fact that we are over, even though I don't want that, but I *need* to have regular visits with Peyton," he says, dispensing with niceties and cutting straight to the point. "It's like a hole in my heart has opened up. You have to let me be a part of her life."

I don't have to do anything, I remind myself. I stay quiet and stare at him.

"You know, I'd love to be back in your life, too. We had

some great times, but I know that door has closed," he says. I can't tell for sure if he's been crying, but I'd bet he has been.

I take a deep breath. "We did have some great times, but we didn't work as a couple. Clearly you agree, since you've been sleeping with someone else." Saying those words out loud still stings. I realize his mother's sentiment about my appearance was correct. I have let myself go a bit, after Peyton was born. But I'm working hard to get back to myself again. And *I'm* all I need, so take that, Marian and Evan.

"I keep saying that it didn't mean anything. I love you, you are the true love of my life. And I love Peyton." He reaches for my hand. I pull away. "I was weak. You seemed, well, uninterested. It will never happen again. Please, forgive me."

"Oh, I'm sure you're sorry now, but I can never trust you again. Ever. You need to move on. But I have a proposal. If you'd like to see Peyton, if you'd like to be part of her life, I am going to need something in return," I say. "You were a terrible partner to me as you know, but maybe you can still be there for her."

"Just tell me what you want me to do," he says, wiping tears from his eyes and kicking the ground as a swirl of leaves and dust blows past us. "Remember how much I helped you recover from Paris? I'm a good guy, I am."

"I do remember, of course, and I'm forever grateful that you were there for me. Let's go sit by the pool. I think it's a little more protected from the wind," I suggest, leading the way. The air is dry and scratches my throat as I walk in front of him. Evan doesn't seem threatening, just sad. I glance up to my bedroom window and see Lizzie sitting on the window seat as promised. I smile.

"Do you have the nanny watching me?" He looks uncertain and then waves cautiously at Lizzie. "Like I'm going to hurt you or something?"

"The last man I thought I loved did. Look, I know, you're

not Paul. I do wish it could be different between us," I say. "But I don't trust you anymore, for obvious reasons."

"I'm sorry, so sorry," he says. "But what about Peyton? What do you need me to do? I have to see her. On a regular basis."

I sit at the outdoor table, and he sits across from me. I study him thoughtfully.

"Name it. Anything," he says.

"I need you to sell the office building I bought you, and as much of the equipment from the commercial kitchen as you can," I say. "We'll split the proceeds. I need cash."

His mouth drops open. "How am I supposed to run my business without an office?"

"Rent space like you used to. With the sale, you'll have plenty of money," I say. "That's what you did before I bought the building for you, remember?"

He folds his arms over his chest, thinking. "It's been nice having my own space," he says. "But I'd rather have a relationship with our daughter. You knew I'd agree."

I feel myself relax. "I knew you would. Plus, the money won't hurt. Maybe move out of that apartment and buy a place for yourself? Move on, Evan."

He nods and takes a deep breath. "Ok, you have a deal."

I smile at him across the table. "Ok, so let's do this. Maybe you could see Peyton tomorrow afternoon, for a start. In the meantime, I've reached out to the real estate broker who sold us the building. He said it will be easy to find a buyer."

Evan looks at me then, and I can see the twinkle in his eye that made our friendship so fun. For the first time in a while, I can remember the good times, not just the stress of the last two years. I remember we were a team, that he helped me try to get over Paul, he helped me heal.

"I'm so glad you've changed your mind," he says. "I'm not the enemy."

"No, you're not." I can't help but sigh as I decide to tell him the truth. "Paul's out of prison. I'm afraid of him. I'm afraid of him finding out about Peyton."

"Oh my god, he's going to want to kill me when he finds out about Peyton," he says. "You all are still legally married, right? What are you going to do?"

I don't know, not really. "I have attorneys, and we are making plans." That's a lie. I have no plan. I feel my heart pounding. *I need a plan.*

"Well, I'm here." He looks a little embarrassed. "I've been watching you, and Peyton."

"I know. I've sensed that you've been lurking around. You need to stop doing that. Promise?" I say. "You are no match for Paul."

"I'll stand up to him, or at least I can try. I want to help. I care about you both. If Paul does show up, and you need me, I'll be here," he says.

I look up to my bedroom window. I don't see Lizzie but I'm sure she'll check on me soon. This time, I don't need her help.

"Thanks, but I can take care of myself, and Peyton. So, tomorrow say three to five with Peyton? I'd like for you to be here with her, keep her in her familiar surroundings. Lizzie will be home, but she'll stay out of your way," I say.

"Sounds good. Can my mom come too?" Evan asks. "She was hoping to celebrate her six-month birthday."

"Can we just get you and Peyton on track and then involve Marian, later?" I ask. "She's so overbearing."

"Tell me about it. I grew up as her son. She means well, though, despite what you think, and she loves Peyton," he says. Evan stands to leave as another gust sweeps through the yard. "Fire winds."

We both pause to think about the terrifying fire that chased all the people living here at the time from their homes, some barely surviving. Things can change in an instant.

"I know. They're scary. A spark can create a firestorm. It only takes one mistake to ruin so much." I look down at my hands. The air is dry and my skin feels like it's cracking. I can sense the threat of fire in my bones.

"I am so sorry that I ruined everything," Evan says as the winds howl. "I was stupid. But I'm here now, whatever you need. And if there is a fire, I'll come get the three of you. No matter what. I'll be watching."

I look up. He's a good guy, all in all. "The three of us?"

"Well, the nanny, too, of course," he says. "I know she's only the nanny, but I'd need to save her as well."

"Of course," I say, eyeing him. Including Lizzie in his heroic fantasy is odd, but whatever.

"See you tomorrow, Cecilia." He nods at me. "Thank you for this, for letting me see my daughter. I'll be a great father to her. I will. I won't let you down again."

This is more like the Evan I knew. And this is the Evan Peyton will hopefully get to know. I know we'll need to formalize an arrangement at some point, but for now it's a start. And with the sale of the building, a welcome infusion of cash that Paul will not be able to touch, it's a win-win.

I unlock the front door and hurry inside, disable the system and then turn it on again. I climb the stairs and I'm surprised to see my bedroom door closed. I knock and then turn the handle. Locked.

"Lizzie? Open up," I say, knocking harder.

I wait a full minute before the door swings open, Peyton on Lizzie's hip. "How'd it go? He looked calm."

"It went great. He's coming over tomorrow to reconnect with Peyton," I say.

"Oh, ok, wow, that's nice of you." She's unable to hide the surprise on her face.

"Why did you lock the door?" I ask.

"You told me to," she says. "An extra layer of security in case he went ballistic."

"No, I didn't tell you to lock my bedroom door," I say. "I'm sure of that." I look around the room. Lizzie has created a play area for Peyton on the plush white rug. Her toys are scattered about. The baby yawns.

"Well, it looks like you've had fun, Peyton," I say.

"We did. Of course," Lizzie says.

Peyton reaches her arms out for me, and I hold her while Lizzie picks up the mess she's made with Peyton's toys in my bedroom and carries it all to the nursery. She's efficient, and kind, and I think I trust her... but why did she lock my bedroom door?

"Time for bed," I say to my precious little girl as we start to walk across the hallway to the nursery.

Lizzie stops and stares at me. "Um, no, it's not bedtime, it's bath time."

I don't have the energy to give Peyton a bath, not tonight. But I need to try. "Oh, right, the schedule," I say wearily.

I turn on the bath water, and then carry Peyton back into the nursery to pick out her pajamas. There are so many cute options. I finally select footed PJs with little lambs on the front. *My little lamb*. I put her on the changing table and take off her daytime outfit. I wrap her in a towel and carry her into the bathroom.

"Stop! That bath water will scald her," Lizzie says, suddenly appearing behind me and pulling me out of my haze. She's right. The steam has fogged up the mirror in the bathroom.

I would have tested it first, right? Peyton starts to cry, unsure of what's happening.

"Maybe you should handle the bath tonight," I say, jiggling Peyton on my hip. And then Peyton reaches for Lizzie. Lizzie will comfort her. Not me. I take a deep breath. Peyton loves Lizzie.

I've grown suspicious of people given what happened with Paul, I suppose. I had a healthy dose of lonely mistrust growing up as an unwanted orphan in the foster system. I kiss Peyton's head, nuzzle her soft hair before I hand her to Lizzie. Another gust rattles the house and Peyton startles. I hope the weather dies down or she could have a restless night.

"I would have tested the water," I say. The look on Lizzie's face tells me she doesn't believe me. "Good night."

I walk across the hallway to my room. I tell myself everything is fine. I just need a good night's sleep. It's hard to sleep when the wind howls, even if that's the only terror lurking in the night.

My phone pings with a text.

<TEXT MESSAGE>*You are an unfit mom you know it. We all do.*</TEXT MESSAGE>

The unknown number haunts me again. I delete the text, toss the phone on my bed and burst into tears.

TWENTY-EIGHT

LIZZIE

I don't like the way Cecilia looked at me when I opened the door. She made me feel like I was guilty of something when all I've been doing is taking care of her daughter, even though she said she would be taking care of her all night and told me to go out. Seems like she should be more grateful. I mean, I'm certainly thankful for everything she's given me, directly and indirectly, and I've told her so.

Of course, I still need more. Doesn't everyone? I saw a TV show that explains why people who own super yachts upgrade to mega yachts and giga yachts. It's like a drug for these guys who buy them. Because once you get a taste of that luxury that very few people can afford, you can't resist buying larger and larger yachts. More, more, more. It's the American way.

After we finish her bath, Peyton takes her bottle and settles easily, until another gust of wind shakes the house and wakes her up. *Ugh.* This is going to be a long night. For me at least. Not for Cecilia. I remind myself that this is my job, and if the baby needs me all night, that's the price I must pay.

I carry Peyton, sleeping for now in my arms, over to the

window and look out over the driveway and out to the darkness beyond. The winds make everyone on edge, everything tense.

I freeze. I see something, someone, moving in the shadows. I'm sure of it. There is a person in Cecilia's backyard, someone who ran toward the pool area, just out of my line of sight. I don't want to scare Cecilia, but I know I'm going to need to tell her. I'm not sure what else to do. I carry Peyton to her crib and nestle her in. I slip across the hall and down the stairs. I see the alarm is on, and I'm sure the doors are locked. In the darkness, I hurry into the kitchen and the family room, with a clear view of the pool area beyond.

I'm sure of it now. There is someone crouched down by the pool. My heart races as I try to decide what to do. Cecilia and Peyton are both sleeping. If I call the cops, all hell will break loose. What if it's just in my imagination, what if I'm tired and creating scary people running through the yard?

I blink and stare at the spot where I thought I saw someone, and now there is no one there. I know what I need to do. I search the kitchen drawers and find a flashlight. I hurry to the alarm pad and disable it, and then run back through the house. I slip outside without making a sound and step into the backyard garden. I train the flashlight on the pool and the far corner of the property.

"Hello?" I call quietly into the night. No one answers. I keep moving the flashlight back and forth across the yard. Did Evan sneak back into the backyard after Cecilia left him? Is he lurking out there in the shadows? No, he wouldn't do that. Why would he need to now? My hands shake with the adrenaline rush as I turn and run back inside, close and lock the door behind me before rushing to the front to reset the system.

My breathing is fast and jagged as I walk back into the kitchen. I look again through the kitchen window. *Whoever was out there, whatever they were doing, they are gone now*, I tell myself, but how can I be sure? I check the sliding glass door and make sure it's locked. In the morning, I'll tell Cecilia we should install cameras out back, just so we can make sure nobody comes onto her property. Maybe one at the driveway gate, another near the front door, some more in the back. She might not want to pay for it, but I'm going to tell her how important it is. I mean, you can't trust people these days.

Back upstairs, I check on Peyton, who is sleeping soundly in her crib. I pull the nursery door closed and tiptoe to the end of the hall to my bedroom. I lock the door behind me, just to be extra safe. I remember to pull a few things from my pockets and admire the sparkles as I display them on the top of the dresser.

After staring at the jewels for a bit, I open the top drawer and pull out a velvet pouch and slip everything inside. I tuck the pouch into the pocket of my oldest jeans and fold them, putting them away in the bottom drawer of the dresser.

I wonder why Cecilia thinks I wouldn't know about Paul or their misadventure in Paris? I mean, she was in all the newspapers for a time, and she even gave an interview to a true crime podcast that I listen to religiously. That's when I first became a little obsessed with her. She was the beautiful victim, the poor gorgeous rich wife on her anniversary in Paris when evil snuck up on her. At least that's what everyone says. Paul's letter—of course, yes, I read it because she left it in the nursery and I'm the nanny—confirmed what I thought all along. It was an act of rage, in the moment. He never meant to hurt Cecilia, not really. Or so he says.

I think it's best the two of them stay far away from each other. I mean, Cecilia's finally getting her act together thanks to me. Look at the state I found her in, and she was neglecting her own baby. She was a mess, sort of still is, but at least I can help her. Now that he's out of prison, Paul should focus on moving on in life. Forget about Cecilia. There are plenty of fish in the sea, as they say. I wonder if he knows about the baby. That's not going to make him happy.

Before I get ready for bed, I look out my window toward the street. Trees bend and sway in the wind, but I don't see anyone out there, not anymore.

TWENTY-NINE

CECILIA

The monitor sounds and I sit up quickly, disoriented for a moment. Finally, I had a good night's sleep, despite the howling winds. I feel like a new person as I hurry across the hall to greet the baby. I'm happy I arrived first to her cribside and had planned it this way. I turn off the monitor and hope maybe Lizzie will sleep and leave the two of us alone. With money being tight, I'm starting to wonder if I should let Lizzie go. I've learned a lot from her when it comes to taking care of Peyton, but some of the things she's done have left me a bit unsettled.

I've decided at the very least I do need her to take some time off, to give me and Peyton a little more time together alone. Anyone would get on your nerves if they were around 24/7, and that seems to be the case with my feelings toward the nanny suddenly. That's the other thing. I need to keep a little more professional distance between us—she's my employee, I'm her boss. And with Evan coming over this afternoon to play with Peyton, it would be nice to have some privacy.

I change Peyton and carry her downstairs to the kitchen, slipping her into the highchair. I grab a smoothie from the fridge for my breakfast, strawberry, and take a big drink. The winds have died down, and the air doesn't seem as dry or electric. As I prepare her bottle, I stare out at the backyard. Something looks off, but I'm suddenly too tired to focus on what it could be. Disappointing because I had a good night's sleep, or so I thought.

Peyton starts to whimper, begging for breakfast, so I hurry and hand her the bottle.

Lizzie walks into the kitchen. "I didn't hear her wake up, I'm so sorry," she says, blinking away sleep and clearly in a panic.

"I heard her. It's fine, she's fine," I say. I am the capable, loving mom. I'm in charge. Everything is fine. "I've got her breakfast sorted, if you want to go get ready for the day."

"Sure, yes, I'll do that," she says with a frosty look on her face. And then she walks past me to look out the sliding doors to the backyard. "Oh, oh no." She emits a little moan.

"What is it?" I ask, swallowing. I don't think I can take any more unexplainable events. What does she see?

"It's the pool. There's something floating in it," Lizzie says. "I thought I saw someone out there last night in the wind, but I told myself I was seeing things. But now I think whoever was out there put something in the pool."

"You should have told me. Why didn't you wake me up?" I rush to the security pad and disable the system. "What is it anyway?"

"I'm as in the dark as you are. Let's not panic until we know what we're dealing with. Tell you what, why don't you stay here with Peyton while I go look around?" She slides open the door.

I grab my phone. "I'll call 9-1-1 if you scream." My hand shakes as I hold my phone. I try to smile at Peyton, to reassure her. I close and lock the sliding door. I carry the baby to her playpen and distract her with toys before hurrying back to watch Lizzie investigate in the backyard.

All I can see is Lizzie standing by the edge of the pool. The look on her face tells me it's something nasty. I want to flag her to come back inside. I open the door. "So, what is it?" I call to her.

"It's two dead rats," she says, her face pinched with disgust. She hurries back to the door.

She shows me a photo on her phone and I almost vomit. "What does this mean?"

"I have no idea but it's so creepy," Lizzie says. "Did you ever have fans, like people who heard your story and did crazy things like this to get close to you?"

"No, not really, not since right after the fall," I say. "But I moved. Nobody knows or cares who I am anymore, or where I live. That all happened a long time ago now."

"You were famous when it happened. I remember your story," Lizzie says. "And Paul knows where you live. He got that letter to you."

We lock eyes. "I thought you didn't know about what happened to me," I say. Have I caught her in a lie?

"I didn't, not really. I mean, I've learned a lot about you since," she says, a small smile forming. "At the coffee shop that day, I just knew you were a woman who needed help."

Well, that was certainly true. I can't give any of this too much thought right now anyway. I need to sort out the dead rats in the pool.

"I'll call the pool guy, he'll know what to do," I say.

"Do you think we should call the police? I mean, it's vandalism if nothing else." Lizzie points to the pool.

I think about the gruesome photo Lizzie took of the rats, the red eyes, the bloated bodies. No, I don't want that kind of attention, police cars in my driveway, local reporters chasing me around again, peeking through my car windows, trying to get an unflattering photo to feed to the national tabloids. I have PTSD from the terrible events in Paris, and the police are still a trigger. No, I'll avoid the police and the media at all costs.

"I don't think we will call the police. I'll just get the pool guy to clean it up," I say.

"Oh, Cecilia?" she says. "I had an idea. What about cameras outside, recording the driveway and the backyard? We'd have video of whoever did this if we had cameras."

I wouldn't mind an added layer of security right about now. It's a good idea. "Ok, I like that idea. Do you want to find a company who will install ASAP?" I know it's going to be expensive, but I cannot be too careful for Peyton's sake. Everything I do is to protect her.

"Sure, absolutely, happy to do so," Lizzie says. "And I'm just going to have another look around back there. Make sure we didn't overlook anything. I'll be in for Peyton in just a few minutes."

"Ok, fine," I say as I turn back to the house. I pray she doesn't find anything else menacing. I can't lose my fragile stability, not now that I finally have it back.

I can't help but think Paul could be behind this. Something like putting two dead rats in my pool seems like his brand of psychological warfare, for sure. Maybe this little prank was about control, trying to keep me off balance and afraid, doubting myself. Is this his subtle way of letting me know he's back in Malibu, hiding nearby and waiting to exact his revenge and finish the job he started in Paris five years ago?

I get a jab of panic as I hurry inside to make sure the baby is where I left her. She is.

THIRTY

LIZZIE

Cecilia seemed surprised I knew her story, more than she told me herself in her pool confession, or at least the version of her story that the media told the world. She shouldn't be. The bathing suit saleslady knew the story. Everyone, at some point, likely heard the tale. She's on edge, that's all. I'll help her calm down after I'm finished out here.

Once Cecilia is back inside the house, I take a few more photos of the dead rats in the pool from several different angles. I look at the photos up close. So gross.

I look to the left, from this far corner of Cecilia's yard, and realize the Johnsons' enormous swing set is just on the other side, although it isn't visible from Cecilia's backyard. I spot the kids' tree fort just above the fence line on the other side. So close, but a whole lifetime away, at least that's how I feel now—and little Jimmy aside, good riddance. My heart softens when I think about that kid. Maybe if I have some time off, I'll pick him up and take him out to dinner. We'll reconnect. Just like Evan and Peyton will during her birthday party this afternoon, the party I planned but I wonder if I'll be invited to attend.

I walk over to Cecilia's amazing garden—planted with fruit

and vegetables and herbs and all kinds of things. I cut a few of the white flowers I see growing all over to make an arrangement for the kitchen table and our birthday celebration. I've never seen her tend to it, of course, but I know the gardener does. Cecilia likes to have other people looking after things. It's definitely her thing.

"Hey, Lizzie." Cecilia's calling me. "Can you come watch Peyton? I need to get dressed for the day."

Proving my point. "Sure, yes, coming," I say. I hurry across the yard and the pool area and make my way inside.

"So, why don't you plan on taking this afternoon and evening off?" she says. "Evan and I need a little privacy. What are the flowers for?"

"Um... sure, good, right. These are for the table," I say, and I can't help feeling disappointed. Is she thinking of getting back together with him? I sure hope not. "I can set everything up for her birthday party if you'd like? You two can celebrate her."

"Sure, ok. But I'm not getting back together with him," she says, as if reading my mind. "But I do want their bonding to go smoothly without too many people around confusing Peyton."

Peyton is more likely to be confused by the notion of her two parents finally focusing their attention on her, but what do I know?

"I get it," I say. And then I get the flicker of excitement. It might be fun to have a little time off since I ended up having Peyton duty last night, after all. *Ah, an afternoon and evening off, what shall I do with myself?* I have many ideas. "I have the balloons, and the cake is in the refrigerator. Just need to tie it all together with some colorful plates. The pink six months candle looks beautiful on top of the white cake with pink polka dots. It's all going to look so cute. Since I won't be here, take lots of pictures for me." I know she won't, though. Cecilia is bad at documenting these milestones. I'll snap a few photos before I leave.

"Ok, well, I can help you decorate. I'll get ready and then you can plan on leaving by noon," she says.

She really wants me out of here. *Fine.* "Sure."

While she's gone, I take a few photos of Peyton and I, hooking up streamers and taping pink balloons up everywhere. The kitchen looks festive and happy, and suddenly I'm sad to not be invited to the party I've planned.

When Cecilia returns from getting ready, she looks like I used to imagine her appearing all the time: hair, makeup, outfit perfection. I wonder if she's missing Evan more than she's letting on. I wonder if she is trying to lure him back. The low-plunging red dress makes me think so. And around her neck is a huge diamond pendant sparkling like a dagger.

"Well, say something. What do you think?" she says, obviously noticing my open-mouthed stare. While she's been getting glamorous, I've been blowing up pink balloons and tying crepe paper to the kitchen light fixture. It's starting to look like a party —but I am definitely not going to be ready to leave at noon. Meanwhile, Cecilia looks fantastic.

"Um, I think you look like you should be heading to a cocktail party or a fancy dinner. I mean, you look gorgeous. Evan is going to be sad he lost you. And that necklace, it's just wow." I grab another balloon to blow up. "How many carats is that diamond?"

"I don't remember, but a lot," she says. "It's the first piece of jewelry I ever bought for myself. Anyway, I can handle everything from here. Peyton's party will be great, thank you. You're off duty until tomorrow morning so I hope you find something fun to do with your time."

I drop the deflated balloon onto the kitchen table and hand Peyton to her. The baby, too, is transfixed by the diamond necklace and wraps her chubby hand around it. Who wouldn't be? It's stunning.

"Oh, I'm sure I'll figure out something to do. Don't you

worry, the world is my oyster," I say, hurrying out of the kitchen. I can feel Cecilia's eyes on my back. I've almost reached the stairs when she calls out.

"Lizzie, did you contact someone for security cameras?"

"Not yet, but I will today. Promise," I call back. First, I need to confirm some things, and I will.

Upstairs in my room, I rummage through my walk-in closet to find the perfect outfit. I decide a dress would be nice to wear today. I curl my hair, do my makeup, and in a flash I'm transformed into an elegant, wealthy woman. Well, I'm not wealthy, but I look the part. Cecilia and Peyton are in the living room when I walk back downstairs; Cecilia is mumbling something about art and life and painting. I know she thinks she's a good painter, but to me her abstract paintings look like she threw some paint on the canvas and swooshed it around randomly. But what do I know?

"Look at you," Cecilia says. "I forgot I gave you that dress. Red is my favorite color to wear."

I smile. "It's like we're twins, sort of." I spin around in Cecilia's hand-me-down, blood-red dress.

"Sort of. Have a nice day." She turns her back to me, focusing her attention on the horrible art hanging on the wall. That's when I notice the uninflated pink balloon in Peyton's hand and watch as she brings it to her mouth.

"Peyton, no!" I yell and grab the balloon from her hand. "Cecilia, how could you let her have one of these?"

Cecilia looks stunned, eyes wide. "I didn't realize."

"The baby could choke, or worse," I say. "Are you sure you don't want me to stay for the party? I mean, just in case something goes wrong?"

Cecilia swallows, composing herself. "I'm sure. Have fun," she says dismissively.

"You, too," I say and hurry out the front door. I don't lock it behind me, though, because even though she's shaken by the balloon, I know paranoid Cecilia will be on it as soon as I leave. I'm about to slip into her BMW when I notice something on the ground. It's a blue earbud. I grab it.

And then it dawns on me. I've just realized who was creeping around in the backyard last night, who tossed the dead rats into the pool. It's my first stop.

THIRTY-ONE

CECILIA

I lock the front door and watch Lizzie drive away. Why did she choose to wear a red dress so very similar to the one I'm wearing today? It's odd, but maybe I should be flattered that she's trying so hard to look like me—and even to act like me, I've noticed.

I don't know what to make of it all, but I guess it's fine. Like she said, she came from a normal, boring household and now she's thrust into a wealthy enclave, first with her old family and now with me and the baby. I wonder if she's jealous of everything I have or whether she's satisfied with hand-me-downs and an occasional new bathing suit, along with a steady salary and a free sports car to drive?

Is that enough? I think about if the situation were reversed. Would it be enough for me? I'd like to think so, but my life is so far removed from the simple one I led before Paul, I can't really be sure if I could be satisfied with a normal life anymore. I think money does change people. I think it has changed me. I still have my painting, of course, and it's been nice not having the pressure to sell my work—although that may change now the money is starting to run out. Now I'm determined to focus on it as a career again. I still dream of having a gallery show someday, adoring art collectors from around the world vying to own an original Cecilia Strom.

Peyton is playing with the necklace around my neck, specifically the diamond. I remember the fury in Paul's eyes when he saw it for the first time when I dressed for dinner and stepped out in a red dress, much like this one, wearing the stunning necklace. The look of shock on his face was priceless, although he soon covered it with a fake smile, of course. He'd assumed when he said no to buying it at the elegant Parisian jewelry store that he would have the last word. He didn't. This necklace was a symbol of defiance, and it's a tangible reminder that I can and will take care of myself when push comes to shove. *Ok, bad choice of wording.* I lean against the wall to calm the feeling of falling and take deep breaths to still my racing heart.

Standing up for yourself can have near-deadly consequences when you're married to someone like Paul, I learned. But I'm still proud of myself. And I almost got him, before he got me; I almost killed him first. Just one more dose of the poison would have done it.

I really hope he isn't lurking around here in the shadows. I'll do anything and everything to protect myself and my baby.

"Lunchtime, Peyton, and then we will have your birthday party," I say and carry her into the kitchen. Peyton loves the pink balloons dotting the kitchen table and floor, and the streamers hanging from the chandelier. She reaches for them and giggles. I still cannot believe she had a balloon in her hand. *How did she get it?* My blood runs cold. I need to pay better attention, and I will.

We're finishing up when the doorbell rings. Evan's early, but I don't blame him. I look into my baby's tiny face, her beautiful green eyes, and say, "Daddy is here." I hope I'm doing the right thing for her and for all of us. I must believe I am.

When I open the door, Evan's eyes fill with tears. "She's gotten so big. Hi, baby."

"Come in." I lead him through the house to the kitchen and family room. The room is bathed in light pouring in through the large windows, offering a view of the sparkling pool and the sun-kissed ocean beyond. Inside, pink balloons dance gently in the air, tethered to chairs and countertops. The long kitchen island serves as a focal point, adorned with the same pink and white polka dot decorations, including the centerpiece—the exquisite half-birthday cake. It's like a perfect dream birthday party for a little girl.

"It looks amazing in here." Evan turns toward me. "And wowza, you look gorgeous. Just like when we first met. You used to always dress to kill. Is this a sign you've changed your mind about us?" He's smiling like it's a joke but I can detect a genuine note of hope in his voice.

"I'm just reminding you of what you lost when you cheated," I say with a smile.

"Touché," he says. "Look at these decorations! I'm impressed. I love all the pink balloons. You've really gone all out for our baby. This is for you, by the way." He hands me a small gold gift bag. "To say sorry," he adds. "And this is for you, baby girl."

Peyton coos over her new stuffed giraffe as I open my gift. It's a gold bracelet with a heart and *Peyton* engraved on it. I used to be able to count on him to be thoughtful like this. But never again. Still, it's a nice gesture.

"Thank you, it's beautiful," I say.

"Just like you," he says and touches my hand.

I don't feel anything, no tingles, no sparks. Just friendship and a shared love of Peyton. I pull my hand away.

"You need to stop that, please." I decide to get down to business. "So, the building is ready to go on the market, correct?" I point to the highchair and Evan slips Peyton in. He sighs as he sits down.

"It is. The broker thinks it will go fast and for the asking price. He has two interested parties already." I can hear the sadness in his voice but then Peyton giggles at him and pounds her fists on the highchair tray, and he smiles. "It'll be worth it to have her back in my life. Should we make visitation arrangements formally? Have you thought about that? And I'll need my name on the birth certificate."

"Sure, yes, that's no problem, and as for a schedule, that's what I was going to ask you about, too. I mean, you work full-time," I say.

"But I dictate my schedule, and most of the evening events I just pop in, show face, and duck out," he reminds me.

"Oh, I know you're Mr. Big Time now," I say. "I'm proud of you." A small pang of envy washes over me. I miss my job there, and I have a lingering annoyance that he fired me. But still, I was in no shape to be working after the baby was born, and truth be told, working with the person you live with is a tough task indeed. It's better this way, for all of us. I'll pave my own way with my painting career. I hope.

"You helped me get here," he says. "But anyway, what works for you?"

I have thought about this, how the future will unfold with shared parenting, but I guess we'll work through it together.

I stand up. "It will all work out. I'll just grab the cake, and we can sing to her!"

I carry the white cake with pink polka dots and a pink candle that reads *6 months* over to the table. Lizzie added some white daisies around the glass cake stand to match the centerpiece she created, and I have to admit it looks good. I light the candle. "Happy birthday Peyton!"

Evan and I look at each other, each wanting the other to start singing first. Finally, he starts and I join in. Peyton claps her hands together.

"It's time to blow out the candle!" I bend down so my face is touching hers as Evan holds the cake close. I blow and Peyton laughs with glee. Evan grabs his phone and takes photos. I realize that anybody looking in at the scene would think we were an adorable happy family.

I walk to the kitchen and grab a knife and three plates. I know Peyton can't really have cake, only a small taste of the icing, but I'd like a photo of her with the cake in front of her. I cut a thin slice and place it on the glass serving plate, and then cut a large slice for Evan and a smaller one for me.

I swipe my finger through the icing and offer it to Peyton, wondering if she'll even like the taste or texture.

"Oh my gosh, look how cute she is," Evan says as she tries a tiny taste.

And she bursts into tears.

"It's ok, baby, no need to eat any," I say, hurrying to grab a bottle for her. On my way back from the refrigerator, I see her push the plate off the tray. It hits the floor and shatters into a million pieces.

"I'll grab a broom," Evan says, rushing to the front closet.

Peyton is crying harder now. I'm not sure what's wrong but I notice her face has bright red splotches all over it.

"Oh my gosh, I think she's having an allergy attack! Food allergies run in my family. I thought I told you that! We're really sensitive to additives." Evan drops the broom and runs over to inspect her face.

"That's why everything I feed Peyton is organic. I don't know why this is happening. I don't know what to do. Should we call an ambulance?" I'm panicking. I pull out my phone and Google which ingredient in a cake could cause a reaction like this. The answer: *Red 40. Also known as Allure Red, the color comes from coal tars and petroleum distillates.* Oh my gosh. I've poisoned my baby. Where is this cake from anyway?

"Where did you get the cake?" Evan asks, picking Peyton up out of her highchair and consoling her.

"The nanny got it. I thought from an organic bakery," I say. "She knows I only buy organic."

"Clearly it's not from there." I watch as he carries Peyton into the kitchen, runs cold water over a washcloth and holds it to her fiery cheeks. "It's lucky she didn't have much. Hey, Cecilia, stop crying. She's going to be ok. She's breathing fine. My reactions were always skin splotches like this, I never stopped breathing or anything."

I can't help it. Tears stream down my cheeks. "All I do is try to be there for her. I keep messing up."

"It's ok. You didn't know the cake wasn't organic," Evan says. "She'll be fine. I grew out of my allergies. She will, too."

I take a step toward them, and Peyton reaches for me. Me. Her poisoner. I take her into my arms and squeeze her. "I'm so sorry, baby."

"Let's go sit in the family room," Evan says, and I follow him there, still holding the washcloth on Peyton's face.

We sit on the couch as I pull myself together. Peyton has settled down and seems back to her normal self, albeit with a few red splotches still dotting her body.

"Ok, I told you she would be fine. She will be. But now I need to know how often do I get to do this?" Evan says.

"I think after this birthday, it's just once a year," I say.

"No, I mean visit her. Be with her?"

I haven't really thought this through yet, but Evan spending time with Peyton could be a way for me to cut back on Lizzie's hours, and my expenses, too. "Well, um, maybe you could take her a couple afternoons a week, so I could get some painting done?" Lizzie likely wouldn't approve of this arrangement.

"I'm going to need more than that. I mean, I am selling my entire building, relocating my business to LA," he says. "I need more time."

"She isn't a business transaction, she's our daughter," I say. I pick her up and begin pacing the family room. I'm such an idiot.

I thought I could control his entire access to her, but I realize now I can't. He'll have demands, too. I take a deep breath. "Maybe this was a bad idea."

"Stop it, Cecilia. It is the right thing, you know it, even if I have to bend over backwards to make it happen. I have, and I will, but I should have equal time," he says.

Over my dead body, I think. But I don't want to tell him that, not yet. I need the money from the real estate sale in my new personal banking account before I can draw my line in the sand. "Ok, sure, you're right, we can do that. Equal time," I say.

"Maybe we should get an attorney involved?" He holds out his arms for Peyton and I give her to him.

There will not be an attorney involved. Ever. I will get the money and he will get a smidge of Peyton time but only when I say so.

"Not necessary, and so expensive." I paste a smile on my face and flip my hair over my shoulder. "You and I will work this through. See, we already are."

"So, every other day?" he says.

I swallow. I can't imagine sharing her like that. *No way.*

"Starting after the building sells and the funds transfer," I say. "For now, until that happens, you can come here every other afternoon if you'd like."

He looks at me, blue eyes sad again. "Ok," he says. "We'll do it your way, work into this slowly. Look, the welts on her face are calming down."

"Thank goodness. Well, after all this excitement, it's time for her nap. Would you mind seeing yourself out?"

"But I just got here!"

"Not really. You've been here over an hour. She's on a schedule. It's important," I say, taking Peyton from his arms. "Say bye bye."

"You know what, you're a piece of work, Cecilia." He's kept his voice fairly quiet, for the baby, but it's full of anger.

"You know what, Evan," I say, "you're a piece of shit. And you know it. So if you'd like to see her, be a part of her life, you will do it my way. Understood?"

And with that, I walk out of the room, and carry her upstairs to the nursery. I look out the window and see Evan getting into his car and driving away. *Good boy.*

The truth of the matter is I have decided I really don't want to share her, not with anyone. Yes, that's a change and I'm proud of myself. I do realize Peyton may benefit from having Evan in her life, but that will get too complicated. I don't want my baby to be one of those kids shuffling back and forth between parents. And I can already tell with the way Evan acted today, if you give him an inch, he'll want a mile. That's not going to happen, not with Peyton.

As I change her into PJs, I have a realization. I *do* have a plan. I will get the funds and then I will block Evan from our lives again. I decide it's time to sell this house, too, and move somewhere Paul can't find us, somewhere too far away for Evan to be able to make regular contact. I won't need Lizzie much longer, either. My back is feeling so much better and I'm ready to be the mom my baby deserves. I'll take care of myself so I can take care of her. We need a fresh start.

As I settle the baby in her crib, I start imagining possible destinations. We aren't going back to Florida, that's for sure. What about somewhere charming, up or down the California coast? I imagine us in a small house by the sea, a swing hanging from a tree, with a painter's studio out back.

Soon, I'm going to make that dream a reality. But I know I need to act fast, as fast as I can. I feel like somebody's out there who would like to make my dream a nightmare. Once Peyton settles in her crib, I hurry downstairs to lock the door and turn on the alarm.

THIRTY-TWO

LIZZIE

I ring the doorbell at the Johnsons' home and wait for an answer. Nobody comes. I knock on the door. Nothing. I ring the bell again. I know the kids are home from school by now. Finally, Mrs. Johnson herself answers. She's more disheveled than I've ever seen her, mascara smeared under her eyes, hair wild and unbrushed, and the smell of alcohol on her breath is strong. It's getting worse.

"What do you want?" she asks.

"I need to talk to the boys," I say.

"Lizzie!" Jimmy runs down the stairs and rushes straight at me for a big hug. "You're back."

I give him a hug back, then bend down to his eye level. "I'm not back, but I did want to tell you I got your message," I say.

His face lights up with a smile.

"What message?" Mrs. Johnson says.

"Oh, it's our little inside joke," I say, standing up and patting his head. "But I don't want any more messages from you, or Johnny. I'll let it go this time."

I look up to the top of the stairs and see Johnny is listening.

He doesn't rush down to give me a hug. On the contrary, his eyes are dark and angry.

"Will you stay? Please," he begs.

I know he put the rats in the pool to get my attention. He wants me to come back. Poor little guy.

"I can't," I say. "But you know what, I'm going to call a service, get someone to help over here. For you, and for Johnny, and the girls. And your mom."

Mrs. Johnson doesn't say anything. She knows the truth.

I look up at Johnny. He nods. "We need help."

"Message received," I say. "I'm sure you will have a bunch of qualified applicants. Don't worry. Help is on the way." I kiss the top of Jimmy's head and head back to the car.

I also decide I'm going to call Mr. Johnson. The ringtone tells me he's still abroad, but he answers after only one ring.

"Lizzie, how wonderful to hear from you. I'm glad you're not still upset about our little misunderstanding," he says. The background noise suggests he's at a bar, probably in one of the private clubs he's a member of around the world.

"Misunderstanding?" I take a deep breath. "You have four children and a wife to take care of. You need to grow up and take responsibility. Life isn't always about you."

"Whatever," he says. "Are you back, helping?"

"No," I say. "I quit. But your family does need help. Especially the kids, and most especially little Jimmy. Come home. For him."

"Will you be there when I do?" There's a suggestive note in his voice. He's such a creep. I cannot believe I stayed as long as I did.

"No. I won't be. Do the right thing, Mr. Johnson. Goodbye." I hang up. Yes, he's a horrible man but he has responsibilities to the four of them. Darn it, I do have a heart, at least when it comes to Jimmy. Poor boy.

As I drive away, I call the nanny service through the car's

Bluetooth and explain the situation. They are eager to fill the position and assure me they will be on it today. Next, I call the security company that's responsible for the alarm system at Cecilia's home. I ask them to install outdoor cameras, and they say they will be by as soon as possible, maybe this afternoon but for sure in the morning. I park up on the street to finish my calls, and I'm surprised when I see *his* car pulling out of her driveway so soon.

Things must not have gone as planned. I pull out behind him, following wherever he is headed. Evan turns into the small shopping plaza on Point Dume, and I do likewise. He parks and heads into a juice bar. I park and follow him over but stand outside. I pretend to busy myself on my phone, my back to the door where he'll be exiting.

"Whoa?" Evan does a double take as he walks out the door.

I turn around. "Oh... Evan, hi! Sorry, did I startle you?"

"Wow. No, it's just that you have an uncanny resemblance to Cecilia. I mean, I was just with her, she's wearing a red dress, too." He looks confused, but also a little sad. The overfilled container of juice is spilling over onto his hand, but he doesn't seem to notice.

"How'd your time go with Peyton?" I ask him. He's so cute with his shaggy blond hair, blue eyes and casual beach vibe. But he's successful, so he's no simple surfer dude.

"She's the best baby," he says. "It was so good to see her. The cake didn't go so well, though. She was allergic to it."

"Oh no. Poor baby. Should I go back and help? I knew I should have handled ordering it, but Cecilia wanted to do it," I say.

"Well, whoever got the cake, Peyton was allergic to it. But she'll be fine. Besides, Cecilia needs to learn to deal with her. Right? I mean, she is the mom. But this is all so hard." He almost looks like he's about to cry.

"Do you want to talk about it?" I ask. I point to a table

tucked away next to the juice bar. "I'll go grab you a napkin. Go sit down."

He does as directed, and I duck inside the bar, buy a water bottle, grab some napkins, slip a small healing candle from a display by the door into my pocket on the way out, and join him.

"I think I might be in shock," he says as I hand him the napkins. "It's like, such a yoyo with her."

"You don't deserve that." I tilt my head, flash a smile. "I'm sorry. Here, I bought you a candle, for healing. You need to clear your heart. She's over you, and you need to be over her, too. You'll have more room for Peyton."

"Thanks, that's so sweet." He sighs and accepts the candle absentmindedly. "I want to be part of Peyton's life, so much so that I'm willing to do whatever Cecilia asks, but she offers me things and then she changes her mind. It's so hard to know what to do."

"She's like that with me, too. And unfortunately, also with Peyton. It's tough, because babies need consistency and constant attention," I say. "I worry, too."

"I'm glad you're there helping. I'm glad you get it," he says.

"Don't worry. I will always be there for Peyton." I give him a reassuring smile.

"Thank you. Anyway, let's change the subject," he says. "Tell me about you. Distract me. You know far too much about my sorry life now."

"Oh, I'm not that interesting." I look down at the table.

"Let me be the judge of that," he says.

I'll get him talking about himself again in a moment. First, my usual. "I really am boring. I grew up in a normal Midwestern household, two parents who loved me and gave me everything they could. Country club swim team, sleepovers, all of that," I say, painting the perfect picture.

"How'd you end up out here in Malibu, then?" he asks. "Let me guess. You wanted to be an actress?"

I am going to be a Malibu housewife someday soon and spend the rest of my life taking care of my husband and children. We will have a happy, traditional home. I'll bake cookies with my kids and puffs of flour will fill the air. I'll swim with them in the backyard pool and be ready and dressed up again by the time my husband returns home, his favorite drink in hand as he walks through the door. I think of my beautiful mom holding a drink for my dad in her hand. She did everything right, everything was perfect, except she chose the wrong man. I won't make that mistake. Her dream will come true through me.

Evan is kind and caring. I've never seen him angry, only frustrated by Cecilia keeping Peyton from him, which is understandable. That's why I'm auditioning now for the homemaker role, although he doesn't realize it.

"No, I always wanted to care for kids. To be a nanny, and then someday have a family of my own." I bite my bottom lip. "I know that's lame. Not many women will admit to wanting the role of stay-at-home mom, traditional wife these days. But it's my dream. Truth be told, it's my mom's dream for me. And I will make it come true. To be of service, to care for my family."

"Lame? It's so sweet, so selfless." He's looking at me earnestly. "Taking care of a child is the most important job there is. I think you're amazing."

I drop my chin as my cheeks flush. "Well, thank you. I think you're amazing, too. I've seen some of the photos of events you've done, in the news and online. You're the best in LA. You must know so many famous people and the fact they trust you to handle their events is so impressive."

I might be laying it on a little too thick, but his ego has been wounded by Cecilia, so he needs a little boosting.

He smiles, a real smile for the first time. "The thing is, once you get to know them, famous people are just people, and they become friends. So yes, I do know a lot of them, and do private events for many of the top names, but it's because we're friends," he explains.

"You should be so proud of yourself and all you've accomplished." I push my blonde hair over my shoulder. "You deserve to come back to a peaceful home after how hard you work. I know that hasn't exactly been the case with Cecilia. And now her money seems to be running out so she's even more stressed. Poor Peyton."

Evan nods. "Yes, she's a bit panicked about money, it seems. All in all, she's really into Peyton, happy about being a mom. You've really helped her a lot. I realize I didn't. I feel bad about that."

I nod in agreement. "It's my job."

"Well, thank you," he says. "I knew I liked you the minute I saw you on the beach with the baby."

"That was you? Watching us?" I ask, noting the confirmation of my suspicions. "You scared me. I barely knew who you were."

"Sorry about that. I just missed Peyton so much, and when I saw you walking her to the beach I couldn't help following. But you didn't know me yet, so I kept my distance. You two looked so cute on that blanket." Evan says with a smile. "I want that. A traditional family, too. I realize I screwed it up with Cecilia. It won't happen again."

Music to my ears. He could be just what I'm looking for. Dependable, handsome, romantic and he loves kids. He wants love and commitment, I can tell, and he's learned his lesson with how he treated Cecilia. And if Cecilia starts wanting more time alone with Peyton, I might just have time to get him really into me. I could sort of be his replacement Cecilia. I mean, she doesn't want him, so he's fair game. We'll need to spend more time together, of course, but that shouldn't be a problem. When I decide what I want, I move fast.

"I believe you," I say.

"So, what are you doing for dinner? I have some time before I need to drive to LA for an event," he says.

"Well, I'm starving, and I'd love to have dinner with you." I reach out and touch his hand, with fingernails painted the same color as Cecilia's, if he notices.

He grins and takes my hand in his. And we've begun. How fun.

Ah, it is now time for our journey together to come to an end. I just want to thank you again for keeping my spirits up during my long days of incarceration. Your notes, and updates on life on the outside, made me realize all the more what I have to live for; the plans we made together gave me a goal to keep in mind even on the darkest days in this place. You will always have my gratitude, my dear, but that, I'm afraid, is all. My heart belongs to someone else, that much has become crystal clear. You and I have a big age gap, my dear. I never date older women. But I wish you good health and a good life. I am sure our paths will meet again someday soon.

With gratitude,

Paul

Perhaps I haven't made myself clear: don't text, write, or call me again. We've both gotten what we needed from each other. Fuck off. Or else. Paul.

THIRTY-THREE

CECILIA

I know I shouldn't do it, but I can't help myself. Peyton is napping and so I'm going to take this opportunity to look through Lizzie's room, search for things—something, anything—to either help me believe she is what she seems, or to confirm she's not.

When she sauntered down the stairs wearing a red dress, one of my red dresses, it was a wake-up call, I realize now. Sure, I gave her the dress, but why would she choose to wear it today when she saw me wearing a red dress? She chose it on purpose. The sparkle in her eye was a challenge.

I take a deep breath, turn the knob and walk into my guest room, Lizzie's room. She keeps it tidy is the first thing I notice. The bed is made, and the entire room is spotless. I walk over to the dresser and pull open the top drawer. Items are folded and stacked as they should be. And now I'm beginning to feel guilty for being in here. I close the drawer and make my way into the bathroom. Also spotless, with not so much as hairbrush on the counter or a washcloth on the sink. Almost too tidy, too perfect in here if you ask me.

My phone rings and I pull it out. Unknown number. I answer. "Hello?"

There's no one there, it seems. My blood runs cold. *Maybe it was a wrong number*, I try to convince myself. But no, even though I've blocked the number every time he's texted, the number changes, and he still gets through to me. I dial this number, and as always it rolls to a generic voicemail. I hang up.

I remind myself to focus on exploring Lizzie's room. I walk into the closet and here, too, it's organized impeccably. The clothing items hang by color, a rainbow of options, most of them from me. I pull open a built-in drawer and discover bathing suits, the ones I bought for her, three out of four of them with the tags still attached. I take a breath and think about what this means.

So what, she lied about taking the tags off? I reason with myself to calm the alarm bells. She'd fallen in love with the suits and wanted to keep me from returning them, and that's understandable. They do look great on her. I close the drawer. I'm not going to fire someone for wanting to keep the gifts I bought. I feel ashamed for rummaging in here.

I pull open the bottom drawer and blink, surprised by what I find hidden inside. It's a framed photo of Evan and I, one that was on the bookshelf in the living room until I put it away in the cupboard. I pick up the photo. Beside it is a bottle of my favorite nail polish, the color I'm wearing today, Passion Red, and next to it is the antique dish with my bath salts. My favorite cozy white bathrobe is in the drawer, too, along with my sexy red bra, something I haven't worn for a very long time so I hadn't noticed it was gone. I stare at the stolen items with a mixture of anger and sadness. But most of all I feel betrayed. I've given her so much, took her in, trusted her with my baby. Why would she steal and lie to me? What would make her take these things, hide these things like a shrine in her closet? I just don't understand.

I leave my things in the drawer where I found them, hurry out of the room, and close the door behind me. Hopefully, I didn't leave any signs of my search. I need to figure out the appropriate way to bring this up with Lizzie. Maybe it's just as simple as telling her goodbye. I can't trust her, not anymore. Peyton is sleeping soundly as I pass by her nursery, so I have time to call my realtor. If I give her my house to sell, maybe she can find a buyer, quietly, and we can execute a quick transaction before anyone finds out. I dial her number, and she answers on the first ring.

"Hello, Morgan. It's Cecilia Strom. I need to sell my house," I say it as quickly as I can so I don't really need to think about it too much. It breaks my heart that it has come to this, but it has, for many reasons.

"Oh no, Cecilia. Why would you sell it? It's perfect for you. And you made it your own with the decorator's help." Morgan Snyder is the realtor for high-end Malibu estates. I know she's thrilled about the thought of me selling, I just caught her off guard.

"I love the house, but it is what it is. I need to sell it. So, a pocket listing? Does that work? I can't have any showings, though, but I can send you the photos from the magazine shoot a couple years back. Nothing has changed," I say. *Well, except everything has.* "We could do a virtual tour if you'd like?"

"Brilliant. Perfect." Morgan sounds far more enthused now, as I knew she would. "I know the house well enough. I'll find just the right person. I have a client in mind. As long as you're sure—I don't want to start the process and then have you change your mind. People always ask about your street, especially if the home comes with a coveted beach key, which yours does. I mean, you could make a killing selling right now. There are very few quality houses on the market."

"Great. And don't worry, I won't change my mind. As much

as I love this home, I'm ready for a change," I say. "Thanks for your help."

That call out of the way, I take a deep breath and tell myself not to cry. It's for the best, it really is. I think of Peyton splashing in the pool, my dream of her growing up here, hosting pool parties for her friends. But it's ok. We will make new memories in our new home. My thoughts return to Lizzie. I decide to search my bedroom, and then the entire house, and try to figure out if anything else is missing. First, I need to search the rest of the drawers in Lizzie's room while she's still out of the house. There may be more of my things tucked away. I hope not. But I'm afraid there could be more.

The doorbell rings, jolting me out of my thoughts. I walk to the door and my heart drops when I see who it is.

"What do you want, Marian?" I open the door to Evan's mom. "This isn't a good time."

"There's never a good time with you. But here we both are," she says, stepping inside. She's wearing a turquoise top and white jeans. With her bright red hair, she's quite technicolor. "I've decided that you need help and I am making myself available to you, free of charge. I need to get to know my granddaughter. I want to know her. I've even quit my bridge club. For her."

"Wow," I say. "Now that's what you call a sacrifice."

"Don't be clever," she says. "I'm trying to be helpful. I want to be helpful. Please let me into your lives."

I take a deep breath and soften toward Marian a bit. She does seem to truly want to be a part of Peyton's life.

She blinks at me, searching my face for a clue as to how I'm going to respond. "I know you have everything money can buy. I mean, that necklace you're wearing must be worth a fortune. But family is important, too. Let me be that for you."

I cover the diamond dagger with my hand and try to ignore

her comment, hoping she doesn't notice the tears that spring to my eyes. I look down at the ground.

"This isn't a good time," I repeat. "Look, we'll work something out. Later. Right now, the baby is sleeping." I fold my arms across my chest, hugging myself. I'm shocked by how much the mention of family stirred up such strong emotions. My mom's face pops into my mind before I can push it away. I take a step back, unnerved.

Marian touches my shoulder and I startle. "So, this is nap time? What is her schedule, exactly? I should know it if I'm going to be spending more time with her," she says. "Just tell me when you'd like me to stop by and play with her."

"Ok, I'll figure out a time." I manage a smile. "Soon. Once things calm down."

"Honey, with kids, things never calm down. I'm here for you right now if you'll let me be," she says. "I know I haven't been helpful or kind like I should have been, but I'm going to make up for that. I'm sorry I didn't try harder before. You just seemed so, well, perfect."

"I'm hardly that." I sigh. Maybe I was, once upon a time, before the fall, before everything changed. Before Peyton. Now my whole life is devoted to her.

"I've been focused on the wrong things, helping the wrong people," Marian says quietly.

I shrug and try to believe she's changed, that she cares. I'm still just not quite sure I believe her. "Ok," I say. "We'll try to make things work. For Peyton." *For now,* I don't add, *because soon, we'll be gone.*

"That means a lot, honey. Now go take a rest while the baby is sleeping. You don't look so good." She pats my shoulder.

"I will. Thank you," I say, feeling calmer around her than I ever have. I hold the front door open as she leaves in a burst of color. I feel my shoulders relax, just a little. It's nice to have someone on my side, even if it will only be until I leave town.

I give her a small wave when she turns around to climb into her car, still wondering about her change of heart, and close the door behind her, lock it and turn on the alarm.

I decide to change into jeans and a sweatshirt, put my necklace away in the jewelry cabinet, and lock it. I walk back through my bedroom as a text pings to my phone.

Dreading to read it, I look down at the screen.

I need to see you. I will see you. I have seen you. I can't believe you're a mother.

I cover my mouth to keep from screaming and scaring Peyton, but I'm shaking all over. I keep blocking these random numbers, but his texts keep coming. I run across the hall to the nursery and open the door, peeking inside. Peyton is fine, still asleep. Thank god.

I stand in the doorway to my bedroom, frozen with fear. The doorbell rings, but I ignore it. It rings again. I swallow and walk slowly down the stairs. I peek through the half-window and see a man in a baseball cap. It could be anyone. It could be Paul.

"Who is it?" I yell.

"Atlas Security, ma'am, about the exterior cameras. We handle your security system. We had a cancellation, so we moved your appointment up. It's our last stop of the day. But I can go home if we're here too late," he yells. "You wanted to add exterior cameras, right?"

Yes, cameras. I need cameras. It's unfortunate that I'll need to spend money to install an elaborate security system for a home I plan to vacate sooner rather than later. But I remind myself that I can't take the risk of not installing security given the mysterious, threatening texts. I'm sure they're from Paul even if it's an unknown number displayed. I turn off the alarm and open the door.

"Thank you for coming," I say. "I have a question. Is there any chance a person can come into my house when the alarm is on without tripping it?"

"No, not without tripping it," he confirms.

"What about through a window?" I ask.

"Well, sure, if the windows aren't wired, somebody can get in that way," he says. "Do you have motion sensors or cameras inside?"

"No, I don't." I'm shaking all over now. I step outside into the sunshine, trying to get warm. I want to run and hide. I feel violated. I feel as if Paul is just outside my house, waiting for a chance to strike. To finish what he started in Paris.

"Are you in danger, ma'am?" he asks. "You look like you've seen a ghost."

I swallow and tell myself to breathe. But I can't stop trembling. Could Paul have snuck in sometime when the alarm was off, and hidden himself in here, somewhere in my house? *No, no way*, I tell myself. I would hear him, see him. Sense him. I let out a puff of air. But maybe I didn't. What if I'm wrong? I need to go to Peyton.

"I'm fine. But I do need exterior cameras, as soon as possible. My pool was vandalized last night," I tell him, trying to keep my voice steady. Of course, that is the least of my worries.

"Sorry to hear that," he says. "Mind if I walk the property? I can make recommendations."

"Sure, please do," I say. Peyton is waking up. I hear her beginning to cry. "But I must go get my baby. Please just install them where you think is best."

"I will. Since you already have an Atlas system, you'll be able to monitor the cameras in real time on the app on your phone. I'll get it taken care of, and they'll be operational in a few hours. Take care, ma'am. I'll be right outside if you need anything."

I close and lock the door and hurry to Peyton. My heart

beats fast, despite my attempts at deep breathing. I suppose it's a normal reaction—I'm scared. And there's no denying the fact I am in danger, and so is my baby. Threatening texts that just won't stop coming, rats in the pool, who knows what he plans next. Should we leave, get out tonight, move to a hotel? Would that be safer or leave us more exposed? I don't know what to do.

THIRTY-FOUR

LIZZIE

Sharing this meal with Evan is one of those moments I've been preparing for since I moved to Southern California. The late summer sunset is spectacular, dazzling orange and purple and pink, and our ocean view table for two is glowing in the light. So are we. I really think he likes me. It's the way he smiles at me, the way he listens to my stories. The way he leans forward and talks to me as if I'm the only person in the world. I take a bite of my baked potato, the cheese and butter melting in my mouth.

Evan smiles at me before taking a sip of his red wine. I'm not a big red wine fan, truth be told, but I pretended to like it because he was so excited about his choice. I noticed the price and figured it must be good. But it's not, at least not to me. It tastes like thick, wet dirt.

"This is so amazing," I say to take my mind off the wine—I mean all of it but that.

I agree," Evan says. "You look spectacular in that dress."

"You keep telling me that," I say. "Thank you. I'm glad you like it."

"I wish I didn't have the event tonight. It's a sixtieth

birthday party for an important client and I handled all the details, so I need to drop in," he says.

"I understand, I really do. Would I recognize your client? Is he famous?" I ask.

"She is very famous, so yes," he says. "Want to come with me? You said you have the night off, right?"

"I do very much want to come with you, but I can't tonight," I say. "I'd love a raincheck." I'm so disappointed I have to say no. Darn it. I'd love to spend more time with him, and I'm already starting to imagine us as a couple with a home of our own, but tonight I have other plans.

"Ok, I get it. But I'd love to see you again," he says. "I've wanted to get to know you since the time I watched you on the beach with Peyton."

"The feeling is mutual." My heart is beating hard in my chest. Peyton, Evan and me. A perfect little family, a perfect life. I think of my mom and my baby sister and know they want this for me, too. And this is for them. Always for them.

"When are you off work again?" he asks. "You should ask Cecilia for a regular schedule, with time off and the like."

"Yes, I know, I will try. She's hard to pin down these days," I say. It's true. I feel Cecilia changing, slipping away from me somehow, but I don't know why, and I don't know how to stop it. I'll figure it out though, I must.

"Well, get her attention. I mean, she needs you, so you have the upper hand," he says. "It worked for me—finally. She needed money from me and now I have her attention. I just have to make sure I keep it and formalize my relationship with Peyton." I notice a fleeting look of concern pass over his face.

"You're right. I'll stick up for myself," I say. "Oh, and Evan, I don't think she should find out we are spending time together."

"Why not? We broke up. She kicked me out and made it quite clear we are over and I should move on, so I am," Evan says, clearly not over the hurt. "And then she tried to keep my baby from me. *My* baby. This is not someone I'm worried about upsetting."

I reach for his hand and give it a reassuring squeeze. "Peyton needs time with her daddy. I'm sure you're a natural with her. And I know you're not worried about her finding out about us, although you don't want her to have any added ammunition to keep Peyton from you, but she's my boss, for the time being at least, so I'd appreciate it if you didn't mention our date tonight." My phone buzzes with a call. It's her. "Speak of the devil, it's Cecilia. I need to take this. Excuse me."

I walk to the front of the restaurant and step outside to talk. I can't risk Evan saying something or Cecilia overhearing anything. "Hi, is everything alright?" I ask when I finally answer.

"No, not really," she says. "Could you come back to the house? We need to talk."

Uh-oh. I don't like the sound of that. "Actually, I made plans when you told me to take the afternoon and evening off. I'm at dinner right now. And I have another engagement after this."

"Reschedule it," she says. Her tone suggests she means it. "Peyton is fussy, I have to go."

"Fine," I say. "I'll be back in a couple hours. I'm in LA, on the West Side."

"You should be back sooner than that. I know where you are, you're at Gordon's restaurant, in Malibu. You're ten minutes from home, at most," she says.

Now I'm the one to be freaked out. "Are you tracking me? How do you know where I am?" I look around the restaurant parking lot. I'm the only one outside, aside from the valet.

"See you soon." She hangs up.

I'm furious. She *must* be tracking me, but how? I look at the phone in my hand. I've never let her have access to it, and she doesn't know my passcode. I look across the parking lot to her car. It must be on her car. I'll have to search it later, after dinner.

I hurry back into the restaurant and to our table. Evan is watching me closely as he pulls the chair out for me.

"Everything ok?" he asks as I sit down. "You look a bit rattled."

"I am. Cecilia wants me home. Now."

"Is something wrong with Peyton?" he asks, worry creasing his brow.

"No, she's fine, I'm not sure what's up," I say. "She urgently wants to talk to me for some reason."

"Well, too bad, you're busy," he says with a smile. "She needs to learn that she cannot always get what she wants when she wants it. My mom keeps telling me that, to give her boundaries. She calls her the princess. The princess can wait. So, relax, finish your meal."

I take a deep breath. "You're right. I don't have to jump just because she called. But the creepy thing is, she knows where I am. She must have a tracker on the car."

"She should have told you that up front," he says. "I mean, I suppose it does sort of make sense. You're driving my precious baby around."

"I'm not tonight," I say.

"No, you're not." He reaches for my hand. "You're with me. And it's lovely. Let's finish our dinner, and then we'll both head off to our obligations. But I'll look forward to seeing you again soon."

We finish at a leisurely pace and when he asks for the check, I'm filled with dread. I don't want to go back to Cecilia's house, not when she's in a mood. And she is. Evan waits for my car to be pulled around, pays the valet and helps me inside. He's such a gentleman. And when he leans in for a kiss good night, I feel sparks, genuine tingles, run down my spine. I'm not acting.

"I can't wait to see you again," I say. The sun has fully set, and stars dot the sky. Ocean waves crash onto the shore in the distance.

Evan runs his finger down my shoulder to the tips of my fingers. "The feeling is mutual. Call me tomorrow when you can. And good luck with Cecilia. She's really something when she gets into one of her moods. I know from experience."

"Thanks, I'm afraid I know those, too." I pull the car door shut. I plan to stop along the side of the road in front of the house, find the tracking device and remove it. As I wait at a stop light, I search the internet: *My car has a tracker. How do I find it?* And I soon realize it could be as simple as an AirTag she's put in the glove box or hidden under the carpet in the trunk. Those are so small, I might never find it. Shoot. I pound my steering wheel in frustration as the light turns green.

I wonder how long she's been tracking me? Is this a recent thing? I hope so. I will simply tell her it's unacceptable and she has to remove it. She can put the tracker on the baby and track her when we're together. That's a solution and it makes logical sense. I can't have someone tracking me. I won't.

At the next light, I type in, *How do I find an AirTag in my car?* Oh, yes, there's a free scanner I can download, and it will provide a list of Bluetooth devices my iPhone can detect near me. The light turns green. Now I'm on Cecilia's street, and I pull over to the side of the road, download the app, and how helpful, it tells me the AirTag is in the backseat. Oh, in the car seat, under the lining. Clever, I'll give her that much.

I drop it on the road outside and stomp on it with the heel of my shoe. Then I pick it up and toss it into the middle of the street. A car drives by, and I imagine I hear a satisfying crunch. Hopefully, cars will continue to run over it. At least I'm rid of it for now. I hop back in the car and drive the short distance to Cecilia's house. As I pull through the gate, I see something new, a camera suspended from the tree branch just above me. Brilliant.

She should have thanked me for getting that done for her, instead of demanding I return here. But here I am. I really hope she's calmed down for both of our sakes, and for Peyton. But I doubt she has. The anger and dread I'm feeling has upset my stomach, ruining the perfect meal I just shared with Evan. I think about Evan, the look in his eye. He's already fallen for me and the feeling is mutual. I would have liked to relax over our dinner instead of hurrying to finish eating.

This better be good, Cecilia, I tell myself. Because now I'm angry, too.

As I walk up to the front door, Cecilia pulls it open. She isn't smiling, but then again neither am I.

"Glad you finally made it home," she says. Although I wouldn't describe her expression as one of gladness. In fact, it's the opposite. And she looks terrible. She's wearing jeans and a sweatshirt, her makeup is smudged, and it looks like Peyton spit up on her shoulder.

"Did I have a choice?" I ask with a hint of sarcasm, stepping inside.

"No." She pulls the door closed, immediately locking it. "Who were you with at Gordon's? That's a nice, romantic restaurant. Evan and I went there all the time when we first got together as a couple."

"A friend." I cross my arms in front of my chest. I take a deep breath and wait for her to make the first move.

THIRTY-FIVE

CECILIA

I don't say anything else but walk slowly toward the kitchen. I know Lizzie is following me. I can feel her stare, her suspicion. And something else. Is it hate or more mild anger? I'm not sure. I don't know why she's done the things she's done.

"Have a seat." I point to the kitchen table. I wait until she sits, and then I do the same. Her teeth look stained, I note. "Were you drinking red wine tonight?"

"I was. Not much, though," she says. "I really prefer white, but it's what he ordered."

"He?" I guess I shouldn't be surprised. She's gorgeous and she parades around Malibu like she owns the place now. It was only a matter of time.

"Just a friend," she repeats.

"Sure. The thing is I worry about you drinking and driving. Have you done that with Peyton in the car? That's poor judgement," I say. "But so are several other things you've done."

"I've been nothing but helpful to you." She crosses her arms again. "The cameras were installed as you requested, I see."

"Yes, that was helpful," I say. *Where to begin?* I decide to cut to the chase. "Did you steal my bathrobe and my red bra?"

I watch her face flush and then harden in denial.

"*Why* would I do that?" she says.

"I have no idea," I say. "I've given you so much since you arrived. Everything you're wearing tonight is from me."

"I know that." She pauses. "I didn't take anything from you."

Why would she lie? Doesn't she know I have access to her room? I will keep my discovery to myself for the moment. I have more questions. I don't know what's going on, but I do know knowledge is always power. "I don't believe you."

She swallows and lifts her hand to the back of her neck. I realize she's imitating me. I drop my hand to the table. I watch as she pulls out her phone, taps the screen.

"What are you doing? We're having an important conversation," I say. She is unbelievable. I reach across the table and grab her phone.

"Hey, that's mine!" she yells as I stare at the screen.

"Oh my god. These are all photos of you and Peyton. Online? You have a whole account of you and my baby?" I'm shaking as I scroll down the screen. "'Malibu Trad Wife'? What does that even mean? Oh my god."

My heart thumps in panic. She's violated every part of my life—my bedroom, my things, and now my baby is forever online. I've been trying to hide from Paul, and she's practically been leading him to us. To me. To my baby.

"Traditional wife, you know, like housewife," she says. "It's my dream. My mom's dream for me. She always told me the best things in life were having a lovely home and lots of children. Oh, and a doting husband who is proud of you and your role in the family."

"But she's not your baby!" I yell. "And you're not a wife!"

"Well, you know nothing is real on social media." She stands up. "My phone, please. I'll delete it all."

"You know what's worse? You've exposed Peyton and my

home to the world. Why would you do this? You know I guard my privacy and Peyton's. Do you want Paul to find me? Try to kill me again?" I stare at her. I really cannot believe this is happening, after all I've done for her. I trusted her with everything.

"Oh gosh, no," she says.

"You know he's out. He's not in prison anymore. He will try to get to me." Another chill rolls down my spine. I close the social media app and start scrolling through her camera roll. It's hundreds of photos of Peyton, of Lizzie and Peyton in matching outfits.

"I didn't know," she says. "You should have told me you were worried about him coming here, to find you."

She's right, I should have told her, if only to protect Peyton. "I should have but now you know."

"That's scary," she says. Her eyes are wide, as if this news has shocked her. But maybe she already knew. It's clear I can't tell when she's lying and when she's telling the truth. My heart is still racing.

"Yes, I suspect he is making his way here. It could explain some of the strange things happening, some of the eerie feelings I've been having of being watched," I say. "But so could the fact that you aren't who you seem to be." I hold up her phone as evidence. But I have so much more.

"What do you mean? That's just social media, it was stupid, but I love Peyton. I really care about both of you," she says. She drops her gaze to the table. "You know, you can trust me, you really can. Give me my phone and I'll delete that account. You need my help, you need a nanny, and we like each other. Everything is working just fine."

"I did need a nanny, and I thought you were qualified. I thought that because you already worked for a family, and you passed the background check," I say. "I thought you were only a nanny, but you're a thief and a liar."

"I am not," she says, and we lock eyes.

"Why don't we go upstairs, I'd like to show you something." I begin to walk up the stairs and I sense her behind me. "Let's go to your room, shall we?"

"Sure, why not?" she says.

My heart pounds in my chest. I'm furious, and something more. As we walk, I begin deleting the photos of my baby and her nanny.

"Hey, don't do that, I'll do it," she says, coming up more closely behind me.

"I wish I believed you would, but I don't," I say. We reach the top of the landing. I turn around and face her. "@Malibu-TradWife," I say. "How dare you post photos of my baby? I demand you take that account down immediately. And delete all the rest of the photos of Peyton and my house from your phone. Right now, so I can watch you do it."

"Fine," she says. I hand her the phone and stand over her, watching.

I'm so angry I'm shaking but I tell myself to breathe. I need to remain in control here. "All of them," I say. "Now."

She looks up at me and seems almost on the verge of saying something, but then thinks better of it and focuses on her phone. She highlights the rest of the photos and presses delete.

"Now delete your Instagram account." I watch as she does. "Why did you do this? Were you trying to hurt me? What was the purpose of the Malibu Trad Wife account anyway?"

Lizzie looks at me again and I'm horrified to see she's smiling now. "I want what you had. That's all I've ever wanted," she says. "You took it for granted, couldn't handle it I guess, but I never would. Anyway, it's all deleted. Satisfied?"

I don't sense any remorse, though. It's like she felt entitled to pretend this is her life, her house, her baby. I stare at her. "Good."

I walk down the hallway and into her room. I march to the

drawer with all the stolen items and pull it open. I turn and face her. "All of these things are mine. My bra even? And this box of happy mementos from the early days with Evan—a concert ticket stub, a postcard from Hawaii that we sent to ourselves on our first little getaway, a coffee mug from my favorite hotel in LA. What could you possibly want with these things? And that." I point to a Gucci shoebox that I discovered that's filled with someone else's treasures: a love letter, a Polaroid photo of four smiling children in a swimming pool, an empty chocolate box from a fancy confectionery in Paris. "I don't know who these things belong to, but I'm certain they aren't yours. Now, tell me who you really are and what you want from me."

"I'm only Lizzie, your nanny. I do sometimes take things, but you can have them back, all of them." She seems to be fighting back tears now. "I didn't mean to make you mad. I just... Sometimes, I just can't help it. Ever since my whole family died, well, I've been grabbing things to fill a hole inside. It doesn't last—the feeling of happiness I get when I take something. I know that. But I can't stop. I mean, the thing is, everyone has something, and that's my thing. It's harmless addiction, really. I mean, once I make my mom's dreams come true with a family of my own, I'll stop, I know I will. You can forgive me, can't you? I'm a lonely orphan at heart, just trying to make my way in the world." She's smiling at me again now, an odd smile as if she thinks everything is just fine.

I look at her and really see her for the first time. I don't like what I see, not at all.

THIRTY-SIX

LIZZIE

I stare at Cecilia. She wants me to tell her the truth. Obviously, that is not going to happen. I force the tears out of my eyes and down my cheeks. She should take pity on me, shouldn't she? Besides, I've allowed her to win with the photos and the social media nonsense, although I have backups, so none of that matters. I'm playing the long game, and I still have moves to make. So what if she found my little stash of her things, and the box of Mrs. Johnson's things? They both have too much for any of this to cause that much distress. And once I take it, once the high is gone, it's just stuff that helped me feel better. Helped me feel less empty, less alone. I just know that once I'm married, once I have a family of my own, I'll stop. I won't need other people's happy memories. I'll create my own. But right now, I need Cecilia to calm down.

"You know, I've helped you a lot. I'm good at being a nanny, and we have a good thing going. We're friends, almost like sisters," I remind her. I stifle a yawn and check my phone for the time. I allow my tears to run dry. "It's late. I'm assuming I have Peyton tomorrow, or are you making a new schedule?"

"You're fired. Pack your things and go," she says.

"But it's the middle of the night. I don't have a car, I don't have anywhere to go," I say. "Please. I'm sorry. I won't let you down again."

"I'm afraid I can't trust you, not ever again."

"But I don't have anyone else, anywhere else. Please." I'm genuinely a bit panicked, and right now I'm telling the truth.

"Fine, you can stay the night, but I want you gone first thing in the morning. Do not go near Peyton while you're here. Just get out. I'll leave your final check by the front door."

It appears I am coming to the end of my time here, darn it. I need to stall, behave. I am not ready to move on yet. I need Evan to see me as a loving, valued nanny. A vital part of Peyton's life.

"Cecilia, please give me another chance," I say. I realize I sound a little desperate and I hate that.

"No," she says. "By the way, I know you disabled the AirTag in the car."

"I did, but only because I don't like people following me," I say quickly. "But I get it if you want to track the baby. I do, and it's absolutely your right to do so. Let's just be transparent about it."

"I don't need to tell you anything, not anymore," she says.

She's beyond mad at me, it seems. I don't know if I can charm my way back into her good graces. I think I've pushed her too far. So, I only have one more night to soak up a bit more of Cecilia's perfect life. She's so spoiled, so lucky, and she doesn't even appreciate any of it. She is a princess, just like Evan's mom says.

"I want you packed and out of here in the morning," she repeats as she walks to the door of my bedroom.

I'm going to miss this room. "Ok, sure, yes, I'll pack but I really hope you change your mind," I say with a soft smile. "Maybe in the morning things will look different. Maybe you'll forgive me for all of this, and we can move on. Your ex hasn't tried to be in touch with you, has he?"

She turns back to me, and I can tell from the look on her face that comment pushed a button or two.

"It's really none of your business."

I watch her walk away down the hall. She pauses in front of the nursery, pressing her ear to the door before opening it and stepping inside. *Well, shoot.* I look at the stash of the things I've borrowed, well, stolen, and realize I've blown it by keeping these things where she could find them. It's take, sell, repeat... not hold on. In most cases, that's what I've done, but no one buys personal things like these. I suppose I saw these things as having a connection to the kind of life I want: Mrs. Johnson's minus her husband, Cecilia's plus Evan.

I look back down the hallway as Cecilia walks out of the nursery. I give her a little wave, but she glares at me. My guess is that she thinks she can handle the baby on her own. She can't, she just doesn't realize it. What if her back goes out again? What if she needs to get a job because she's spent all her money? What if she finally realizes she's a terrible mother? What if other people do, too? What happens then?

I close the bedroom door and lock it. I head straight to the pile of items Cecilia left on my bed, scoop them up and put them on the floor by the door. I'm surprised she didn't take them back. Maybe she has so much she wants me to keep them? Who knows? I can always take more. It's been my thing since they all died. A doctor once said I have kleptomania and that it meant I had a mental illness. I disagree. I'm fine. I just like collecting things. Most of this stuff has little value, and I could afford to buy myself any of these things, especially now, but it's more fun to take them. These things are my connection to happy lives, to full lives. The life my mom and Sally were supposed to have, the lives my dad took away, the monster.

When I came home from school that afternoon after the

spelling bee, I was surprised my mom wasn't in the kitchen making one of my favorite after-school snacks. It never ceases to amaze me how life can change in an instant. For that moment in time, before I knew the truth, I was whole. I'd never had the urge to steal anything. Not ever. That only began after the shock of their deaths wore off and the emptiness replaced it. The emptiness I can only fill when I become what my mother was, what she always wanted to be.

I close my eyes because all I see is blood whenever I try to picture my mom's beautiful face. Because he'd smashed it with his fist and that's the image that always races to my mind. Opening that bedroom door, and finding her in bed in a pool of blood. He beat her, and then shot her, to be sure she died. I don't know why. I never will.

And then, like now, my heart races wildly. I screamed, "Sally!" and ran through the house, trying to find her. But she was gone. My baby sister and my mom, gone in a flash. I ball my hands into fists and allow my fingernails to dig into my palms. I open my eyes, back in Cecilia's beautiful guest room, no blood in sight. And there it is again, the urge to steal, to calm myself, to fill the hole deep inside.

I have a lot of urges, truth be told. Self-control is not a strong quality of mine—in fact, I don't have much at all. I have trouble resisting temptation, too, like if I see something pretty, I want it. I'll take it. It's healing, at least for a short moment. And, I must admit, it's a turn-on thinking about what I'll steal next. I already have my mind set on a particular item of Cecilia's. I'll grab it tomorrow, perhaps, on the way out. I know it's risky, but she's already fired me, so what's she going to do if she catches me? Call the police? I doubt it. She still has fears about the paparazzi revisiting the story of her fall in Paris. She doesn't want the negative attention. She's trying to lay low. I've never been caught, not since I was a kid.

The first time I was caught shoplifting, it was a year after my family died. I was honest. I told the security guard I couldn't help it. He looked at the 10-year-old me and said, "You're broken. You need fixing."

"Yes, sir, I agree," I'd said, not knowing quite how that was going to happen. But I did realize my kleptomania wasn't normal, although I didn't know the word for it, not yet. I'd only just begun.

"I'm gonna let you go with a warning, but you can't do this again," he'd said, taking pity on me.

I'd blinked and pretended to cry. It wasn't a total bust—after all, I still had five pairs of earrings shoved in the front pocket of my jeans. He thought I'd only lifted the purse in his hands. I stared at the purse for a minute before meeting his eyes.

"Thank you, sir. I'll get fixed," I said. "I promise."

"I should tell your parents, you know," he said.

"You can't. They're dead." I knew my words would have an impact.

He took a moment to recover, then patted the top of my head and walked away. I was so exhilarated by the entire episode that I ran all the way back to my aunt's home.

"Lizzie, why are you out of breath?" my Aunt Sally asked when I burst through the door. "And where did you go after school?" She was my mom's younger sister, but the opposite of my mom in every way. She worked full-time as a paralegal at a law firm, never wanted kids, and was suddenly stuck with me. We both knew I'd need to leave as soon as I could.

"Nowhere, I wasn't anywhere. Just hanging out with a new friend. I ran home so you wouldn't worry once I realized what time it was," I said, trying to calm down. I was still high on adrenaline.

My uncle walked into the room. "Did you really make a friend?" he asked.

They both thought I should have friends by now since I'd been with them for almost a year. But the thing was, I didn't like any of the kids in this small Southern Tennessee town, and they didn't like me, either.

"Yes, I did," I said. "Sir," I added.

I'd become a bit wary of men since I'd seen what my dad was capable of. After seeing he was the root of all evil. How did I know Uncle Dave wouldn't do the same thing my dad did someday? I mean, if I was honest, I had started to grow suspicious of my dad toward the end, started to realize just how awful he was. And I'd been standing up to him a bit, standing between him and my mom as often as I could when he started to berate her. But that didn't stop him.

He didn't appreciate my newfound strength. I didn't appreciate how he smelled of alcohol and sweat.

"Dave, just let it go," my aunt said. "Poor girl has a friend. That's great. Go wash up for dinner, Lizzie."

"Yes, of course, go on, Lizzie," Uncle Dave said. I stared at him a little while longer. Would he ever hit me, hit Aunt Sally? He didn't seem like the type, but I couldn't really tell. I hurried out of the room, trying to run from the memories—the sound of my dad slapping my mom, my mom crying out in pain. In my bedroom, I crawled into my bed, put the pillow over my head, hoping the flood of memories would stop. Little did I know then, they never would.

Nobody really cared about me after my mom died. And I missed Sally in the core of my being. Every time I saw a baby, especially a baby girl, my heart would break for her. For the life she didn't get to live. I babysat for the people who lived next door to my aunt and uncle, their baby girl. It was my only outside activity and I loved it.

My aunt and uncle said I was a natural, and so did the neighbors. I loved taking care of that baby, and even stayed in town longer than I'd planned because of her. But when I finally decided it was time to move, I also knew a job I could pursue.

I'd take care of children, the way I wished I'd taken care of Sally, the way I wish I'd protected Sally.

I also perfected my other calling. My journey across the country, Tennessee to California, gave me a lot of opportunities to steal, from fellow passengers on buses to big-box stores in every state I passed through.

My first job in Malibu was waiting tables, and let me tell you that is not the right job for a person like me. The opportunity to grab things is limited at best, and really, at a restaurant you're only stealing from coworkers, some of whom have even less money than you. Working as a nanny though, the opportunities are plentiful, I discovered, as long as I had control and knew where the nanny cams were aimed. That was my first step, finding those little cameras. Parents are so predictable when it comes to their kids. And their stuff. Of course, the richer the family, the more there is to swipe. Mrs. Johnson's things were fine, I suppose. I have an antique clock, a gold locket with Jimmy's photo in it and a decorative box they bought on a trip to Italy, back when they were happy. I stole a pair of Mr. Johnson's cufflinks, too, and sold those for a good price. Wish I had taken more from him, the jerk. I'm not a scary criminal, I just have fun with it. Stealing makes me happy. It's a dopamine rush. It makes me feel like I'm connected, I'm someone, I'm here. For a moment, while it lasts, I also feel worthy of love. Worthy of having the things other people have, the things my father took away from us all that day.

Lately, I've been focusing more on items that will also make me rich, building up a nest egg for the family I'm creating someday soon. Hopefully, a family with Evan and Peyton. That would be wonderful.

I grab the black and white photo of Evan and Cecilia and carry it into the bathroom. I open the frame and remove the photo from inside. I use my tiny nail scissors to cut it up, to eliminate Cecilia from the picture. Pieces of her fall into the trashcan at my feet and all that's left is Evan. Evan smiling at me. He is looking for love, he as much as told me so, and I can give him that. I look at the bits of Cecilia in the trash. *That's better*. I mean, clearly she's finished with Evan, she didn't even care enough about the photo to reclaim it. So now it's mine. He's mine.

I change into pale pink silk pajamas, yes, formerly Cecilia's, and climb into bed. I place the photo of Evan, yes, formerly Cecilia's, inside the top drawer of my bedside table. If Cecilia comes snooping around again once I'm gone, she'll get a big surprise. And of course she'll come snooping around.

I look across the room at the dresser. My heart thumps. I jump out of bed and hurry to open the bottom drawer. I reach to the back corner, find my old jeans, still folded as I left them, the satisfying lump in the front pocket still there. I'll get rid of that tomorrow afternoon. But then the reality hits me: she fired me. How dare she fire me? I'm the only competent caretaker in this home. Peyton needs me, hell, Cecilia needs me. And if I'm being honest, I need them. I want this, I want what Cecilia has. I want a home, a baby, a life. I'm realizing I need to stay one step ahead of Cecilia, and I need to keep her happy, make her believe I am who she and Peyton need in their lives. I need to get her to forgive me. I can't have Evan think less of me because of Cecilia. I won't. I know she'd be lost without me. Just look what's happened to Mrs. Johnson.

I climb back into bed and open my photo backup drive. All the photos are still here, password protected, when I need to relaunch my MalibuTradWife account. And then, if things keep going well with Evan, I'll eventually shut it all down and be an actual traditional wife and mother.

Imagine, I could be Peyton's mom someday soon. Well, stepmom officially, but mom nonetheless. And then if Cecilia has issues again, well, maybe she'll be considered unfit to be a mother? I mean, when I met her, she was totally incapable of caring for Peyton. I have photos of her falling asleep while she held the baby. She almost put Peyton in a scalding hot bath. I have so many examples of how it's so dangerous for Cecilia to be alone with a child. She told me once she never even wanted to have kids, that Evan talked her into it. What's changed, really, except for me coming along and taking over? What would happen to Peyton if I left tomorrow morning?

Interesting, isn't it, how quickly a person can come undone? Especially if they have a little help from a friend. I smile just thinking about it, and for good measure send a little text.

THIRTY-SEVEN

CECILIA

I feel so alone.

"Once again, you picked the wrong person," I say, looking at myself in the bathroom mirror. I even had Jim, my attorney, do a background check on Lizzie and there were no red flags. How could this be when she's obviously a thief? And a liar. I guess Lizzie has never been caught until now, so there wouldn't be anything on her record. I begin to realize I should probably file a police report. She shouldn't be able to get away with this any longer.

Another text pings on my phone.

You should just face it. You're a failure. At everything.

Why is Paul doing this to me? When is he just going to reveal himself, demand the money, instead of torturing me? I delete the text and block the new number. I haven't been sleeping well again, ever since I learned Paul was released. It's like I'm just waiting for him to appear in my life at any moment, but then he hasn't, so I'm constantly on edge. Meanwhile, during the day I'm exhausted.

I spoke with Charles Reed, my financial advisor, who let me know Paul has not contacted him, nor has he made a withdrawal from our joint account, which is great, since there isn't much money left. That means he must have money stashed away someplace I didn't know about. I wonder how I can prove that, and I wonder how I can get my divorce attorney to get me half of whatever he has hidden away. He had to declare all his accounts in the prenup agreement, all his assets. If he hid anything from me, there are big penalties. Well, if I could ever find it, that is. Paul knows more about hiding money than I ever will, so I should probably just forget about ever finding his secret stash. The only good news is it must be enough that he hasn't even wondered about the account I've almost depleted. What a mess I've made.

My phone pings with another text and I dread finding another threat. But this time it's from my commercial real estate broker.

We have an offer on the office building. Asking price!

Thank goodness. As much as I feel guilty about Evan having to move his catering business, this sale means I don't have to rush into selling my house but I still know it will go fast. Both of these transactions will give me a chance to build a new future for myself and for Peyton. I will learn to budget and stick to it. I spent most of my life poor, scraping by. I can do it again. I will. I text back.

Great news. Expedited closing?

Yes!, comes the reply.

Well, that's one thing that's gone right today. I feel a little of the weight lifting off my shoulders as I get ready for bed. I pull on my favorite white silk pajamas. My phone pings again with a text.

> *You've been busy since I've been gone. A child with another man? How dare you.*

The message is from an anonymous number, but I know who it is. Again. I delete and block the sender, mark it as spam like I've done with every one of his texts. Somehow, he keeps changing numbers, he keeps getting through.

Almost immediately another text comes in: *Now that you've had a practice baby, you're ready for ours, right darling?*

My hand shakes, but I manage to text back: *Leave me alone or else I'm calling the cops.*

> *But you won't, darling. Because then I'd have to tell them the whole story. See you soon xoxo*

He's here. In Malibu, circling me like a shark, hiding just beneath the surface of my life, ready to strike at any moment. He knows about Peyton. I swallow and try to push away the panic I feel, but I can't. Instead of deleting the last text, I take a screenshot of it. I'll need to give it to the divorce attorneys when the time is right. I need to prove he was threatening me from the moment he was released from prison, although he's choosing his words carefully, acting like we're friends or lovers. It's clear he's still obsessed with me and now it seems he's obsessed with my baby, too.

I will call the police and report Paul as soon as Peyton and I are safely away from here. It is the cops' fault he's out early anyway. They allowed him to find me. I've decided I need to run now, not tip anyone off before I go. They'll try to make me stay, be the bait to Paul's shark. I won't do that. Not with a baby. It's too dangerous. I don't trust anyone. I can't, not even the cops. My timeline has just been condensed again. I need to sell this house immediately.

I rush downstairs and check the alarm is on. I pull up the cameras on my phone. There is no motion detected on any of them. The camera facing the pool area gives me goosebumps on the back of my neck, as I remember the dead rats. I don't know what Paul was trying to accomplish with that one, but I'm sure it was him.

As I walk up the stairs I think about his latest text, the presumption we will be together again, that I will have a child with him. He's delusional, but is he dangerous? Has he changed in prison, like he professes, or is he just toying with me? Has he forgotten the truly horrible things we did and said to each other?

Everything I know about Paul tells me he hasn't changed, cannot change, and that he is gaslighting me, giving me a false sense that he is someone I can trust, but the reality is that he never will be. It's almost like he's erased any memory of his bad behavior and he's trying to portray himself as a perfect husband.

I know different. I survived him once, got away from him only when he was sent to prison. I will not be his source of narcissistic fuel, not ever again. I'm stronger now, I know more. As I climb in bed, eyes wide open, I'm not sure if my pep talk to myself is working. I think at this point my only hope is to close the deal on Evan's building, sell this house, take the money, and *run*.

THIRTY-EIGHT

LIZZIE

I wake up after a spectacular night's sleep and realize that I'm actually relieved that everything is out in the open. I hope I can convince Cecilia to forgive me so I don't have to leave this luxurious place. She won't forgive me. I know it. And I'm going to miss Peyton, I really am. But it won't be for long. It really is like having my own baby girl when I'm with Peyton. We are so close because we had so much time to bond, especially in the beginning when Cecilia was barely functioning. But now her back is better and she is spending more time with Peyton, she thinks she can handle parenting, especially since she's not working yet. We'll see. Either way, I've realized I have to leave here, at least for now.

One thing is for sure, without me drugging her with her own prescription sleeping pills every day in her smoothies and homemade juices, she will have more energy. I only used a quarter to half a dose each day, but it was enough to keep her tired, needing naps, off balance. And I refilled the prescription so she never noticed any were missing. That might be why she's starting to come around. I wasn't able to dose her yesterday. It might also be why she's starting to see me in a terrible light. I saw the look in her eyes last night. She thinks I'm a traitor, a thief. She's wrong, she really is. But I know what it looks like.

I hop out of bed and do a few stretches. I filled my own suitcase with as much as I could, and filled the other three Cecilia gave me, and I still have more stuff left to pack up. I can't believe all the clothes and accessories and shoes Cecilia has given me. I hope I can figure out a way to hang them all up properly in the cheap hotel room I'm moving to this morning.

The thought makes my heart drop. I carry the first suitcase downstairs. I'm careful not to wake Peyton as I know that would set Cecilia off. I'll spend my time settling into my new digs this morning, and then this afternoon I'll run some of my errands, maybe I'll visit a department store and steal a few things just to distract myself, to make myself feel better about this situation.

I'm not losing Peyton. I'm not, I remind myself. It's temporary. Evan and I will get her back.

To distract myself, I focus more on my planned afternoon shoplifting spree. I so enjoy the high that comes from getting away with it. I've never been caught by the authorities again, not since I was 12, so I've got an impressively spotless official track record of theft. Of course, some people, like Cecilia, have discovered my crimes, but these people don't want cops involved in their lives as much as I don't.

I walk back upstairs to grab another suitcase, thinking back to how it all started, this habit of mine. I remember the first time I stole from a person. I'd been living with my aunt and uncle for 6 months or so and they made me go over to a "friend's" house for a playdate because they both had to work late.

The girl wasn't a friend, and she hated the idea as much as I did, but her mom was nice and so I hung out with her in the kitchen.

"I'm so sorry Emma has to do homework instead of playing with you," Emma's mom said, averting her eyes with the lie. "Maybe you can help me set the table for dinner?"

I'd smiled at the kind woman who was doing her best. But inside, I was empty, hurt, alone, and I found myself filled with the urge to take something from this home, take something from this woman who had what my mom wanted.

I slipped a silver spoon into my pocket as I moved around the dining table. "Oh, we're short a spoon," I said to her when I walked back into the kitchen.

"That's strange, I could've sworn I gave you five." She turned toward a drawer. "No worries. Here's another."

As she handed me the spoon, my heart raced with excitement. It was just too easy.

Emma never had me over again, and nothing was ever mentioned about a missing spoon. I mean, what 12-year-old girl steals a spoon from a kind mom who is just trying to help her fit in?

This one did. And that was just the start. Out in the world, I prefer stealing from chain stores instead of boutiques—that only hurts the big man not the little shop owners—and I love to steal from people I don't like. Cecilia's quickly shifting into that category. Mrs. Johnson got there quickly, too, along with her absentee husband. They all have more than enough anyway.

With all my things stacked by the front door, I take some time to get ready for the departure. I refuse to look the part of someone who has just been fired. As I morph into my role model, another head-to-toe Cecilia outfit—tight black jeans, white button-down, black ankle boots, black Gucci purse—and style my hair into blonde waves and put on shimmering sun-kissed makeup, I turn up Peyton's monitor. So nice that she's sleeping later these days. Good baby. I've trained her well. I swipe my lips with Cecilia's favorite lip gloss—this one stolen from her purse—and admire my reflection in the mirror.

I'm ready to take on the day. I walk out of my room, and close the door behind me, quite aware that Cecilia may rummage around in there again after I'm gone. Cecilia is still asleep it seems, no doubt with the help of the ground-up pill I slipped into her wine last night, and so I decide to take a moment and pop into the nursery, say a silent goodbye to Peyton as she sleeps. I crack the door open and walk in, only to find Peyton wide awake, staring at her mobile. *Shoot.* Well, this isn't good.

"Good morning, sunshine! How's my baby girl?" I say quietly, and she smiles at me and waves her arms. How different she is from when I started. So much calmer, on a schedule, growing and thriving. I pluck her out of the crib and change her into a matching outfit: cute black and white tights, a white sweatshirt dress and darling little black shoes. We are adorable. I snap a photo of the two of us in the nursery, as usual. Of course, I can't post the photo, not right now with Cecilia watching my every move, but I will save it for later. There will be a time when my MalibuTradWife account will be back online, along with the other accounts I run. And, of course, I'll officially be a Malibu traditional mom someday. It's my dream and I will make it come true.

Cecilia appears at the door, looking terrible, like she hasn't slept at all. "I told you not to say goodbye to Peyton," she says, reaching for the baby.

"I was just going to watch her sleep, but she was awake when I snuck in. I'm sorry. I'm going now." I hand Peyton over and back away.

"You never do what I say," she says. "But this time you will. If you don't leave this moment, I will call the cops. I will do it, Lizzie. I know I've told you how I don't like to have them and the resulting press in my life, but I'll do it. I'll call them." She holds up her phone as proof.

I take another step back. "Ok, ok. Don't call the cops. You don't want them racing over here, scaring the baby. I'm leaving. Now. But you're tired. You aren't thinking clearly. Are you sure you don't want me to stay? I could make you a smoothie?"

"Oh my god, get out. Now," she yells and Peyton starts to cry.

As much as I want to stay and comfort the baby, I know I can't. *And here I was thinking we were one happy family*. She's just so edgy and sensitive these days.

"Goodbye, Peyton. I love you," I say and dash out of the room before Cecilia gets any more worked up. I pause in the hallway, snap a quick photo with the nursery scene in the background, and then hurry down the stairs.

I know the photo will be proof, once again, that Cecilia is unfit, unworthy of Peyton. It's too bad I couldn't drug her one last time, just for old times' sake. I have made sure all the remaining smoothies and juices in the fridge are drugged. But I wonder if Cecilia might have started to figure out the secret ingredient I've been adding to her smoothies every morning. *Whoops*.

My Uber driver deposits me and my stuff in front of the shabby motel I booked online last night. It's going to have to do until I figure out my next move. And I'll never let Evan, or anyone else for that matter, know I've fallen into this sort of living situation. I won't be here long. I can't be.

At least Cecilia didn't contact the cops, even though she found my stash of her things. Although, this morning I think she was on the brink of it, despite her overwhelming desire to stay out of the press. That's why I left in a hurry. So far, it seems I'm in the clear. And I'm not that threatening, am I? Maybe she thinks my little habit is cute, or sad, or pathetic. Maybe she has bigger things to worry about, like Paul.

I guess I was obsessed with her, too, in my own way. I stalked her, watched her, climbed to the top of the Johnson kids' playhouse just to catch a glimpse of her sunbathing in the backyard or working in her garden. It was a fortunate placement of the playset in the corner of their yard. A great observation tower for me. I saw in Cecilia and her home, her life, everything I ever wanted. Everything my mom wanted for me. It was like I was drawn to her by a secret force, like it was meant to be. And now I've learned so much from her, taken so much from her. But I want more. I want it all. Her entire life.

It's time to call Evan now that I'm in the privacy of my cruddy hotel room. He answers on the first ring.

"Hey. I just wanted to let you know that Cecilia fired me," I say with a sigh.

"What? No. Is she out of her mind?" I can hear hammering in the background. "Sorry, we're building a stage for an event tonight." I wait as he moves away from the sound. "Look, I'm going to see her today, I'll tell her this is unacceptable. Peyton needs you."

"You're so sweet, but please don't do that," I say. I cannot have Cecilia tell Evan why she fired me. "She'll know we've been talking and feel like we're ganging up on her. For Peyton's sake, we need to keep Cecilia calm."

"Ok, but we're a team now," he says. "So, what are we going to do?"

My heart swells with happiness despite my new surroundings. "Well, you'll see her and the baby today at the real estate closing," I say. "See how she is, how she's acting. I'm worried," I pause, as if hesitating, "that's why I put some cameras inside and around the house, so I can make sure Peyton is being cared for. I'll check them today and this evening. Cecilia doesn't know about them, of course, but it's important. If I see anything awry, I'll come running and I'll let you know, too. I care about the baby, I love her, I really do."

"I can't believe we have to spy on her to protect Peyton. Shit. Lizzie, she needs you, Peyton does, we all do," Evan says. "Where are you now?"

"Oh, I'm staying at a friend's house. I'll have to make permanent arrangements if Cecilia doesn't change her mind," I say. "I miss Peyton already, so much. My heart is breaking."

"I know the feeling." Evan sighs. "Ok, I'll call you after I see her. We'll make a plan. Oh, and I miss you, too."

That makes my face flush. "Let's get together," I say. "Tonight?"

"Yes, I'll call you after my meeting."

As we hang up, I am filled with emotions. All of them hopeful. I might get what Cecilia has, what she takes for granted. I look around the dump of a hotel room, threadbare magenta bed cover, stained carpet and beat-up furniture. I do not belong here. I never have.

THIRTY-NINE

CECILIA

I'm driving too fast, I realize, and lighten the pressure on the gas pedal. It's because I don't feel comfortable about having Peyton in the backseat and being on a freeway and not being able to do anything if she cries. What can I do? How do parents handle this? I check the rearview mirror and she's still asleep, thank goodness. I can only hope the drive back goes as smoothly. I pull into the parking lot of my real estate broker's office and look around. I hope Evan is on time for once. My attorney is set to join us, too, so he can draw up the legal papers that make it possible for us to split the proceeds of the sale of the office building. I've also asked him to put in vague language about shared custody to be decided in the near future.

There won't be any shared custody, but Evan doesn't need to know that. I get out of my car and am relieved to see Evan, right on time.

"Hey, Cecilia, how are you?" he asks. His attitude is cool, almost frosty, and he's staring at me with a strange look.

"I'm great. Let's get this deal closed, shall we?" I walk around the other side of the car, popping the door open. I reach in and grab the baby carrier.

"You brought Peyton?" Evan says. "That's so nice of you. I've never seen you out and about with the baby."

"Yes, well, I knew you'd want to see her, and she's been such a good baby recently." I stifle a yawn. "Just don't wake her up."

"No, never wake a sleeping baby," Evan murmurs as we start walking toward the building, then he touches my arm. "Look, I know this isn't any of my business, and I'm not saying this because I'm trying to get back together, because I'm not. I'm happy, and I have hope for the future. But you look like you don't feel well. Do you need a doctor?" he asks.

He's happy? He has hope for the future? He was just declaring undying love a day ago. *Men.*

"No, I don't need a doctor. I need this deal closed, the money transferred, and that's all," I say. I also need to not be broke, and then I need to run. Paul is circling, I can feel it.

"Ok, whatever," he says, holding the office door open. "We'll put the paternity and shared custody in this agreement we're signing, agreed?"

"Yes, that's why my attorney is meeting us here." I force a smile. *Whatever you want, dear*, my smile says.

The meeting lasts a couple hours as we hammer out the details, sign documents and celebrate the closing with a champagne toast courtesy of my real estate broker. Peyton was perfect, only fussing when she needed to be changed, and generally enchanting all the men in the room.

I only had a sip of the celebratory champagne, but driving home my eyelids feel so heavy that it's a struggle to stay awake. I may need a short nap when we get home. I don't want to fall asleep when I'm supposed to be watching Peyton, but I don't think I can help it.

I pull into the driveway, exhaling a sigh of relief. I climb out of the car and hurry to retrieve Peyton from the back. She babbles at me as we walk across the driveway. I unlock the front door and step inside. I don't plan on going anywhere else until the real estate sale funds hit my new bank account, but then we are gone.

I carry Peyton to the family room and slump onto the couch. I'm not going to look in the mirror right now because I'm exhausted, stressed out, and I know what I'll see—a washed-out mom who needs to sleep.

I look at the homemade green juice I took out of the refrigerator earlier. I've had half a bottle today, and instead of invigorating me, I think it's just making me dizzy.

"Ok, baby, I'm going to get a bottle for you, and you're going to take a nap in your nursery and I'm going to take a nap in my room. Sound good? Of course it does." I struggle to get us off the couch, head to the kitchen and grab a bottle. I don't have the energy to warm it up. I carry Peyton upstairs and walk into the nursery in a fog. I pull down the blinds, hoping she won't complain about an unscheduled nap.

"Mommy needs you to be a good girl so she can take a nap," I say, changing her diaper through a haze. "I'll just be twenty minutes or so." I place her in the crib. She makes some cooing sounds and seems to be fine with the idea. *Thank goodness*. I stumble out of the nursery and shut the door behind me. I cross the hallway and enter my room in a daze, shutting and locking my door. Why am I so exhausted? I resolve to never let this happen again. I will take control of my life, and Peyton's, and the anxiety will dissipate.

I climb on top of the comforter, not bothering to pull it back, and fall instantly asleep.

FORTY

LIZZIE

I check the cameras in the kitchen and family room. Cecilia and Peyton were on the couch, but now they've disappeared out of view of the camera. I hope maybe they're out back swimming, but that's unlikely. Cecilia's totally suffering from all the symptoms of sleep deprivation. She simply can't get a restful sleep with all the meds I've been giving her. I looked it up: anxiety, anger, tension, disordered thinking, increased irritability and she's doing that microsleep thing where she sleeps for like 30 seconds while she's talking to you. She doesn't even know it's happening, because every drink in her refrigerator is laced with something. Not the baby's food or bottles, of course. I'm not a monster.

I hope Peyton will be ok this afternoon. I made sure the bottles were ready for today, and everything is set in the family room. If all else fails, she can put Peyton in the playpen and sleep on the couch, like she used to do when I first arrived. I wish she'd do that so I can watch them.

Cecilia is a disaster, but she has good taste, I think, as I pull into the shopping center filled with pricey boutiques. Despite the fact she fired me, I can't help but appreciate her sense of style, especially in jewelry. I wonder where she hid the necklace she bought in Paris. I mean, I wouldn't swipe that, no, she'd notice right away, but it isn't in her jewelry closet. Fortunately, there were plenty of other sparkly things to choose from, as usual. Her vast jewelry collection is a gift that keeps on giving.

I'm meeting Evan for a late lunch and I'm excited. We've been texting all morning since his meeting with Cecilia and the anticipation, well, it's almost the same feeling I get when I steal something. Exhilarating. For lunch we're meeting at a cozy beach café. If all goes well, and it will, he wants to take me to dinner at a new restaurant in town that's impossible to get a reservation for, unless you run LA's most successful event company, that is.

I'm running ahead of schedule, so I detour to one of the jewelry stores where I've been selling Cecilia's things. I rotate, going to different stores and pawn shops so no one is too suspicious. Cecilia's Rolex watch was a fan favorite. I always tell them my grandmother died and left me these pieces. They are always impressed by her generosity and wish me condolences as they underprice the piece. *Ha.* But they soon find out I'm a savvy seller. I know the value of the things I swipe.

These two pieces, a thick gold and diamond necklace and stunning drop diamond earrings that match, have fetched a good price from the jeweler, which I accept immediately. I know when to barter and when to take the money and run. So I do, and I'm only 5 minutes late when my Uber pulls into the beach café parking lot. I think about the other jewelry items I plan to sell nestled in my purse, and as I walk into the café I wonder if any of them were gifts from Evan. Ironic, if so.

I spot Evan waiting for me at the front of the café holding a bouquet of sunflowers. "Lizzie, you look beautiful as always," he says. He hands me the flowers and kisses my cheek. "It's so lovely to see you. I haven't been able to stop thinking about you since our date last night. And I'm sorry, again, that Cecilia fired you. She's impulsive sometimes. It's the same way she treated me."

"I know. I'm sorry for you, too, but at least we have each other, and Peyton," I say. A surge of happiness runs through me. I really like this guy. What a plot twist. *Or is it?*

"Our table is ready." He places his hand on the small of my back, guiding me past the other diners. "And here we are."

The table literally sits on the sand, and is very private and romantic, tucked just inside a thatched roof cabana. "How did you arrange this? It's lovely," I say. Another bunch of sunflowers are in a vase on the table, and there's a gift wrapped in yellow paper sitting on what I assume is my charger plate.

"Allow me." Evan pulls out my chair. "Open your gift, if you'd like?"

"This is too much, you've gone overboard," I say. "But thank you."

I tear off the wrapping paper and open the box inside. It's a ring, a sparkling yellow center stone with diamonds surrounding it. It's gorgeous, and unique, and I'm totally speechless. This is only our second date. He's too good for me. I mean it, he really is. Darn it.

"Evan, oh my gosh, this is exquisite," I say, when I finally get over the surprise, slipping it onto the ring finger of my right hand. It fits perfectly.

"Business has been great lately, but meeting you has been even better. It's a rare yellow diamond. It reminded me of you, the way you've brought sunshine back into my life, and Peyton's," he says.

"My pleasure," I say. "I love Peyton like she's my own. And I love the way you are with her. You're a good dad, I can tell."

"That means the world to me," he says. "Do you have an agreement now with Cecilia? Did she give you any severance?"

"No, she didn't offer anything," I say with a sigh.

"Well, that's not right," he says. "I can talk to her."

"No, don't. It's over," I say. I really don't want him mentioning me to her, not when this is going so well. I pivot. "How about you? Did you get an agreement with Cecilia, do you have parental rights?" I ask. If they get their deal finalized, then Evan and I are free to make our own plans.

"As of today, yes, we signed legal papers after the sale of the building went through. I mean, she sort of treated it like a business transaction, I guess. I traded my building for a chance to see Peyton, to be part of her life. It's totally worth it. It's a miracle, actually. We don't have a schedule yet, and I'm not relaxing until we do," he says. "But I think it's going to work out. But, enough of that, let's talk about us."

Ok, not so subtle. "What do you mean?" I ask. I tilt my head and bite my lip like Cecilia would do. I might have even winked, but I'm not sure. My heart is racing, and I'm not even thinking of stealing.

"Like I said, you gave me a lifeline to my daughter all these months and that has been the kindest thing anyone has ever done for me." I see the tears in his eyes, and mine get misty, too. For real. "And then, last night, I felt it. I know this might seem sudden, or too fast, but I truly believe we were meant to be. God put you in the coffee shop when Cecilia needed you, when my daughter needed you, and now he's let me realize that you are what I need, too. Who I need."

"Oh... wow," I say, not at all certain that god had anything to do with all this, but Evan does seem convinced.

"Oh no, I blew it, didn't I?" He drops his head into his hands.

"Hey, no, this is the most romantic thing anyone has ever said or done for me, ever." I reach for his hand. Fabulous. *Malibu Hot Step Momma coming up soon.* Oh, and Evan's great, I mean look at how romantic this is. I stare at my ring and it flashes in the dappled sunlight. I won't be selling this ring, not ever. I stand up and lean across the table to give him a kiss.

What a rush. There's nothing better than a relationship based around the love of a child. Oh, and I can tell we will have so much fun together.

"Can you see a future with me, me and Peyton?" he asks after another kiss. "We both already love you."

I smile. See it? It's my dream come true. To become an official Malibu trad mom. I have the weirdest feeling in my chest, it's like warmth and happiness swirling into places in my heart usually reserved for plotting and stealing.

"I can, I really can," I say. "But Evan." I've turned serious now. "You should know that I'm worried about Cecilia's ability to care for Peyton. I mean, even today I worried about leaving them. I told you about the cameras, didn't I? So I can rush back if anything goes wrong."

Evan blinks. "Cecilia is doing better though, right? She'd never hurt Peyton."

"No, not on purpose, it's just that she's a bit unstable, as you know, and she has daytime drowsiness, dizziness, headaches, problems with attention and her memory is slipping." All side effects of taking too many sleeping pills for too long, I don't add.

"Oh no," Evan says.

"Yes, it's not a good set-up for successful parenting," I explain. "Sometimes she falls asleep sitting up, or even in the middle of a sentence talking to me she forgets what she was trying to say."

"Oh, that's not good. She looked dreadful at the signing today, come to think of it. Why isn't she sleeping?" he asks.

"Stress, I guess. I think motherhood is pushing her over the edge," I say, injecting a sorrowful tone into my voice.

"Seems like it, for sure," Evan looks concerned. "What should we do?"

"We stay vigilant," I say. "She won't be able to handle Peyton alone. Trust me. I know." I pull out my phone and check the hidden camera in the family room. No one is there. I must assume all is well. For now. "All seems fine right now, though."

"How do you know? There's no one there." Evan leans over to look at my phone.

"Yes, that's good, she's likely taking Peyton for a walk, or playing in the backyard. Healthy mom behavior," I say.

"As opposed to?" He raises his eyebrows questioningly.

I take a deep breath, thinking back to that day I'd given Cecilia a double dose of pills, and it showed.

"I'm running out to do a few errands," I'd said. "Are you ok with the baby?"

"Sure, ya, fine, fine," she'd slurred.

"Are you sure? You sound really tired." I held a shopping bag in one hand and my phone in the other, with the camera app on.

"Go, go." She sat down on the family room couch, the baby propped on a cushion next to her.

And then, as if in slow motion, I watched as Cecilia toppled over. Luckily, she missed landing on the baby—just. I rushed over and picked Peyton up off the couch. "Baby, you and I will go shopping and let Mommy rest."

I exhale at the memory and shake my head. "I have photos, and a video, from just one of the many times I've caught her sleeping when she was supposed to be caring for the baby."

"Oh my god." Evan's eyes widen.

"I was there, so the baby was never in harm's way," I say reassuringly, reaching for his hand.

"Thank goodness," he says. "But that's terrible and dangerous. Poor Peyton. Thank god you were there. But I'm... I'm starting to think I might need to take the baby away from her. I mean, she fired you. Who is going to make sure Peyton is ok?"

I look at Evan, a tear artfully forming in my eye. "That's the same thing that keeps me up at night. I've been worried, too, but I've documented everything. You know, in case you need it. I'm glad to help, of course. I love that little one as if she were mine." I can tell I'm seriously worrying him. He's frightened for his daughter. But I'm also showing him that together we can save Peyton, take Peyton. "Anyway, let's fix this together, shall we?"

"Yes. That's what I want to talk about," he says, squeezing my hand.

This is so wonderful, so absolutely what I was hoping for, that I'm grinning from ear to ear. I've finally found a home and a family, and no one, and nothing, will ruin it. Believe me.

FORTY-ONE

CECILIA

The only reason I even open my eyes is I because I suddenly sense it's almost dark outside. A jolt of panic hits my heart and I leap out of bed.

How long have I been asleep? Oh my god, Peyton!

"Peyton, Mommy's coming!" I yell as I unlock my door and yank it open before hurrying across the hall. I'm moving fast but it's as if I'm underwater, as if different parts of my brain are having trouble communicating with each other. I'm hungry, too. I cannot remember the last meal I ate. When I walk into the nursery, I jump. I swear someone just ducked behind the curtains. I don't scream, I stand frozen in the doorway, staring at the place where *he* was.

"There's nobody there, Cecilia," I tell myself and take a deep breath before walking further into the room. My brain is playing tricks on me. My body just needs food, fuel.

"I'm so sorry, Peyton," I say, knowing that she will need a diaper change. And she's likely just as hungry as me, poor baby.

The crib is empty. I pat the bedding irrationally, looking for her. I hear a scream and realize it's mine. I check Peyton's bathroom and open the closet. *Where is my baby? I need help. I need to find my baby.*

My heart thumps with fear and dread as I race across the hallway and grab my phone, dialing 9-1-1. Who took my baby? *Peyton, where are you?*

"What's your emergency?" the operator asks.

"Someone has taken my baby from her crib," I wail, struggling to get the words out coherently.

"Calm down, ma'am. Did you say your baby is gone?" the operator asks.

"Yes, my baby girl. Six months old." I crumble to the floor.

"Ok, I have a squad car on the way. Stay on the phone with me. I have your address as 22583 Fernwood Drive, correct?"

"Yes. Please hurry. Who would take my baby?" I cry.

"I don't know, ma'am, but try to take some deep breaths as the officers will need your help. I'm sure you have photos of your little girl on your phone, right? They'll need those," she says.

I'm in a nightmare. I can't be awake. This is a terrible dream. I pinch my arm and feel the pain. This is real.

I hear a siren in the distance.

"Ma'am, the police are almost there. Please go and meet them at the door," the operator instructs me. "Stay on the phone with me. You sound like you're hyperventilating. I need you to breathe."

I pull myself up to standing. I don't want to leave the nursery. I picture Peyton in her crib, her big green eyes, her smile, her fuzzy blonde hair. But I must move. I must find her. I hold onto the banister as I rush down the stairs, taking them two at a time, and fling the front door open. I run out to the driveway as the police cruiser pulls in.

It's just then that I realize the alarm didn't sound when I opened the door. *Oh my god, this is my fault.* My knees give out and I fall to the gravel driveway as everything goes black.

FORTY-TWO

LIZZIE

Evan and I reluctantly part ways after lunch, the yellow diamond ring sparkles on my finger, reminding me how much he likes me and how much we have to look forward to.

We're talking about a future together. It's fabulous. It's just what I dreamed of—a happy blessed life in Malibu. But first, I need to help Evan get what he wants: Peyton. Challenge accepted. My Uber pulls into the parking lot of my favorite pawn shop masquerading as a jewelry store, located an hour away from Malibu in a run-down strip mall. People like Cecilia would never come to this part of the valley. She's never left the coast since I've known her. The driver will wait for me as arranged.

A bell jingles over the door as I walk in.

"Bonjour, Ms. Bates," the old man behind the counter says. He's bald and wears round, black glasses, and a tight smile. We've become quite familiar over the last few months. I appreciate his lack of curiosity about me, his laser-focused attention to whatever I bring in to sell him.

"Bonjour, Mr. Claude," I say, returning the smile.

"What do you have for me today from your poor, dearly

departed grandmother?" His eyes twinkle with anticipation. We both know he's underpaying for what I'm bringing him, but we also both know he's expedient and discreet.

When I hand him the last of the jewelry I've swiped from Cecilia, a fabulous gold cuff bracelet encrusted with diamonds, he whistles.

"Oh, *très bien*," he says, turning the bracelet around in his hands. "As always, your grandmother had great taste."

"*Oui*, she did," I agree. I watch as he writes an amount on a piece of paper and slides it across the dirty glass display case. When I see the number, I nod. "We have a deal."

He disappears with the bracelet through a curtain behind him and comes back with my money in $100 bills. As I walk back out the door to the jingle of the bell, I'm filled with hope.

I drive to the closest branch of my bank and make a deposit. When the teller hands me the receipt with my current balance, it's almost a shock. I have more money in my bank account than I've ever had before. Enough to help start a real life, set up a real home.

As I drive back over the canyon road to Malibu, I decide to kill some time shopping at a small boutique in the impossibly upscale shopping center near Cecilia's house. As I walk inside, I feel the saleswomen size me up, and for once, they seem to like what they see in me.

"Welcome," the tallest, skinniest woman says. She has a bright pink scarf around her neck but otherwise she wears all black. "Just let me know if I can help you find anything."

"Well, I have a special date tonight," I say.

"Special, you say? Well, we have just the thing." She leads me to a display rack bursting with colorful dresses. "How's this one?" She holds up a pink skimpy dress, too short, too suggestive.

"No, that's not quite right. I don't want him to think I'm

desperate. This is the man I'm going to marry. I need something sophisticated," I say.

She raises her eyebrows but smiles. "How's this one?" She holds up an elegant light blue gown, and I know before I even try it on that it's the one. "A flattering cut, not too revealing, but sexy, too. He'll want to propose immediately."

I laugh. "I'll take it." And I do, and a shiny gold bracelet from the display case, too. Although, I don't pay for that little bangle.

After leaving the boutique, I'm walking on the sidewalk, enjoying a beautiful late afternoon in paradise, when I get a strange sense that someone is watching me. I stop and turn around, but there's no one there.

My mind is playing tricks on me, I tell myself, slipping my new bangle on my wrist. I admire the way it sparkles in the sun and bask in the thrill of taking it. My ride is here.

As I slide into the car, I'm torn. I'm thinking about Cecilia, about how she fired me. And I'm missing Peyton a lot. That baby girl has stolen a piece of my heart. And then I think about Evan and how we'll make the perfect family with little Peyton, and one day perhaps another baby girl of our own. The family of my dreams, or my mom's dreams recreated without the violence. As I think about this, some of my mom's words come back to me: *I picked the wrong man, but otherwise my dreams have come true. You will pick right, you will live the life of my dreams.*

I will, Mom, for you. And Sally.

My phone rings and I answer.

"Do you have Peyton?" Cecilia says as soon as I pick up.

"No, you fired me, remember?" I sound sarcastic but I'm actually a little worried. "Where's Peyton?"

"I need you to come to the house. Now," Cecilia says, her voice frantic.

What has she done now?

"Is the baby ok? What's wrong?" I say. To the driver I say, "Please head to Fernwood Drive. Cecilia, take a deep breath, I'm five minutes away. What's happened?" My heart thumps in my chest. She's such a bad mom. If anything has happened to precious Sally... I mean, Peyton, I don't know what I'll do.

"She's gone," Cecilia says and begins to sob.

"What do you mean?" My hands are shaking. "You lost her?"

"Just come over now, the cops need to speak to you." She hangs up.

I swallow the dread I feel. I knew she shouldn't have been left alone with the baby. Now, everyone will know what I knew all along: she's unfit to be a mom.

I've told her that so many times, in so many ways. My heart shatters. *Peyton, I'm coming.*

FORTY-THREE

CECILIA

The cops stare at me across the kitchen table, a mixture of pity and suspicion in their eyes.

"We found a Wi-Fi jammer in the bushes next to the house. That's how they disabled the alarm and the security cameras. But still, the baby's room is across the hall from yours. I'm surprised you didn't hear anything. How long were you asleep, Mrs. Strom?" the cop with the sideburns asks.

"I told you, I don't know. My alarm didn't go off. I slept too long, maybe three hours," I say. *Oh my god. I'm the worst.*

"Who else has a key to the house?" the cop with the baby face asks.

"My nanny. That's it. Oh, and my ex, Evan Dorsey," I say. I can't believe I didn't make them give me back my keys. I'm such a horrible mom.

Sideburns notes something down. "Where's the nanny?"

"I fired her," I say. "Last night. But I called her. She's coming over right away."

They both look at me. Deep frown lines form on baby face.

"We're going to need to talk to her, and your ex. Describe what the baby was wearing, again," sideburns says.

I've already done that and I'm getting frustrated. "Can you do something? Someone took my baby!" I stand up. I can't take this anymore. "While you're sitting here questioning me, someone has Peyton." I pull out my phone and call Evan.

"What are you doing, Mrs. Strom?" Baby face moves as if to try and stop me. "Put the phone down."

"I'm calling my ex-boyfriend. Evan, do you have Peyton?" I say, ignoring the cops when he picks up.

"What? No, of course not. I'm at work, in LA," Evan says. "What's happening?"

I take a deep breath and burst into tears. "She's gone. Someone has her."

"Oh my god, no," Evan says. He sounds as frantic as me. "I'm coming. I'll help find her. I'm running to my car now. It's going to take me an hour or so. Call the police!"

"They're here now," I say, glaring at the two sitting at my kitchen table. "But they aren't doing anything."

"Mrs. Strom," sideburns says. "We need your full attention. Hang up the phone."

"Is Lizzie there?" Evan asks.

"No, she's on her way, but she doesn't have the baby. Please come, hurry," I plead.

Lizzie wouldn't take Peyton, would she? She couldn't. She took stuff from me but my baby? I have to believe her. But maybe I shouldn't.

"I'm on my way," Evan says.

I hang up the phone. "The nanny is on her way and so is my ex, the baby's dad. He doesn't have her, I'm certain. But I want you to question my ex-nanny. She's a thief, that's why I fired her. Although I can't imagine she'd harm my baby," I say, but then I reflect on how Lizzie has pretended to be Peyton's mom, how she often dressed them alike, how she has a social media account pretending to be a mother and implying she is a wife, too. "But you should talk to her, for sure."

"We've seen it all, Mrs. Strom," baby face says. "Look, I want you to know we put out a missing persons bulletin and an Amber alert. We'd like your permission to wiretap your landline and your mobile phone."

"Yes, fine," I say.

"Ok, we'll get the process rolling. It should take a couple hours," he says. "In addition, we are organizing searches for this neighborhood and all of Malibu. We're certainly not doing nothing. Also, can you tell me about your ex-husband? He went to prison for attempted murder for trying to kill you, according to our files."

"He did, yes, and now he's out," I say. I know it's not baby face's fault Paul is out, but I cannot help blaming everyone in law enforcement. "But I haven't seen him."

"We're going to try to locate him. We need to talk to him," he says.

I nod in agreement and wrap my arms around myself. I am not going to tell him about Paul's threatening texts. I don't want the attention off of Peyton. And besides, I don't know where Paul is, only that he must be in Malibu. I feel him nearby.

"Is your ex-boyfriend the baby's father?" sideburns asks. "Is he involved in her life?"

"Yes, he's the father, but he's not really involved in her life. I told you this already. He never helped with her from the day she was born. He's coming here from work in LA. But he doesn't have her, I know he doesn't," I say. "Where is my baby? You have to find my baby!"

FORTY-FOUR

LIZZIE

I walk through the open door of Cecilia's house and into the kitchen, busy with four cops milling about. Cecilia sees me and runs to me. We hug, a genuine heartbroken hug.

I can't believe this is happening.

"Mrs. Strom," an officer with big sideburns says. "We're going to head out on the search now. Please stay here. Answer any phone calls. We are in the process of setting up wiretaps on the landline and your mobile, as we said. Once they're set, we'll record any calls. If a ransom request comes any other way, or before we're set up, notify us at once. We will be in touch as soon as we find her. And we will find her. We've left an officer here with you, and two more squad cars are patrolling the streets around the house."

"Where do you think she is?" I ask.

"And you are?" He stares at me.

"The nanny... I mean, former nanny. I love Peyton," I say, real tears spring to my eyes. I cannot lose another baby. I won't.

"We'll need to take a statement, but right now we're doing the search before night falls. Stay here, ok, miss?" he instructs me.

"My name is Lizzie," I say. "And I will stay with Cecilia. Go find the baby. It's getting dark and the fog is rolling in thick."

Cecilia and I stand side by side as the officers file out of the house. They leave one young-looking guy standing in the foyer by the front door. Cecilia appears to be in shock, and I'm not sure if I am or not.

"Tell me what happened," I say.

"I fell asleep. I slept too long. Didn't hear the alarm. When I woke up, she was gone." Cecilia is sobbing. "Her crib was empty. Oh my god."

I start walking back and forth the length of the kitchen. I've already checked the cameras. There is nothing visible on the inside of the house. But I don't have the outside footage.

"Did you check the cameras outside?" I say. "They could've recorded something."

"Whoever took Peyton used something called a signal blocker to jam the Wi-Fi, the cops said." She sniffs and starts to cry again. "It jams everything linked to the Wi-Fi—cameras, alarms, everything."

"Sophisticated," I say.

"No, you can buy one online, they told me," she says. "You just need to know about it. Criminals do, but so do regular people. It could be anyone. What if Paul took her?"

"Why would he? He wants you, not her," I say, although a chill rolls down my spine.

"He wants money, that's all," she says, seeming to agree. "But maybe he's using Peyton to get to me, to the money? I just don't know. I want my baby back."

I can't sit around here just waiting. I need to move, to do something. "Would you mind if I go help with the search? I just got an alert on my phone. They need help canvassing Point Dume," I say, swallowing my fear. I'm starting to imagine Peyton discarded somewhere on this rugged point, alone, cold, crying. And the fog has rolled in, making the neighborhood seem much darker and gloomier than normal.

"Go ahead. They told me I have to stay here," she says. "Find her. Please." Tears begin rolling again.

I wanted her life. I did. But not this part. Not at all. I nod and run out the door.

FORTY-FIVE

CECILIA

All I can do is pace around the kitchen, touch her highchair, her DockATot, cradle the giraffe Evan got for her. I cannot believe I've let this happen to my baby. This is all my fault.

My phone lights up with a text from a new number. I know it's Paul.

Darling, having a rough evening I presume?

I stifle a scream.

"Ma'am, are you alright?" the young police officer from the foyer appears in the kitchen and stares at me.

"I'm fine," I manage to say though my hands shake. "Just thought I heard something. It's ok."

"I'll be just inside the front door if you need anything," he says and slips away.

I text back: *Paul. Do you have my baby? The police are here. I will tell them you've taken her.*

If you do, you'll never see her again. I promise you that, darling. Do you miss me? I know you do. It seems we both might have something the other would like.

My hands are shaking, and I move to the kitchen table so I don't drop to the floor. Paul has taken Peyton. Paul has my child. Oh my god.

Another text pings up.

There are too many cops around for us to meet in person, although we will again someday soon. I'm going to call you. Do not tip off the cops or you won't like what happens next.

My hands fly over the phone keypad.

Do you have her? My baby? Please don't hurt her. I'll do anything you say.

My phone rings and I answer quickly.

"Paul, tell me what you want, and make it quick. The cops may be listening," I say in a whisper. The cop in the foyer doesn't seem to hear me. They said the phone line would be tapped, but I don't know if it's set up yet.

"Darling, I want a lot of things from you, but for now pay me $500,000 and I'll give you your little brat back," he says calmly.

"Oh my god, have you hurt her?" I say.

"Cecilia, stop. Get a hold of yourself. I'm not here to hurt you or your baby. Why would you even think that?" Paul says. "Calm down already. I need you to transfer the money immediately into my account, at the same bank, and we'll take the next step from there. I've texted the account number. Hurry, there isn't much time. Hang up and do it. Call me back when you've finished."

I hang up, take the phone from my ear and open my

banking app, beyond thankful that the money from the building sale has landed in my account. With shaking hands, it's hard to make the transaction, but I do it. I call Paul back and relief washes over me when he answers.

"Is she hungry, cold? Is she crying?" I ask. "She needs her mom. She needs me." I see Peyton's favorite stuffed animal, a sea lion, smiling at me from the playpen. She can't sleep without it. I can hardly breathe.

"From what I hear, she'd likely be better off without you, darling, but that's just what I hear." He gives a short laugh. "Did you make the transfer?"

"Yes," I say, stifling the fear and the tears. "Give me back my daughter."

"Oh, yes, there it is. Wonderful," he says. "You know, you owe me so much more than this."

"I don't owe you anything," I say, and realize I spoke too loudly.

"Everything ok in there, ma'am," the foyer cop calls.

"Yes, fine, all is fine," I say, hiding my phone in my lap. I wait for him to walk back to the front door before picking up the phone again.

"No, Paul, I don't owe you anything, but I've given you the money, so please tell me where the baby is," I say. "I'm begging you."

"Right, well, I do quite enjoy it when you're desperate. But I'm hurt, deeply. Did you really think you'd gotten rid of me forever?" he asks. He's taunting me now. "Oh, darling Cecilia, how could you want to forget me like this? It's very disappointing."

"Paul, I need my baby. Where is she? How can I get to her? I paid you the money," I say.

"Well, yes you did, and I just swept it into another account so you can't take it back," he says. "I know how clever you are, my darling."

"Please just tell me where I can find Peyton." Tears run down my cheeks. I stand up and walk to the sliding glass doors leading to the backyard and step outside. The fog has settled over the point like a thick, cold blanket. It's chilly and damp. *Oh, Peyton, I hope you're not outside in this weather*. "At least tell me she's safe and warm. Please."

"It is a foggy evening here in town, I agree. You do know I've been here in Malibu watching you since I got released from prison?" he says. "You have a lovely home, not as nice as the one we shared, but nice. I enjoy checking in on you, seeing how you've chosen to live without me. You should have stayed in the house we shared. It was paid off. And you do know by now that security alarms only provide a false sense of security? Anyone can breach them."

And he has. I have nothing to say to him. Except this: "Where is my baby? I'll do anything to have her back."

I hear him laughing on the other end of the line.

"Paul, please," I beg as I look at the pool still glowing blue as night begins to fall.

"Why would I ever want someone else's baby? Think about it," he says.

"To hurt me, that's why." I take a deep breath as a thought pops into my head. "Did you put the rats in my pool? Was that some kind of sick joke?"

"Why would I do that? You're a little crazy, Cece, you know that? I've heard you're unwell, not sleeping, and then alternatively, sleeping all day, not taking care of the baby the way you should."

"I went through a hard time, recovery was long and painful thanks to you, and then pregnancy and having a baby. You wouldn't understand, Paul, but you almost killed me," I say. "But here I am. I am a survivor. I am taking care of my baby. I'm a good mom. Please, I beg you, tell me where my baby is. Bring her to me. Please. Or tell me where you are, and I'll come get her."

"Oh darling, I don't have your brat. I really have no idea who took her, not really," he says.

"What? Are you telling me you didn't take Peyton?" I ask, my heart thumping again. "But you just said you had her. I paid the ransom. Oh my god."

"Well, sorry. I might have told a tiny white lie," he says.

"You know who took her, don't you?" I say. I'm grasping at straws. He must know something. "Please tell me. Please."

"Like I said, it's fun to hear you sounding so desperate. Tell me you miss me," he says.

I swallow. "I miss you. Tell me."

"I love the sound of that, darling. Well, turns out I did have some conversations with someone while I was in prison. I thought she was going to help me get back together with you, but I was wrong about her," he says.

"Who? Who are you talking about?" I say, pressing the phone against my ear, holding on for Peyton.

"I'd rather keep that private. It's personal. Anyway, thanks for the money," he says. "I should hang up now as I'm sure the cops are listening. I'll be in touch."

"Wait, don't go, you know who has my baby! Wait! Paul!" But he's gone. I hear a scream, it's loud, and desperate, from a pain deep inside. It takes a moment to realize it's me.

The young cop appears and wraps his arm around my shoulder, walking me inside.

"Mrs. Strom, what is it, did something happen?" Concern is etched on his face. His phone buzzes and he answers. "Yes, sir. I see. I'll talk to her."

He turns to me, his face now stern, serious. "Did you just receive a ransom call? Do you know anything new?"

"I don't know where my baby is, I thought I did, but I don't,"

I wail. Once again, I've been a fool. "Please, you've got to find her."

"Mrs. Strom, I need you to tell me what just happened," he says. "We haven't been able to install the listening device on your mobile phone yet, so I need you to tell me the absolute whole story here. What just happened?"

I drop into a chair at the kitchen table and try to decide what to say.

The cop brings me a glass of water and I do my best to settle down. I'm going over the conversation with Paul in my head, trying to piece together what he was saying. He's been talking to someone, someone in my life, while he was in prison. Who would do that? Who would betray me like that?

"Ma'am, what did the caller say?" the cop asks.

I take a sip of water and wonder if Peyton has had anything to eat or drink all day. I wonder what I can tell the cop about Paul, about where to find him. I know he's in Malibu, but I am also now convinced he doesn't have my baby. Who has Peyton?

FORTY-SIX

LIZZIE

"Where's Peyton? Did you find her?" Cecilia asks as I walk into the kitchen. She's crazed, manic. I don't blame her. I'm cold from searching outside in the thick fog for the past two hours, and there is still no sign of the baby.

"No, not yet, but we will," I say, touching her shoulder. "The whole town is out looking for her. You made the local news, too. Peyton's photo is everywhere. She'll be found."

Cecilia stares at me. "I need you to tell me the truth. Did you talk to Paul, go visit Paul in prison?"

"No, of course not," I say. It seems she really is losing her mind. "I've never met your husband. I don't want to."

Cecilia begins to pace the kitchen. "Someone has. Someone led him to me, to my baby."

"Wait, do you think Paul has the baby?" I ask.

"No, I thought he did. I just paid him a ransom, because I believed he had her, but he doesn't," she says. "I'm such a fool."

"Oh my gosh. That's beyond evil. I'm so sorry. Sounds like he's taking advantage of you, of the situation," I say. I almost feel a pang of sympathy for her as I watch her pace the kitchen. I know Peyton will be found – I can't imagine any another scenario. And when she's back, Cecilia needs to realize this is no way to raise a baby. Paul is never going to leave her alone, he's made that quite clear. At some point, Cecilia's just going to need to accept the facts.

"Should we tell the cops what happened?" I ask.

"They know. I just told them everything. I'm just worried about taking their focus off Peyton, in case they start chasing down Paul instead," she says. "I'm so ashamed I believed him."

"Don't be ashamed. Did you tell them he's been stalking you, threatening you? It might help." I nod at her encouragingly. "You're desperate and he knew it. The news of Peyton's kidnapping has spread across town. Officer? Can you come in here, please?" I call.

The officer from the foyer walks into the room. "Yes, ma'am?"

"Mrs. Strom has something to tell you." I pat Cecilia's hand. "Go ahead. For Peyton."

"My estranged husband, Paul Strom, called as you know and told me he had taken Peyton," Cecilia says, taking a deep breath. "I paid a ransom, and then he said he didn't have her. The truth is, though, he's been stalking me, threatening me since he was released. I should have reported him sooner."

The cop nods. "Thanks for telling me. Anything else?"

"He said he met with someone while he was in prison. Someone who he thinks may have my baby," she says.

This is news to me. "Oh Cecilia," I say. "Who?"

"Mrs. Strom, do you have any idea who that could be?" the cop asks.

"He didn't give me any names." Cecilia starts to cry again.

"Ok, ma'am, we'll get on this right away," the cop says and hurries out of the room.

I look at Cecilia with something that might almost be pity, but I also know she is a formidable foe. "Ok, you need to sit down, you look like you're going to faint."

Cecilia nods and drops into a chair at the kitchen table. She probably won't be able to handle another ultimatum tonight. But too bad. Paul's had his fun. It's my turn now. Poor Cecilia. She's created a bit of a mess of her life. She wanted all of this—the money, the big house at the beach, the perfect baby—and now she's got it, and it seems to me she's doing a good job of ruining it all by herself.

"You need to stay strong, for Peyton," I encourage her. "Can I get you anything to drink?"

"No, I'm fine. And I know, I'm trying." Tears are still running down her cheeks.

I pull out a bar stool and sit. I'll give her a minute to compose herself before I tell her what is going to happen now. What my demands are. I scroll through my phone, find the album I've been creating. A text comes in from Evan.

Come to my apartment. #7b at the beach apartments on PCH and Grasswood Drive. Come now.

I text back: *I'll be right there. Is this about Peyton?*

I wait for an answer, but none comes.

I wonder why he isn't here already, out searching for his daughter. I turn to Cecilia, uncertain what's happening with Evan, but the knowledge he needs me makes my heart sing. I need to have a little convo before I head out, though.

"Look, Cecilia, I'm afraid I've seen overwhelming evidence that you're an unfit mom. Like when you constantly fall asleep on the couch with the baby next to you. She could have suffocated if she'd fallen between the cushions, or if you'd rolled on top of her." I hold up the photo evidence.

"How do you have that photo?" Her tears have stopped now. "Delete that. What are you doing to me? Peyton is missing. What is wrong with you?"

"There are so many more very incriminating images of your

poor parenting skills. Your negligence, like this one, Peyton wailing in her playpen, desperate for a feeding, and you were where? I'll tell you. Upstairs getting ready," I say. "Oh, and what about when you forgot her in the backseat of your car? She's strapped into her car seat, screaming, locked inside your car while you're inside doing god knows what. She could have died if I didn't find her that day. Don't deny it. You know the facts. And I have the proof. What about when she almost swallowed the pink balloon you gave her?"

She looks at me with crazed eyes. "I didn't give her that balloon. How dare you? You were supposed to be helping me. But more than that, I helped you, too. I took you in and I've been more than generous giving you gifts and taking you under my wing. And this is how you choose to repay me? I just cannot believe it. The baby needs us focused on bringing her home."

"Well, it's time you faced reality for once. I tried to help you. But you're beyond help," I say. "When Peyton comes home, and she will, more than ever she'll need a stable, loving home. And you can't provide that."

"You're so wrong. I'm her mother. She has everything she needs with me, she always will," she says, her tone darkening.

"I have grounds. And proof. For you to lose custody of Peyton," I say.

She stares at me, frozen in place, fury furrowing her brow. "No one is taking Peyton from me again. No one. Why haven't they found her yet? Oh my god."

"They will find her. I know it. But I also know her father can take her away from you," I say. "And he will. Now that he has all that he needs to make his case."

"Peyton doesn't have a father. Just me," she says.

"You're delusional, you know that? Remember, you agreed to give him shared parenting as part of the real estate agreement you just signed to get all that money?" I see the shock in her eyes as I reveal what I know. "Or did you lie to him just to get the money?"

"How do you know all of this?" she asks, a flush on her cheeks. It's clear I've surprised her but she's trying to act like I haven't.

"Evan is such a wonderful guy. He didn't deserve to be treated the way you treated him. But I guess I should thank you. You kicked him out of your life, and now," I pause for dramatic effect "we're in love." I smile. "But let's focus on Peyton. On getting her back, and then when she's home, she'll have me to watch over her, to love her, like a mom. A good mom."

I see Cecilia swallow. "Once Peyton is home, you will have nothing to do with her. Do you understand me? You will not take my baby from me. No one will. Not ever again."

And if looks could kill, I'd be dead. Somehow, despite all my photos of her endangering her child, she thinks she has the power here. She's wrong.

"I've got to go. I'll be back soon, and we can finish our talk. I know they'll find her." I turn and walk confidently out the door.

My Uber pulls into the apartment complex and I jump out, finding Evan's place immediately. I knock on the door.

He answers it, clearly in a panic. "Why haven't you called me? What took so long for you to get here?" He grabs my arm and pulls me inside, closing the door behind us.

I glance at my phone. That's when I realize I've missed five calls from him. "I'm sorry, I was with Cecilia. Evan, what is it?" I ask.

Evan's breathing hard and fast. "It's my mom. She's lost her mind. She took the baby."

Oh my god.

"Yes," he says.

"Is she alright?" I ask.

"She's fine. Confused, maybe, but she's asleep right now. Meanwhile, there's a full-blown search out for her. I don't know what to do," he says, his eyes flashing with the terror of it all, the reality of what his mother has done.

"Take me to her," I instruct him. He leads me down the hallway to a bedroom and opens the door. I rush to the side of the crib. It's her. She's fine. Oh my gosh. I touch her tiny head and feel myself relax for the first time since I heard the news of her disappearance. We walk quietly out of the room and close the door.

"What do we do?" Evan asks. The poor man is shaking in the hallway.

"Ok, we take a deep breath and make a plan," I say. "Where is Marian?"

He points down the hall and I hurry to confront her.

Marian sits on Evan's couch. Mascara stains her cheeks, and her red hair is a wild mess. "I was trying to save her, protect her," she says, blue eyes blinking rapidly at me.

I stand in front of her trying to keep my rage under control. "Protect her? By grabbing her from her crib while she slept?"

"No!" Marian says. "She was awake, poor little thing, and fussy, and Cecilia was ignoring her as usual, asleep in her room. I just... I needed to protect her."

"From Cecilia?" I ask. Evan grabs my hand.

"No, from Paul," he says as Marian nods.

"I visited him in prison, I was trying to get dirt on Cecilia, I'll admit it. I didn't like her, didn't think she was right for Evan, and then, with the baby, well, I knew she was too much of a princess, too self-centered to have a child, and I thought..." Marian stands up slowly and looks as if she could topple over at any moment. "I thought Paul was a good guy. I thought he was on my side. But he wasn't. He's horrible."

"Mom took the baby so Paul couldn't, right Mom?" Evan says, prodding her.

"Yes. I felt so bad I led him to Cecilia, told him where she lived," she says. "And about the baby. I was afraid he'd do something to Peyton. He was so jealous that Cecilia had a baby without him, without his approval, with another man. He got super angry about Evan, too. I needed to protect my son and my granddaughter. And what with Cecilia being so unreliable, such a bad mother, well, I had to do something."

I shake my head. "How could you? I agree she's a bad mother, but still. This is over-the-top."

"I know, and I'm ashamed now. It was a really bad idea. It was a spur-of-the-moment decision," she says.

"You carry around Wi-Fi blockers, Marian?" I ask, shaking my head. "Was this Paul's plan?"

"No, he just was obsessed with the technology. I just listened during one of our visits. He told me that it was designed so you could hide the blocker next to a house in the bushes and disarm a system," she says. "Paul scared me at the end. He sent me a threatening note. I had to protect the baby."

"Or you could have told us, or the cops," Evan says.

"I know, son. I know. But I had a copy of your key so I just let myself in. And it worked. I snuck up the stairs and walked into Peyton's nursery. The baby was awake and she smiled at me, waving her little arms. I picked her up and snuggled her. She needed a change, so I did that, and then I took her home with me. It was an impulse, only because I love her so much. I put her in her little car seat and we drove to my house. I realize now I've been a fool. That Paul played me, put the entire notion in my head. But the baby, she's ok. I've fed her and changed her. I know I need to give her back."

Evan takes me in his arms. "Will you help us? I don't want my mom to go to prison. She's a good woman who made a big mistake. Peyton is fine, she giggled when she saw me. And she finished a whole bottle. She's doing great, and, well, can we try to work this out? We need your help. I need your help."

"I'm so sorry for what I did." Fresh tears run down Marian's cheeks.

"We know you are, Mom," Evan says. "It's going to be ok. Lizzie will help us. We all need to stick together here."

I imagine Cecilia's reaction, her rage and need for revenge. But then I imagine her relief, her joy at having Peyton home safe and sound. I take a deep breath, take out my phone and call Cecilia's number.

She picks up immediately. "It's Lizzie. Look, can you step outside and talk?" I ask.

"What is it?" she whispers frantically.

"Are you outside?" I ask. "Is this line being monitored?"

Marian has sunk back down on the couch and is wringing her hands. Evan stands next to me.

"Not yet. Do you know something?" she says.

I put the phone on speaker, then turn to Evan and nod.

"I'm so sorry, Cecilia." Evan's voice is shaking. "My mom took Peyton, but she's safe, sleeping here at my apartment now. It was a big mistake. She's so sorry."

"I'm so sorry, so very sorry," Marian sobs. "She's unharmed. I love her."

Cecilia doesn't speak for a minute, and then in a strangely calm voice, she says, "Bring her home. Now. How did you even get into my home, Marian?"

"I took Evan's key, I put the Wi-Fi blocker in the garden so the alarm system didn't work. It was easy." Marian's words are barely coherent through the tears. "You were asleep, you're always asleep."

"That's because Lizzie has been drugging me," Cecilia says. "It all makes so much sense now. The smoothies, the juices. I was a fool."

Evan looks at me and I shake my head and shrug as if to say, *Cecilia's unhinged, you know that.*

He nods. Hopefully he believes me. I think he's overwhelmed by the entire situation. In a short time, he's lost Cecilia and then almost lost Peyton. Poor man's heart can't take much more. I'll help him through it, though, I will.

I turn my attention back to the phone. "Look, Marian made a mistake, a big one," I say. "But we're going to bring Peyton home. Just let's do it quietly."

"Why should I keep quiet about this? Why shouldn't I tell the cops right now?" she says.

"Because the baby has been through enough. The police would be traumatizing—lights, sounds, yelling. Any good mom would know that," I say. Evan nods in agreement.

"You know what's traumatizing? Being kidnapped," Cecilia says.

"Please, just let me bring the baby home. Then you can do whatever you'd like. Tell the cops or not. It's your choice. But just let me bring her home quietly. I don't want her to go through any more traumatic events."

"Ok, fine," she says, ignoring my dig. "But if you don't bring her to me now, this minute, I will tell the cops. They're here in my house, as you know. Bring her home or I'll send the cops to Evan's apartment. You have five minutes."

"Give me ten, please. I'll come right now. Just don't tell the cops. We'll do whatever you say. I need to protect my mom. She's lost her mind. She thought she was protecting her, from Paul, and from you, that's why she took the baby," Evan pleads. "Don't worry. I'm on my way. I'll bring her to the back gate."

"Yes. Hurry. And she better not be harmed in any way, or I'll tell the cops everything," Cecilia says, her voice tense and angry.

"She's perfectly fine," Evan says. "We're leaving now."

I let out a deep sigh as I hang up the phone. Evan and I stare at each other. And then, despite everything, I smile with relief. "I knew the baby would be ok. I never suspected this, though."

"I just wanted to protect her. I'd been a fool to talk to Paul, to answer his questions, to tell him about Cecilia and her child. I had to take her so he couldn't. You have to believe me." Marian looks at us, pleading.

"I know you were trying to do what you thought was right," I say, because the poor woman is a wreck, and I love her son. "But you can't just take a baby, even if it's out of love."

Marian nods and dabs her eyes. "I don't know what I was thinking. I almost feel like Paul was watching, smiling, when I drove away with the baby. I think he's watching Cecilia's house. You should tell her that. And tell her I'm so sorry."

"It's going to be ok, Mom," Evan says. "Let's go, Lizzie. And thank you so much for helping us."

"Of course," I say and follow him down the hallway and into the nursery he's created for Peyton, even though he's never been allowed to have her overnight. It's charming, and sad, and I need to fix that. His mom's actions weren't his fault.

"Did you know Marian was going to take her?" I ask, my voice quiet as I scoop Peyton up into my arms. It feels so good to hold her again. I kiss the top of her head.

"Of course not," Evan says, and I believe him. "But I doubt Cecilia will believe that."

"I know. That's a problem."

"Let's get her back home to Cecilia," Evan says. "Maybe she'll forgive my mom... eventually."

I have no idea what Cecilia will do, to Marian, to Evan and to me, but I'm pretty sure forgiveness is not at the top of her list.

FORTY-SEVEN

CECILIA

I call Lizzie's phone. "What's taking so long?"

"We're almost there. I'll meet you at the gate," she answers.

I hang up and sneak out the back door. I make my way through the backyard and reach the metal gate.

"Hello, darling," Paul says.

In the dark, I can't see him, but I know he's only an arm's reach away. I clamp my hand over my mouth to keep from screaming.

He steps up to the gate, within inches of me. "I know. I've startled you. You look like you've seen a ghost. But it's just little ol' me." Even in the darkness and fog, I can see he's smiling, still taunting me.

"Go away or I'll scream," I say, grateful for the iron gate between us. I step back.

"By now, I'm sure you've figured out who has the baby. I watched wretched Marian take her from your house," Paul says.

"Why didn't you tell me that when I paid your ransom? You put her up to it, I'm sure you did," I say.

"Maybe I had a little something to do with her scheme. Some words of inspiration, let's say, but I didn't tell her to take the brat. Not in so many words, although I may have given her the impression that I was going to swipe her," he says smiling. "Look, darling, I'm going to leave town. I know you've told the cops about me, and they're likely closing in. So, why don't you get your baby back, settle in for a bit, and I'll be in touch? You look tired, Cece. You should get some rest."

Headlights appear on the street behind him and he steps away from the gate. "Goodbye for now, darling."

As he disappears into the fog, I'm shaking all over. I close my eyes, and when I open them Lizzie stands on the other side of the gate.

"Where's Peyton?" I whisper.

"Sleeping in the car. She's fine. I checked," Lizzie says.

"Here's how it's going to go," I say, almost businesslike now. "Assuming Peyton is unharmed, you and Evan will ride off into the sunset, never to have contact with her again."

"No way." Lizzie crosses her arms.

"I don't think Evan wants to see his mom in the slammer, and, well, you two are now accomplices to a kidnapping." I take a deep breath. I just want to hold my baby. I want this nightmare to end. But I also want to be clear that they are out of our lives for good.

Lizzie is dating Evan, of all the repulsive things. My ex-boyfriend and my baby's daddy. How could she? She's my nanny, for heaven's sake. How could *he*? And what's worse is that Lizzie knows about the money we just received from the sale of the building. She also knows about my parenting errors, and apparently has taken photos of me doing things that may make me lose custody of my daughter, according to her. Taken out of context, they all make me look horrible, the worst mom. It's not just that she has picked up on my perceived shortcomings, but she's purposefully painting me in the most unflattering light possible.

But now I have the upper hand. I have proof she's a thief

with the little stash she created in the guest room, proof she's been drugging me with my own sleeping pills – I found the empty bottle in her room confirming my suspicion – and more.

"Should I go tell the officer what's happening? Have them come out here to the back gate? Should I explain that you planned the kidnapping with help from your boyfriend? Oh, and I could tell them about all the things you've stolen from me and other families in town."

Lizzie looks at me, wide-eyed. I know she's thinking about Evan and his mom. Heck, Evan could be charged with kidnapping, too. Maybe he was part of Marian's scheme?

"No, I don't think that would be a good idea," she says. "How about I delete what I have on you?"

"Sure. I knew you'd see it my way. And while you're at it, make sure Evan moves the car forward," I say. "You know, out of the glow of the streetlights. Tell him to bring me my baby. Now."

I see Lizzie frantically texting.

The back gate is hardly ever used but it is always locked tight. There are no cameras facing it. My heart pounds with anticipation at the thought of holding my baby again.

"Here's the thing, Lizzie," I say, through the iron bars of the gate. "We were a good team for a bit, right?"

"Sure," she says. "Whatever. You know I love Peyton like she was my own, like I loved my baby sister, Sally."

"I should have fired you sooner. I should have realized you were drugging me," I say. "It wasn't postpartum depression I suffered from after you started. It was you. You were drugging me."

"I suppose it was," Lizzie says. "But, to be fair, a lot of moms use that stuff to take the edge off, so maybe I was helping you."

"As if. But still, that wasn't enough for you. There's all the jewelry you stole, and sold. Yes, I've been to Mr. Claude's. I will get all of my jewelry back," I say. "You can keep all the clothes and accessories I gave to you and bought for you. Not to mention my former partner you're now dating. When you walk away from this gate tonight, I don't want to see you ever again. Not you, not Evan. Or else the cops will find out who kidnapped my baby. I will implicate all three of you." I pause and stare at her in the darkness. "Remember, I can always do a bit of evidence gathering myself, I can always link this crime to you, Evan and Marian."

She nods and takes a deep breath. Seems she's not so flippant anymore. "Ok. Fine."

I unlock the gate from my side.

"Open it," I say, to make sure her fingerprints are on it.

Across the street, I see Evan get out of the car. The gloomy fog casts a surreal, otherworldly haze over him as he takes a baby carrier out of the backseat.

My heart bursts with a love I have never felt before. I want to run to her, but I can't. There are cops around everywhere and I can't draw attention to what is happening. I tell myself she's almost home.

"Hold the gate open for me," I say to Lizzie, pushing past her. I meet Evan in the shadows along the side of the road, and he hands me the carrier.

Peyton sleeps peacefully, as if nothing has happened. Thank god. I touch her tummy, kiss her tiny head, smell her sweet baby scent.

"Don't ever contact me or Peyton again," I repeat.

Evan nods, tears streaming from his eyes. "I'm so sorry. She's so sorry. Paul told her how to use the Wi-Fi blocker when she visited him in prison. Later on, she became afraid Paul was going to take the baby. He sent my mom a threatening note. It made her do it, grab the baby. My mom was just gullible."

I shake my head in disbelief. Paul. It's always Paul.

"We need to go now, Evan," Lizzie says. "Cecilia needs to sneak the baby back inside."

"I'm so sorry," Evan says again.

Lizzie holds the metal gate open for me and I walk into my backyard with my baby. I don't say goodbye. I hear the gate click closed softly behind me and lock it. I turn in time to see Lizzie taking Evan's hand, leading him away.

I take a deep breath and smile at Peyton. Relief washes over me like a warm breeze.

It's no longer important what the nanny saw, or what she did to me. All that matters is me and Peyton and the future. My baby is home. I fight the urge to wake her up. I know she needs her rest. Because tonight, after I lie to the police, tell them that someone, I don't know who, placed her baby carrier at my back gate, we're gone.

The police stayed for hours, asking me questions, looking for leads, fingerprinting the gate as I knew they would, cancelling the Amber alert. I didn't care. I held Peyton in my arms and decided I would never let her out of my sight again. When they finally left, it was almost two in the morning, but I found myself strangely alert.

I carried Peyton upstairs and into my bedroom, locking the door behind me before putting her in a portable playpen to continue sleeping. We will share the same bedroom from now on, I decide. I pack quickly, only what I truly need for my new life, which when you boil things down to what matters most, isn't very much. Besides, I have plenty of money in my bank account now to buy us whatever we need.

As I pack up my bathroom toiletries, I'm again amazed at how exhilarated I feel now that I'm not being drugged by my own nanny to make me look and act like a bad mom. I lost days, so much time with Peyton, because of Lizzie. And now, she's latched onto Evan, who seems to be happy about being with her. I suppose I really don't care if they end up together, although if I were him, I'd watch my back.

She's a thief and a liar. She drugged me and tried to take my baby from me. Evan was a bad partner once I got pregnant, and a terrible dad once Peyton arrived. All in all, I guess they deserve each other. And Marian? What was she thinking? Visiting Paul in prison like they were family or something. I haven't yet taken the time to research what a Wi-Fi blocker is, but I do know, from now on, my security systems and cameras will be hardwired.

I'm finished packing. I watch Peyton sleeping peacefully. She must be exhausted by the whole ordeal, but I know she wasn't mistreated. Marian was her grandmother, after all. *Was*.

It's time to focus on the future. Yesterday, I made an all-cash offer on a charming cottage by the sea in a small community on the central coast of California. It's the perfect size for Peyton and me, two bedrooms, with enough land around us that we'll have privacy. It even has an artist's studio where I'll paint while Peyton plays on the swing set just outside my door. I'll have a security company hardwire an alarm system, and install cameras inside and out, just to be safe, but I don't expect any trouble, not from Paul, not from Evan or Lizzie either.

And in our new life, I won't be hiring a nanny, that's for sure.

I will purchase the cottage under my new company name, Little P & Mama C, an LLC my attorney set up for me a few months ago. Peyton and I will have a simple life, and I'll learn how to budget so the money from the building sale lasts a long time. And I'll stop trying to get Paul to sign the divorce papers, because that keeps us connected, keeps him in the know about where we are. Someday, when he finds another stupid woman who will marry him, he'll sign them, and my attorney can handle the whole thing without me.

I'm considering myself officially a divorced, single mom

from this moment on. A mom who will do whatever it takes to protect her daughter. Who has done what she could do protect her. I'll do it again if anyone tries to take her away from me.

I stare at Peyton sleeping soundly and take a deep breath. Everything is going to work out just fine for us, and I'm going to be the mom she deserves. And from now on, if someone tries to help us, says they're only the nanny, or only the event planner, or only an old lady's escort, or *only* anything else, I won't fall for it.

I know better now. I'll never let anyone into our lives, our home, again. I'll never let someone watch me like that. Never.

A LETTER FROM KAIRA

Dear Reader,

Thank you so much for reading *What the Nanny Saw*. I truly hope you enjoyed it. If you did and want to keep up to date with all my latest releases, just sign up at the following link. Your email address will never be shared, and you can unsubscribe at any time.

www.bookouture.com/kaira-rouda

Writing this story was a blast because I had the chance to bring back one of my most notorious characters, Paul Strom. He's not a nice guy, but ever since his debut in *Best Day Ever*, he's been in the back of my mind, begging for a sequel. Now, perhaps, he's happy. Only problem is, Cecilia Strom wasn't finished with her story yet. If you enjoyed this novel, perhaps you'd like to check out my backlist of *USA Today*, Amazon Charts and internationally bestselling psychological suspense including *Best Day Ever, The Favorite Daughter, The Next Wife, The Widow, Somebody's Home, Beneath the Surface, Under the Palms* and *The Second Mrs Strom*.

Thank you again for reading! If you'd like to keep in touch, I'm active on social media and would love for you to join me there! I also have a newsletter, and I'd love for you to sign up—you can do so via my website. I promise not to overwhelm your inbox, and I do have special, subscriber-only benefits.

Oh, and since you're a crime fiction fan, please tune in to the Killer Author Club, www.killerauthorclub.com, where we interview bestselling authors every other Tuesday. Join us for the fun.

Your support means the world to me. Thank you!

Kaira

www.kairarouda.com

facebook.com/KairaRoudaBooks
instagram.com/KairaRouda
tiktok.com/@KairaRoudaBooks

ACKNOWLEDGMENTS

To my publishing team at Bookouture, thank you. It has been a joy to work with you. Extra special thanks to my editor Lydia Vassar-Smith who read my novel *The Next Wife*, and loved it, and asked if I had anything more. Yes, I did. Thank you so much for finding me. You're a fabulous editor. Thanks, too, to Kim Nash, digital publicity director, who shares my love of the beach and all things PR. I've enjoyed our chats immensely.

To my agents, Annelise Robey and Meg Ruley, and the rest of the team at Jane Rotrosen Agency, thank you for all you do for me. Thanks to the team at Gotham Group, Ellen Goldsmith Vein and Ross Siegel, for handling my film/TV rights. Beyond excited that *Beneath the Surface* has been optioned for a feature film. To Heather Sadlemire and Tonya Cornish, thank you for spreading the word about my books. I couldn't do this without you. And to all the bookstagrammers and book bloggers and reviewers who share my books with the world on social media, you are the best.

And speaking of social media, if you haven't yet, please check out the Killer Author Club, a biweekly live show hosted by authors Kimberly Belle, Heather Gudenkauf and me. We have a great time featuring the best crime authors in the business and discussing killing, of the fictional kind. Find out more at: www.KillerAuthorClub.com.

Thanks, most importantly, to my husband, Harley, who encourages me daily and inspires me always. I'm so lucky you're my partner. And to my kids, Trace and Annika, Avery and Paul,

Shea, and Dylan—I love you all so much. And to Tucker, my beloved dog, thank you for keeping me company while I write. Our walks together, although slower now, are my favorite part of the day.

And to you, the reader, thank you for reading this novel. I hope you enjoyed it. You are the reason I have the honor of living the career of my dreams. I'd love to keep in touch. You can find me at www.kairarouda.com.

PUBLISHING TEAM

Turning a manuscript into a book requires the efforts of many people. The publishing team at Bookouture would like to acknowledge everyone who contributed to this publication.

Audio
Alba Proko
Sinead O'Connor
Melissa Tran

Commercial
Lauren Morrissette
Hannah Richmond
Imogen Allport

Contracts
Peta Nightingale

Cover design
Eileen Carey

Data and analysis
Mark Alder
Mohamed Bussuri

Editorial
Lydia Vassar-Smith
Lizzie Brien

Copyeditor
Lusana Taylor-Khan

Proofreader
Jenny Page

Marketing
Alex Crow
Melanie Price
Occy Carr
Cíara Rosney
Martyna Młynarska

Operations and distribution
Marina Valles
Stephanie Straub
Joe Morris

Production
Hannah Snetsinger
Mandy Kullar
Jen Shannon
Ria Clare

Publicity
Kim Nash
Noelle Holten
Jess Readett
Sarah Hardy

Made in the USA
Las Vegas, NV
10 November 2024